THE ADVENTURE OF
THE COAL-TAR DERIVATIVE

The Exploits of Sherlock Holmes and Dr. John H. Watson
against the Moriarities during the Great Hiatus

Steven Philip Jones

Hardcover ISBN 978-1-78705-839-2
Paperback ISBN 978-1-78505-840-8
ePub ISBN 978-1-78705-841-5
PDF ISBN 978-1-78705-842-2

Published by MX Publishing
335 Princess Park Manor, Royal Drive,
London, N11 3GX
www.mxpublishing.co.uk

Cover design by Brian Belanger

To Gary Reed
Thanks for the trust and friendship all these years

I am particularly indebted to the author(s) of *Varney the Vampire*, which was invaluable to me in writing the prologue.   S.P.J.

Contents

AUTHOR'S NOTE

YOU NEVER know what the postman might bring.

In the summer of 2012 a package arrived from my friend John Ross who lives in England. John and I met many years earlier when we collaborated on an original graphic novel sequel to Bram Stoker's *Dracula*, during which he became painfully aware of my fascination with Sherlock Holmes, who makes an important cameo in our story. When John chanced across a battered diplomat briefcase purportedly belonging to Holmes's elder brother Mycroft at a market in Sleaford he thought of me and sent it as a gift.

The briefcase came with no provenance, but it was love at first sight. I am the type who hangs on to an antique console radio that has not worked in decades because they don't make 'em like that anymore, and I thought the scruffy black leather bag with battered double gussets was as beautiful as a mint condition 1940s Underwood Champion typewriter. It did not even matter that a slip pocket had pulled away from the back compartment during the briefcase's transatlantic journey, exposing a bundle of manuscripts, letters, and stationery that had been sewn in behind the fraying fabric. Imagine my incredulity when I saw "Mycroft Holmes" in the stationery letterhead and read that many of the manuscripts were written by Dr. John H. Watson. Others were written by a British government agent named Walter Simonson and by Sherlock Holmes himself. All these papers were dated between May 1891 and

March 1894, the approximate period of The Great Hiatus when the world believed Sherlock Holmes was dead after plummeting into the Reichenbach Falls with Professor James Moriarty, the man Holmes referred to as the "Napoléon of crime." If these papers were genuine than the Great Detective had been far more active during The Great Hiatus than he suggests in "The Adventure of the Empty House," and the same could be said for the Good Doctor and the Moriarty criminal organization.

I shall forgo documenting the often laborious details involved with my attempts to authenticate these papers, except to say that I am grateful for the enthusiastic assistance of many American and British Sherlockian groups spearheaded by The Always Available Hansom Cab Drivers of the American Middle West. A scholarly accounting of these efforts and the editing of these papers is in the works, but for the casual reader I offer this manuscript detailing some of the most tumultuous months in the history of the British Empire if not the world. For those readers who may not be Sherlockians or are unfamiliar with Victorian history, I am including footnotes to provide some hopefully helpful explanations. Finally, I have written a companion prologue and epilogue to present what I consider to be essential information that is suggested or mentioned in passing in the transcripts, but I leave it up to each reader to decide if any or all of the following adventures really occurred.

Steven Philip Jones
Cedar Rapids, Iowa -- May, 2021

"The course of events in London did not run so well as I had hoped, for the trial of the Moriarty gang left two of its most dangerous members, my most vindictive enemies, at large. I travelled for two years in Tibet, therefore, and amused myself by visiting Lhassa, and spending some days with the head lama. You may have read of the remarkable explorations of a Norwegian named Sigerson, but I am sure that it never occurred to you that you were receiving news of your friend. I then passed through Persia, looked in at Mecca, and paid a short but interesting visit to the Khalifa at Khartoum, the results of which I have communicated to the Foreign Office. Returning to France, I spent some months in a research into the coal-tar derivatives, which I conducted in a laboratory at Montpellier, in the south of France."

- "The Adventure of the Empty House"

PROLOGUE: PROVENANCE
22 February, 1860

WIND AND rain ushered in the morning.

A mistral that charged down the Rhône Valley under the cloak of night lashed the Mediterranean along the Gulf of Lion as fishermen in the village of Providence gathered in the bay at first light, relieved to find their little barques still where they had been beached at sunset.

"God bless any poor fellows at sea," a Corsican salt named Massallo cried to his young neighbor Herrera. "If they woke and found themselves upon a lee shore they will never get off again."

Waves rolling into the bay edged closer to the boats, so the mariners hurried to drag their vessels high above the reach of the prowling water. When finished Herrera shouted, "I'm for the house. This is not a day to be out in."

One of the other fishermen replied, "Only the most devout will receive their blessings and ashes today. If I do not have the whole house blown down I will consider myself fortunate."

Noticing Massallo studying the sea, Herrera peered out too. "I don't see any ships coming in the horizon. Do you?"

"None. I hope there may be none." Massallo walked away, looking bedeviled. "If you see a flare or hear a gun, let me know."

* * * *

Out upon the rampaging Mediterranean, Cleveland Scout, formerly of Her Majesty's Royal Navy, stood at the helm of the merchant vessel *Kettleness*, his hands clutching the ship's wheel. It did not matter that the rudder was busted and the sails and masts were gone. This is how Scout intended to meet his maker as his mate Jack Pringle, who had served with him since their bluejacket days, reported the pumps were choked and useless. The *Kettleness* was at the mercy of the weather and waves, and with the wind set dead shore Scout could no longer keep her head out to sea. "She strove hard and resisted long."

"Ay, she carried us through most of the day."

"Best fire the guns and flares."

"We cannot expect assistance."

"It may give warning to those on shore. There is no telling how far we may be driven towards the land. We may even be set right on to the beach."

"So we might."

The comrades traded last smiles. "Give the order, Jack."

Thirteen souls were aboard the *Kettleness* not counting the captain and mate: the crew, cook, and seven passengers. The crew, seeing land ahead, obeyed Pringle's command with alacrity, alternating between guns and signal flares every half-minute. Meanwhile one of the passengers emerged from the companion to broach the ship's master. Even under current circumstances the traveler remained a remarkable sight. His emaciated frame was wrapped within a fashionably cut coal-black suit with matching bisht trimmed with gold scorpions and grasshoppers, while a pale and placid wax mask crowned with a lengthy jet-black wig veiled his features. Deep-sunk eyes and cadaverous lips were visible through slits in the false face. Always reserved but gentlemanly, the passenger inquired in a melodious voice that somehow cut through the din, "How long do you think it will be?"

"Until when, sir?"

"Until we shall be wrecked."

Scout admired the man's sangfroid and wished he knew the passenger's name, but the stranger had paid a ridiculous sum to sail incognito with a large box of confidential cargo that had been stored in his compartment since they departed the Port of Varna. "Well, sir, we strike in five minutes, perhaps twenty. If we are forced in upon the shore in a direct line, we expect the shortest time."

"And if we should not meet with any obstruction we may be thrown far on shore."

"Yes. That is the village of Providence. You can just make out the Châteaux de Pelfrey on the cliffline. If we had the time I could tell you stories about that old manse and its smuggler past."

"I would have liked to have heard them."

"I only wish I had the means to steer the *Kettleness* within fifty or a hundred yards of the shore. There would be a better chance of some of us reaching the beach."

"Which is now rather more than uncertain."

"It is so."

"I understand." The passenger thanked Scout and returned to his compartment.

A few seconds later the *Kettleness* rammed a sunken rock.

The jolt toppled everyone deckside as the sea breached over the schooner and carried off Pringle and three crewmen. Scout contrived to lash himself to the wheel, but a second breach dashed him against the stump of a mast. Blood dyed the deck before another wave washed it away and swallowed the man.

The *Kettleness* heeled about in the shallow water. Now and then great waves lifted the ship and pounded it higher on the rocks. Each shock scuttled the keel and tumbled mariners and passengers into the boiling foam until only the stranger remained, emerging from the companion with an object clutched beneath his cloak as he struggled against the indefatigable fury. Lifting his left hand he made as if to wave to someone on shore or to throw something away before a mammoth breach engulfed the ship.

* * * *

Herrera alerted Massallo of the gunfire and red flares shortly before sunset.

The pair roused their fellow fishermen to join them on a crag overlooking the bay.

The sky was heavy and the rain incessant, but the mariners could make out the death throes of the merchant ship. Above the bellowing wind the old Corsican shouted, "There are but bare rocks under her and she will not settle into any place.

"Ay, ay," Herrera acknowledged. "She will be beaten and bumped until she breaks and splits to shivers."

The gathering did not speak again until a loud shriek borne upon the hoarse wind was heard above the roaring ocean. A fisherman clasped his hands and prayed: "Heaven have mercy on them, for I fear the sea will have none."

Massallo led the way towards the beach.

Upon reaching the bay the crash of breakers and the thunderous gales became one strange and awful sound of furious character over which Herrera asked Massallo, "Do you see anything upon the water?"

"Nothing. They are most likely dashed to pieces."

Another fisherman prayed, "God help them, poor fellows. If they are not to be saved, may they soon have an end to their tortures, for the strife after life must be dreadful."

"It is." Massallo watched the sea with eyes that observed nothing outside himself. "Such sufferings are endured under excitement, so they are not so much felt as when a person has been saved. Passing the barrier of life…becoming insensible to all…and then being recalled to life is an agony not to be described."

That same moment the rain and wind softened and the moon peeked out as the heavy clouds incrementally dissipated.

"Well," said a sailor, "I did not expect to see the storm abate so soon."

"I did not," said another, "though the sea will not abate for many hours."

The fishermen kept their vigil a while longer to assure they had done all that was possible, but as it became apparent nothing or no one was going to be carried ashore, each returned home one by one until only Massallo remained. The old seafarer was too beset by memories to abandon all hope yet.

Approaching the waterline, Massallo stopped upon an all-too familiar spot and looked back towards the cliffs where a vast and spacious grey stone mansion overlooked the bay. Massallo first saw the Châteaux de Pelfrey from this spot on a terrible day seventeen years earlier when a storm like this had delivered him to Providence.

Massallo had been in love with a Corsican girl whose relations intended her to marry a rival with more money. Through her intercession Massallo obtained time to increase his fortune, which he invested in a merchant vessel. It was a time for devils to be abroad, however, and a few years later he and his shipmates found themselves chased into a tempest by Algerians. Knowing the best they could hope for if captured was to be turned into slaves, Massallo and his companions sailed perilously close to shore, where they were compelled to pump and cut away the wreck.

All was confusion.

Not a sound could be distinguished over the wind, rain, waves, and thunder.

The speaking trumpet was useless.

Then just before the Algerians could overtake them the pirates sheered off.

Before Massallo's vessel could do the same or run bump ashore lightning splintered the mast to atoms and left the stump burning. The strike killed two of his best hands and rendered the remaining crew senseless, leaving no one to man the pumps and the ship out of control.

Massallo's vessel crashed.

All hands were thrown into the roiling sea.

Massallo thought he had drowned only to find himself lying alone on the familiar spot on the beach. Too exhausted to move his head, all the Corsican could see through the rain was the looming cliffline and the Châteaux de Pelfrey upon its precipice.

With his fortune lost Massallo remained in Providence, where, somewhat like Odysseus on Ogygia, he prospered and lived a tolerably happy life. Massallo hoped he would never see another storm like the tempest that brought him here, but he could not help wondering at a man's ability to adapt himself to unexpected circumstances. Before he wondered very long, he spotted a body thrown up by the breakers, rolled hither and thither, left on the shore by one comber before being withdrawn by another, until a high roller carried the body further ashore and spat it out on the beach.

Massallo retrieved the body and was surprised to find its face covered by a pallid mask. He was even more surprised that the dead man was clutching a metal lockbox with intricate arabesque and a lock with three keyholes. Like most Mediterranean sailors Massallo had heard about such coffers and knew whatever it contained was probably very valuable or important, but he was more curious about the reason for the mask. He attempted to unfasten it but its waterlogged straps refused to be untied, so the fisherman cut them with his whalebone handled knife. Beneath the mask Massallo found the ghastly face of a miserable carcass.

In the same instant a bony hand snared the Corsican's wrist in a furious grasp.

Massallo winced and dropped his knife.

A shadow fell over him and Massallo screamed.

And then he died.

THE FIRST ADVENTURE:
MEA GLORIA FIDES

From the Unpublished Personal Reminiscences of John H. Watson, M.D.

I. *Auld Acquaintance*

IT WAS that dreadful May of 1891.

My wife Mary did her best for me when I returned alone from Switzerland and took a short leave from my practice. As it was, if not for her well-intended insistence and my own sense of obligation, I would have rejected Mycroft Holmes's request to organize his brother's papers and put 221B Baker Street back in order after the failed fire set by the Professor Moriarty gang. I knew such work would occupy me physically, but not mentally, and therefore delay the process of my moving past the death of Sherlock Holmes.

Besides the attempted arson, Holmes had left our old rooms in more disarray than was his habit, which was understandable considering the circumstances prompting our escape to the Continent. It did make my chore more difficult than I had supposed, but with persistence the ship was nearly righted again within a couple of days. The one spot I elected to avoid was Holmes's desk. With the exception of retrieving his personal casebook (which my friend bequeathed to me per the disposition of his estate), I had no intention of going through its drawers, believing it was Mycroft's place to attend to his brother's personal most items.

Late in the morning of the third day Mrs. Hudson stepped into the sitting room to inform me that a visitor was waiting in the foyer. "The gentleman went to your home only to have Mrs. Watson send him here. He claims he went to university with you." Mrs. Hudson stepped closer to present me with the visitor's card. "His name is Lot Morrill." Lowering her voice, she confided, "He's an American."

That was true. Morrill was born and raised in the Delaware Valley before his family moved to London a few years prior to him entering college. Where I continued my training to become an army surgeon at the Royal Victoria Hospital after receiving my degree from the University of London, Morrill returned to America, where for a time he worked with Joseph O'Dwyer.[1] The intervening years appeared to have softened Morrill somewhat, adding a paternal patina to his weather-beaten chestnut face, but Morrill was still six feet of brawn with a forty-four inch chest, testaments to a rugged boyhood working on a farm.

I was overjoyed to see Morrill and just as delighted to accept his invitation for an early lunch at Simpson's, which had been a favorite of ours and several fellow-students. Morrill apologized for calling without forewarning me as we waited for the waiter to bring the carving meat, but I assured him that he could not have arrived at a better time. "I've about reached the end of a difficult task and a meal will do wonders for me. Now what's it been? Twelve years?

"About that, although Bart's seems a lifetime ago."

---

[1] Joseph O'Dwyer (1841-1898). American physician and pioneer in the use of intubation for the treatment of childhood diphtheria.

"And I've kept track of you in the Colonies."

"'The Colonies?' You snob!"

"I'm not! Your work on intubation at St. John's Hospital for Sick Children? Revolutionary!"

"I only assisted Joseph. No glory in that but plenty of satisfaction. Speaking of which, I've kept track of you, too. My condolences on Mr. Holmes."

"Thank you, Lot. Holmes was the best man ... the wisest man I've ever known."

Sadness creased Morrill's brow as dark thoughts appeared to overcome his memory. Stumbling a bit for words, he replied, "Very appropriate. I'm sure Plato could not have held Socrates in any higher esteem than you did Sherlock Holmes."[2]

"I'm sorry if I dampened the mood."

"Not at all. I'm just getting peckish." Morrill looked everywhere else but towards me as he asked, "Where's that waiter?"

The cloud over our heads dissipated as we ate and by the time we finished Morrill seemed his old self. As we walked out onto the Strand I spied a hansom waiting nearby and waived it over. "What would you say for a tour of our old haunts?"

The cab drew up and a gangly, bushy-bearded Cockney driver with grey eyes asked, "Where to, gents?"

---

[2] In *Phædo* (or *On the Soul*) Plato concludes his account of the execution of his teacher Socrates: "Such was the end, Echecrates, of our friend; concerning whom I may truly say, that of all the men of his time whom I have known, he was the wisest and justest and best."

Morrill beamed. "Well, if you're really up for it, John, I wouldn't mind --"

A familiar voice called from behind. "Doctor Watson!"

Morrill turned. "Who is that? A colleague of yours?"

I said, "In a manner of speaking."

Morrill's previous glumness percolated as he contemplated the small, lean, bulldog of a man with ferret-like face approaching. "Oh, a Scotland Yarder. Rough looking sort."

"Lestrade is that."

The Inspector wasted little time. "Sorry to bother you, Doctor, and if it weren't important – "

"You wouldn't intrude, I'm sure. Inspect or Lestrade, allow me to introduce my friend, Dr. Lot Morrill."

Both men shook hands as Lestrade asked if I could come with him. "Official business. I have a four-wheeler waiting."

Morrill patted my shoulder. "Go on, John. They must need you."

"I'm sorry, Lot. Let me pay for the cab so you can use it."

"I appreciate that, but I'd rather walk. I'm just up the street at Charing Cross Hotel anyway and the sun feels good."

"Certainly. Dinner tonight?"

"Sure." To Lestrade, "A pleasure, Inspector."

"Same to you, sir. This way, Doctor."

I tipped the cabman for his time and followed Lestrade. Turning my head, I watched Morrill trudge towards his hotel while the hansom maintained a similar pace as it rambled down the Strand towards Fleet Street.

II. *The Stormy Petrel*

Lestrade brusquely ushered me into a Clarence cab where sat a tall, wiry, unpresupposing fellow dressed in a seersucker suit and Panama hat waiting for us. He appeared to be in his early thirties with hair and mustache blond enough to pass for white. Lestrade said, "Doctor Watson, allow me to introduce my friend, Walter Simonson."

Speaking with a slight Swedish accent, Simonson said, "I can't tell you how much I've looked forward to talking with you in person. I only wish Mr. Holmes could be here, too."

Try as I might I could not recall the stranger's name. "I'm sorry, but have we corresponded?"

"No, but I did correspond four times with Mr. Holmes using the name Fred Porlock."

That name I remembered. "The Birlstone murder! You tried to warn Holmes about it!"[3]

"I did before I tried to warn him off it. Your persistence nearly got me drawn and quartered, for all the good that would have done poor Birdy Edwards.[4] From what I hear, he was a bully trap after my own heart."

---

[3] See *The Valley of Fear*.

[4] Pinkerton agent who infiltrated and suppressed The Scrowrers, a fraternal organization that terrorized the Vermissa Valley in America while waging war against the railroads and iron and coal companies during the 1870s. Likely murdered by the Moriarities. See *The Valley of Fear*.

"Holmes intimated you were working closely with Professor Moriarty."

Lestrade winked at Simonson, who grinned as if sharing some private joke.

"What is it?" I asked.

"Actually I infiltrated Moriarty's organization in '86 for the British government under the aegis of Scotland Yard's Special Branch.[5] The Inspector serves as my liaison. There were times, however, when I felt justice might be better served informing Mr. Holmes rather than my superior about information I learned, but only if he had no idea what I was truly about. But now, Doctor, we need your help."

"My help? Why, certainly."

"Thank you. Before I explain, allow me to beg your patience for a few minutes."

We drove in silence until the cab stopped in front of a four-story house on Wigmore Street where Simonson rented a suite on the third floor. Lestrade forewarned me this was the scene of a crime with a body in the sitting room, but I saw no constables as we entered.

The dead man was sitting upright in a chair Simonson confirmed had been moved to face the suite's entrance. He was a swarthy man in his late fifties with the physique of a person at ease with harsh outdoor living, and even the repose of death could not belie that this had been

---

[5] The world's first Special Branch, it is responsible for matters of national security and intelligence. Originally called the Special Irish Branch, this unit of London's Metropolitan Police (a.k.a. Scotland Yard) was formed in 1883 in response to several dynamite bombings carried out by Irish republicans against the British Empire between 1881 and 1885.

someone best not trifled with. Beside the chair stood a table with a half-filled carafe of brandy and two glasses, one of which had been recently used. Nothing else in the suite appeared disturbed, although I noticed flecks of mud on the carpet around the chair.

As I examined the body Simonson explained, "We have no idea who he is. We found a garrote, a neddy, concealed knives, and a Colt revolver on him. Things being as they are we assumed he was an assassin working for the Professor."

"That certainly sounds sensible." At first glance the body had every appearance of someone who died somewhat peacefully while asleep. There were no signs of struggle or violence and every indication suggested the man had only been in the suite a few hours. "It appears as if he were partaking some of your brandy, Mr. Simonson."

"Oh, Walter, please." Simonson bent close to the carafe. "Judging by what's left, my guess is he had two full glasses."

Lestrade snorted in disgust. "That's a nerve. Enjoying a man's spirits while waiting to kill him."

Simonson shrugged. "Better than no one enjoying it at all."

I inspected the used glass. "Perhaps it made him drowsy." Lifted it to my nose. "Smells all right, I suppose." I sniffed again before asking Lestrade why there were no constables outside.

"Unadvisable under the circumstances, but these premises are being watched."

Simonson elaborated, "Expediently apprehending the Moriarity gang takes precedence over proper police protocol."

I said, "That sounds rather drastic, ignoring the fair-play of British law."

"It is and with cause. The collapse of the Professor's former empire is sending aftershocks through three continents. These past few days have been like going to war. In fact we are sworn to secrecy regarding this matter."

I set the glass back upon the table. "Is that why I was brought here? So you wouldn't have to call a coroner?"

"In part. Not all of the Professor's associates are willing ones, and among other means Moriarty used blackmail and extortion such as purchasing incriminating debts to manipulate people in high positions of corporate and political power. Now Moriarty intends to expose them and inflict widespread harm."

Hearing such a scheme sent a definite shudder through me. "The more I learn about this Professor, the more I understand why Holmes was willing to sacrifice himself to destroy such a man."

"It was Mr. Holmes who informed the government about this plot just before you two left for the Continent. Considerable resources are being dedicated to stymie it, but now my superior needs to see a file Mr. Holmes kept with his casebooks and indexes."

"Oh dear."

"What's wrong, Doctor?" asked Lestrade.

"Holmes kept all those in a large tin box he stored in his bedroom,[6] but it's not there now and I have no clue where he put it.

Simonson waved a hand. "That's all right. Mr. Mycroft has the clue."

"Pardon?"

"Mr. Holmes gave his brother a clue that was to be revealed to you if circumstances dictated."

"What if I don't understand it?"

"There's only one way to find out. The message from Mr. Sherlock Holmes is: 'Not papers. And then my fee.'"

To this day I am uncertain which I felt first: relief or annoyance. "Oh, for Heaven's sake."

Lestrade frowned. "That makes no sense at all."

"Actually it makes perfect sense. I've written an account of one of Holmes's investigations I titled 'A Case of Identity.' In that account I reference an earlier investigation I call 'A Scandal in Bohemia.'"

"The one about Irene Adler? Oh, I like that one! She was more than a match for Holmes."

"And he admired her for it. You might remember that Holmes requested a photograph of Miss Adler from the King as a memento."

"Oh, I see now! Holmes wrote where he hid this tin box on the back of that photograph!"

"No. Walter, I must return to Baker Street."

Simonson was ready. "Let's go. The four-wheeler is still waiting."

---

[6] See "The Adventure of the Musgrave Ritual."

17

"Just a moment. Once we're there, I must go inside alone. I have my reasons.

"Agreed. Inspector?"

Lestrade bobbed his head.

I thanked them and then said, "Before we leave, Walter, I need you to tell me everything you know about this body."

"I have. I give you my word."

"So you have no idea who put hemlock in your carafe?"

Lestrade took hold of the flask. "What's that?" He inhaled. "Everything smells all right."

"I suppose. Walter, prior to this morning, when were you here last?"

"Yesterday afternoon, and the brandy was fine then or I wouldn't be talking to you now. The body was here when I returned and I immediately contacted Lestrade."

The Inspector tapped the carafe. "How can you be sure there's hemlock in here without an analysis?"

"I can't. It could be something similar. Say curare. Except that has a bitter taste this man would have noticed if he drank even one glass. On the other hand hemlock contains coniine. Just 0.1 grams can be fatal and its effects would have been abetted by brandy's natural inebriant action and ability to depress the motor function of the cranio-spinal axis."

"Fair enough, then. It sounds like a quick and painless death."

"Relatively, yet unpleasant. He probably felt cold, but wouldn't know why, followed by numbness, starting with his extremities. Eventually he would not have been able to move and died alone trapped in that chair. Before paralysis set in, however, it looks like he walked around a bit attempting to warm up. That would explain these dried bits of mud about the floor."

"Actually," Simonson said, "that might have been me when I came back."

"Really? I thought I saw mud on his boots." I took another look and pointed towards the dead man's feet. "Yes. Look here. This mud is the same yellowish brown as what's scattered on the floor. If we can identify where it came from, it might help us identify him."

"Wait a moment please." Simonson scuttled to his bedroom and returned within moments carrying a pair of grubby boots and tweed pants. "I haven't cleaned these yet and you can see they're splattered with the same color mud."

"Where's it from?"

"A Derbyshire mine called Blue John Gap. It's been abandoned for years. Locals claim it's the lair of a beast or creature."

"I read about that in the *Daily Telegraph*! Fascinating story! Those folktales got stirred up again by a...uhm...Dr. Hardcastle. I recall he passed away from phthisis which he insisted was aggravated after hunting what he claimed was some primordial monster back in the mine."[7]

"You have a good memory. Hardcastle actually stumbled across an outpost for Moriarty's organization that was playing up the legend to

---

[7] See "The Terror of Blue John Gap."

scare people away from the mine, going so far as making it appear the thing was nicking sheep whenever there was a full moon."

Lestrade said, "Sounds like an excuse for free mutton to me."

"Waste not, want not. Moriarty's men arranged things to look like Hardcastle treed the monster in the mine only to have it double-back on him, then told him to get busy dying or they'd save him the effort."

Another shudder ran through me. "That's outrageous!"

"That's Moriarty's idea of poetic justice, but what comes around goes around. When news about the Professor's death and the search for his associates reached Blue John Gap, Moriarty's agents realized they had better leave the country if they were going to save their skins. Fleeing by road or countryside would be dicey, so they opted to commandeer a train that runs between Derbyshire and London. They would ride it into London where they could scatter into the East End and escape England by ship."

"A sound plan."

"Sound enough that when word of it managed to reach London late last night my superior had no choice but to order me to lead a posse there. We arrived as the gang was moving in to seize the train along a deep trench near the mine, and after a brief gun battle they fled back to Blue John Gap to make a last stand. We didn't disappoint them." Simonson held his muddy boots and pants a little higher. "That's where I picked this up."

"So this stranger had to have been there, too, except he had more sense than to return to the mine. He must have recognized you and found a way to London to confront you."

"Only to poison himself," said Lestrade. "News about your raid must have gotten back to London and another of Moriarty's gang poured hemlock or whatever in this carafe. How could they know about this fellow's intentions? I'd say you had two near-misses this day."

Simonson nodded, nonplussed. "I suppose you're right."

III. *Auld Lang Syne*

Lestrade's hypothesis generally satisfied me as well, so we left for Baker Street. I was grateful to Simonson and Lestrade for understanding that rummaging through Holmes's things in front of anyone struck me as too severe a violation of his privacy. As for Holmes's clue, in "A Case of Identity," I erroneously referenced "A Scandal in Bohemia" as "the case of the Irene Adler papers." Holmes had actually been commissioned to retrieve an indelicate photograph taken of the King of Bohemia with Miss Adler. Holmes never seemed to tire of chiding me about this slip, although it now occurred to me that there might have been a method behind this needling. The photograph of Miss Adler was a reward my friend had requested on the spur of the moment, whereas the fee paid by the King came in the form of a gold snuff-box with a large amethyst on its lid. I was convinced Holmes had somehow left instructions on how to locate his tin box in that snuff-box, but his clue did not seem to include any suggestions as to where he had hidden the gold box.

Since I had thoroughly arranged Holmes's papers and conscientiously put back his belongings I already knew the snuff-box wasn't anywhere obvious, like tucked in the tobacco he kept in his Persian slipper or stashed in the coal scuttle with his pipes and cigars. Doing my best to think like my friend, I suspected he would have selected somewhere sensible yet inconspicuous, so I tried exploring places like the pockets of his dressing-gowns (where a snuff box would hardly be out of place) and on the deal (where it might be lost in plain sight amongst the chemistry equipment) only to come up empty.

The longer I searched, the more frustrating it became.

People's lives depended on me and that weight was pressing upon me.

For a fleeting moment I pondered if Holmes had even left the snuff-box here. He could have left it in his brother's care without explaining why to Mycroft. Then realization inspired by simple common sense struck.

Holmes would have known the last place I would search was his desk, where, to any unobservant eye, the snuff box would be just one more outré item among many.

When I found nothing in the first drawer I opened a second.

"Eureka!"

There it was with the Irene Adler photograph. Holmes had left me a clue.

I opened the snuff box's lid and poked through the powdered tobacco. Feeling nothing, I poured out the tobacco, pried up the bottom, and there was a key! Judging by its appearance, most likely to a bank deposit box.

I bolted down the steps and began to shout for Mrs. Hudson to lock up for me, only to draw up short when I noticed some flecks of dried mud in the foyer.

"What's wrong, Doctor Watson?" Mrs. Hudson asked. "Are you all right?"

"May I ask when you last swept this floor?"

"Why, early this morning."

"And has there been anyone else in here since my American friend?"

"No, sir. Well, that one policeman, Mr. Lestrade, but he's here so often." Mrs. Hudson glanced down and scowled. "Oh, look at that mess on the mat. I'll shake it clean."

"You needn't bother." The events of the past few days came rushing down upon me and nothing seemed to matter any longer.

"Doctor? Are you feeling all right? You seem pale."

"I feel pale. I'm sorry I startled you, Mrs. Hudson. Would you please lock Mr. Holmes's rooms? I have an appointment."

I gave the key to Simonson and Lestrade, leaving it to their resources to divine the bank box it opened. They expected me to accompany them but I begged off under the pretense of needing to get back to putting Holmes's things in order. Once they were out of sight I flagged a passing hansom and requested to go to the Charing Cross

Hotel. Lost in my doldrums, I failed to recognize until later that the driver was the same bearded cabman from earlier.

Getting Morrill's room number from the front desk, I knocked on my friend's door and called his name.

"Come in, John. It's unlocked."

A wiser man might have been more cautious, but I entered and shut the door behind me. Daylight was fading outside. The room was growing dark in the gloaming, but I could plainly see Morrill in a high back upholstered chair turned towards the door holding a glass in one hand. His jacket was draped over the back of the chair and his tie and collar were loose.

"Afternoon," he said. "Or should I say good evening? Time does fly. I'd offer you a drink, but I'm afraid I just finished the last of it."

I rattled from revulsion and horror. I snatched the glass, but it was empty. "Hemlock?"

"Perceptive. Same old John. You know you gave me quite a turn when you paraphrased Plato this morning. Coincidences like that always pester me. I don't believe in them. I'd rather think everything happens for a reason."

"Well, this isn't going to happen! Not while I can stop it!"

"You know you can't. I'll be dead before you can scrounge anything to use for artificial ventilation, and we both know that's the only way to sustain life until the effects of coniine poisoning wear off. Besides, whatever you could find around here would probably be so inadequate you'd end up killing me anyway, and you don't need that on your conscience. So, please, grant me a final request. Sit down and talk with me one last time."

I was not prepared to give up so easily. "Lot!"

Neither was Morrill. "John."

Faced once more with nothing I could do, I brought a chair beside him and sat. "Why?"

"You'll find a letter on the bedside table that explains all this. Just in case." He pointed to an envelope with my name on it. "You can give it to your colleague. Now did I ever tell you about my family?"

"Only that your father died and your mother remarried."

"That's more than I tell most folks. In a nutshell my father was a farmer in the Delaware Valley. A good man. Honest. Strong. A Confederate captain named Harsh Washburne killed him near the end of the War. Harsh had taken a fancy to my mother and she returned the feelings. Only my mother and I knew about the murder and I never could get myself to hate her enough to take Harsh away from her. Don't ask me why. I can't claim to understand it myself."

"I'm so sorry, Lot. I had no idea."

"It's not really something you confide to someone else, except maybe a priest." Morrill stretched his fingers and legs. "I'm starting to get numb. Best hurry."

My frustration rekindled. "Lot, please! I can --"

"Do nothing, John! You'll do nothing!" Taking a breath to calm himself, Morrill went on. "I presume Inspector Lestrade of Scotland Yard took you to Simonson's flat?"

My expression served as my answer.

"I'd say it was a coincidence, but --"

"You don't believe in them."

Morrill's expression suggested he might have been having second thoughts about that. "There wouldn't have been an opportunity for any coincidences if I left England this morning. Who would have been the wiser? I could have gotten away after Simpson's, too, I suppose, but in my heart I knew I could never really escape this, so I paid my call on you." An expression far happier than I would have imagined possible for a dying man spread across Morrill's face. "It's really good to see you again."

"The dead stranger? Is that Washburne?"

"Oh, yes. Like I told you during lunch, my mother died suddenly two weeks ago. Myocardial infarction. Harsh never considered the consequences of that. I was finally free to avenge my father. His murder has been within a hand's reach of my thoughts for most of my life. I couldn't live with myself if I did nothing, but now that I've done it I still can't live with myself. I'm a doctor. 'Do no harm.'"

"I ... I don't know what to say."

"You don't have to say anything. That's the wonder of friendship at times like these." Morrill trembled, unable to stop. "I'd ask for a blanket, but it'd do no good."

"Lot, please forgive me, but with recent happenings I have to ask --"

"'Was I ever part of Moriarty's gang?' No. That was Harsh. He worked for Moriarty for years. That's why we moved to England."

26

"As a paid killer?"

Morrill nodded. Talking was obviously becoming more difficult. "And a good one. Give the man his due. Killing came second nature to him. But the War taught him how to lead men. Plan. Execute raids. I suppose he'd have turned that training to crime on his own. Like Frank and Jesse James." A violent shiver forced a momentary pause. "Moriarty paid well. Mother thought I should be grateful to them both. Father could never have paid for my medical education."

"You would have found a way."

"Thank you. That means a lot." Another violent shiver. "Harsh and my mother moved to Matlock. Last winter. So he could run things at Blue John Gap. Then she died. I couldn't get here for her funeral. Harsh thought it natural I'd want to visit her grave. That was only one reason I came."

"Washburne must have been trying to find a way to get out of the country with his men by the time you arrived."

"Yes. He'd decided to steal the train. I thought, 'If he's killed doing that, that's Providence. '"Murmur not at the ways of Providence.'"[8] I went along with him to the Gap this morning. We made plans to meet in Montenegro. I'd avenge my father there, but I told Harsh I'd get him back to America. Instead Harsh came back to the mine. He'd recognized Simonson. Wanted blood. So I helped him get to London. Helped him find Simonson's place. He never thought twice about my helping him. Then ... when his guard was finally down ... I poisoned him ... and

---

[8] Thomas Jefferson in a February 21, 1825 letter to Thomas Jefferson Smith.

watched him die." Morrill's eyes brightened as tears of bewilderment overwhelmed him. "I wish I could say I'm sorry. Why can't I say I'm sorry?"

I placed a hand upon his shoulder. "Because you're not a liar, and, where it really counts, you're still a good man."

Morrill said nothing. He did not move.

"Lot?"

There was no reaction, not even breathing.

"Lot!"

A tear rolled down his cheek of its own volition.

"Oh, Lot. Now you're gone, too."

For the second time in as many weeks a crushing wave of loneliness threatened to drown me.

IV. *An East Wind*

Night fell by the time I made my way to the lobby to notify the hotel that one of its guests had committed suicide. Identifying myself as the victim's friend as well as a doctor, I consented to watch the body until the police arrived as well as keep the matter confidential so as not to upset the other guests.

I have no idea how long it was before Lestrade arrived with a constable to relieve me. He extended condolences as I presented him with Morrill's written confession. "His parents are dead and he has no brothers or sisters. I believe he was alone in the world. Unless someone else steps forward, I'll attend to his funeral arrangements."

"Thank you, Doctor Watson. And thank you for earlier today."

"I only hope I was of some assistance."

"You were invaluable." Lestrade tapped the envelope. "Any questions I may have after reading this can wait until tomorrow."

"I appreciate that, Inspector."

Outside I found Simonson paying the cabman that had brought me to the hotel. As I approached I heard him instruct the driver, "Fair warning, make sure you deliver that message." Realizing I had joined them, Simonson said, "Hello. You've caught me in the act of commandeering your cab."

"I don't recall asking him to wait." I appraised the driver. "Weren't you outside Simpson's this afternoon?"

"That I was, sir."

Simonson leaned in to inform me, "His name is John Reeves. I've been assured by my superior that he is a trustworthy chap hired from time to time for elementary tasks, such as keeping an eye on certain people."

Reeves smiled a silly smirk.

"If you say so, Walter. Why didn't you come up with Lestrade?"

"I'm afraid there's no time. I'm on my way out of the country until all of the Moriarty gang is in a salt box. Orders from my superior. For my own good, he says. This isn't my style, but what choice do I have? *Mea gloria fides*."[9]

"I understand. Will you be away long?"

"I hope not, but who can ever say how long a war will go on?" Simonson shrugged. "I am sorry about your friend."

"Yes. I've been hearing that a lot lately."

"I'm afraid life is like that sometimes."

"You think I would have learned that in the Army. By the way, Lestrade seemed to suggest you were able to use that key. Hopefully that will speed the war along."

"Hopefully."

"I'd be honored if you visit me when you get back."

Simonson brightened. "I'll do that. And I'd be honored if we could share this cab."

"I'd like nothing better."

Reeves asked, "Taking you back to Baker Street then, sir?"

I almost said yes but realized there was nothing more I really needed to do there. "No. No, take me to Paddington." I gave him my address. It was finally time to go home.

"As you say." I joined Simonson in the hansom as the cabman snapped his reigns and told his horse, "Off with you, Caprice."

* * * *

---

[9] "Fidelity is my glory"

My dear Watson, I leave this letter with my brother Mycroft in case events arise that prevent me from seeing you again. By the time you read this Mycroft should have informed you how I was able to avoid escorting Professor Moriarty into the abyss at the bottom of the Reichenbach Falls. It was a near thing, I promise you, but the lucky opportunity of my "death" proved of invaluable assistance in avoiding the almost certain retribution of Moriarty's most dangerous lieutenants, and it should prove just as invaluable in helping to bring all the Professor's agents to justice.

Mycroft has been my only confidant. I can only hope that you will understand what I am doing is with the best of intentions. To include anyone else—even you—would only bring danger to you while increasing the risk of my continued survival. I would not even risk entrusting Mycroft with this letter if recent events had not prevented me from immediately leaving England. That said, I cannot allow you to continue living in ignorance of the trivial part I played in the circumstances leading up to the death of your friend Lot Morrill by his own hand.

If you are angry with me, perhaps you will find some solace in the scolding Mycroft afforded me when he was asked to meet a cab driver named John Reeves in the Stranger's Room at the Diogenes Club only to discover it was his younger brother. "What in Heaven's name are you thinking? You're known here!" he told me in the closest thing to a holler I have ever heard from him.

"But Sherlock Holmes isn't here. I'm a cabbie baring a vital missive." I explained how Reeves had been working along the Strand when you chanced to waive me over. You have complimented me more than once in your accounts of our adventures by confessing that I have succeeded in hiding behind a disguise even from you, and I prayed such would be the case at that moment for both our sakes. It did, but I thanked the heavens when Lestrade interrupted and you departed with him. When I told this to Mycroft, he attempted to hide his concern that I might have followed after you and Lestrade, but I assured him that had been unnecessary. "I knew their destination as well as you do, so I took the precaution of following Dr. Morrill. His visit to Watson could have been a coincidence, but I felt it wise to verify."

"And did Morrill return to his hotel?"

"Without detour, but for two shillings another cabbie is doing Reeves the favor of watching the Charing Cross Hotel in case Morrill leaves. An ounce of prevention..."

Mycroft, as you are aware, possesses a greater faculty for observation and deduction in comparison to my own, and, at times, I am afraid the younger sibling in me delights in taking advantage of this to try his patience. Such was the case that day, but at last he had had enough of it.

"All right, I have no more energy to bandy words. Blast it, you're supposed to be on your way!"

"And abandon a colleague in peril?"

"Oh, Sherlock, if that's your important message I promise you Dr. Watson is not in peril. I told you I shall see to that, so you surely don't need to hang about playing guardian angel."

"Actually I've been playing guardian angel for your right-hand man, Walter Simonson, although he always communicated to me under the *nom de plume* – '"

"Hush! Even here the walls may have ears!"

I was unaccustomed to my brother showing concern for an underling, but in all candor I had to tell him, "Surely you can see that the time has passed for worrying about that."

I would have remained in England if I had not been certain that Mycroft could keep his promise regarding your safety, so I pray it causes you no pain when I confess that the reason for my delay was to return this favor by safeguarding the man who had written to me as Fred Porlock. However, once the inexplicable and sometimes cruel hand of Fate attended to the matter for me through the actions of your friend Morrill, I made my departure as soon as I was assured that Simonson was himself safely away from England.

So now you know that, while I played no part in the deaths of Harsh Washburne or Lot Morrill, I was in the orbit of these events as they played out. As tragic as they were, I was nevertheless grateful for the opportunity they presented to see you once more, even though I could not personally offer my sincere condolences to you at the time. Please believe I do so now.

As always, I remain very sincerely yours,

Sherlock Holmes

THE SECOND ADVENTURE:
THE CASE FOR WHICH THE WORLD
IS NOT YET PREPARED

From the Unpublished Personal Reminiscences of John H. Watson, M.D.

I. *Mr. Sherlock Holmes*

I HAVE on an occasion referred to my friend Mr. Sherlock Holmes as an automaton,[10] an observation inspired as much by his curious faculties as his almost habitual callousness. His numerous accomplishments in the field of detection stand as testament to his mental talents and on numerous occasions his iron constitution proved the equal to his brain power, but even the most inhuman, two-legged calculating machine is made of clay and all mortals have limits. So, while the weakness of failure much less emotion frequently seemed impossible in Holmes, there were rare instances that revealed him to be as human as any man.

One of those instances occurred after The Great War, which I had served primarily in London on the staff of Queen Alexandra's Military Hospital, although occasionally my duties carried me elsewhere including Malta. Holmes and I kept in touch through correspondence during those years, but we had not seen one another since immediately before my joining the Royal Army Medical Corps,[11] so I was delighted but surprised when he called at my rooms on Queen Anne Street on a warm September afternoon in 1920.

---

[10] See *The Sign of Four.*
[11] See "His Last Bow."

"I have just come from visiting Brother Mycroft at the Diogenes Club. It has put me in a melancholy mood, which, as you know, is sure to turn my brain upon itself. Activity remains the least expedient but preferable antidote. Being a retired detective, my only recourse is recollection, so I believe the time has come to make a serious effort at that textbook on the art of detection I've been putting off."

"That is a marvelous idea! Such a book is long overdue! Can I be of any assistance? I'd be honored to put down any of your undocumented investigations, like you suggested I do with the Cornish horror."[12]

"You might be of invaluable assistance regarding one case, some details of which require some clearing up. I hesitate to ask, however, as it requires you breaking a confidence."

"What confidence is that?"

"Do you recall my once making mention of the *Matilda Briggs*?"[13]

"The ship that was somehow associated with the giant rat of Sumatra."

"A story for which the world was not prepared as the repercussions from its revelation would have been catastrophic. Now with the Treaty of Sèvers[14] I have been wondering if the need for such precaution is past. Perhaps it never shall. Perhaps it never mattered. It seems as if man is destined to trod ground that has been cursed since Adam on a pilgrimage through the valley of violence in the hopes of reaching the

---

[12] See "The Adventure of the Devil's Foot."
[13] See "The Adventure of the Sussex Vampire."
[14] The short-lived Treaty of Sèvers was signed on August 10, 1920 and all but dissolved what remained of the Ottoman Empire by carving its lands into European spheres of influence.

kingdom of wisdom. Before the war I believed we would be a stronger and better race after weathering that storm,[15] and we are in some ways, but our destiny hasn't changed. It never does. There shall come more bitter winds until God's own will be done, and until then even the best efforts of the best mortal can only postpone the inevitable. So, Watson, I suggest you and I decide what we should loose upon our troubled world after exchanging some information. I shall confide all I know about the giant rat after confide what part you and our old comrade Lestrade played in the matter of Ivanhoe ffriend."

This was a name I had not heard in many years. "You ask no easy thing."

"So I supposed. Please believe that revealing what I know places me in the same dilemma. Would it make it easier if I admitted that I am only aware that you were acquainted with Mr. ffriend because of Mycroft?"

"Not especially. When did he divulge this to you?"

"After the capture of Colonel Sebastian Moran. Mycroft was clarifying a few points regarding his own part in the arrest when he mentioned ffriend and let slip he was indebted to you and Lestrade but refused to explain why."

"'Let slip?' Your brother?"

"Perhaps some purpose did cross his mind 'twixt cup and lip."

"Perhaps."

If anyone except Sherlock Holmes had requested such a favor I would have never even considered it, but eventually I excused myself

---

[15] See "His Last Bow."

37

and retrieved some pages from my private papers. "I recorded the events while the facts were still fresh. Force of habit. I'm afraid my notes are rather rough. I never had cause to go back over them."

Holmes thanked me and spent the next few minutes reading as I ran alongside my words and replayed the events in my mind.

II. The Adventure of the Wrong Gentleman

Inspector Lestrade of Scotland Yard had not had called for several months when he visited on a cool and windy night in June of 1893. Two years had passed since the death of Sherlock Holmes and in the interim I had moved my practice to Kensington. Like so many evenings of late I had fallen asleep reading rather than carry myself to bed,[16] so I was more or less presentable when Lestrade arrived at half past twelve to request my aid in an urgent matter.

Our destination was The Photogravure, a private museum dedicated to photographs and modern paintings, housed in a brick three-story villa in Belsize Park. "A lot of West Enders like this new art," Lestrade commented as he unlocked the museum. "Not my taste, I'm afraid. This place belongs to The Honorable Damon Nostrand, a member of what remains of the Moriarty gang. Nostrand's father may be a peer but the son is a genuine toff and a regular nimmer. Buys, sells, and smuggles, all from here. Stolen art is his specialty. Not that we can prove it, so the CID has been sending rotating teams of jacks posing as patrons to drop

---

[16] Watson offers no explanation why he has been doing this, but it is likely that his wife Mary was suffering from the tuberculosis she would succumb to in just a few months.

by and look about to see what they could see. When tonight's pair didn't check in as scheduled we sent a bobby to pop his head in. He found the place closed before hours and all of Nostrand's men gone."

"Any trace of your detectives?"

"None, Doctor. We've searched this building from shingles to cellar three times and haven't found a hint of what happened. We already suspected Nostrand had lit out of the country a few days ago. We don't know why, but if he did then it makes no sense for his men to abandon their base unless they were following orders."

"Or they had no choice."

"Either way my men's lives may be at stake. If they weren't, I would have never disturbed you so late. Could you look around and see if we missed anything?"

"Me?"

"You know Mr. Holmes's methods. He said so himself more than once."

"Well, I'll try, but Holmes trained himself for this. Such matters were his specialty. He saw things I couldn't and knew things I don't." I started off by examining the first floor, during which I inquired where Nostrand might have gone.

"Scuttlebutt has it he's heading to India or Nepal. No notion why. At least not as yet."

I moved to the second floor while Lestrade remained below on the chance fresh word arrived about the missing detectives. While I found nothing beneficial, there was something about the museum bothered me.

Something was out of place, although I had no idea what, but ambiguous feelings proved useful to Holmes in more than one of his investigations, so I kept a sharp watch out for any indication of what might be abrasing my intuition.

Nostrand's office was the last room I searched. It struck me as being smaller than I expected, but as I looked around a growing sense of nostalgia enveloped me. At first I suspected Nostrand's eclectic decorations were inspiring my recollections of the jumbled Baker Street rooms I had shared with Holmes, then I realized my wistfulness was being ignited by the sweet fragrance of a tobacco that was softening by the instant. The next moment I spotted a crumpled piece of paper in a corner behind Nostrand's desk, which turned out to be a ship's manifest. I started to call to Lestrade, then decided the wiser course was to rush downstairs to inform the Inspector that I had found something.

"What is it?" he asked.

"No time to waste! Follow me!"

I dashed to the cab that had brought us to the museum while Lestrade locked the building. Before climbing in I loudly told the driver to turn towards the docks when he reached the end of the street. Once on our way, Lestrade asked, "What's so important at the docks?"

"Nothing. We're not going there."

"But – "

"Indulge me a moment, please, Inspector." I waited until the cab turned before instructing the driver to pull up and park under some trees, then I showed Lestrade the manifest and explained how I had discovered it.

"'Morrison, Morrison, and Dodd.' And Damon Nostrand is aboard! I can't believe we missed this."

"I don't believe you did."

"We must have."

"Not if someone dropped it there after your last search. Someone who needed to lure us away from the museum."

"Who? Nostrand?"

"I can't say. Does he smoke kreteks?"

"What's that?"

"A fairly new cigarette from Central Java. Rather uncommon in England, but Holmes studied it to update his monograph on tobacco. It blends cloves and other ingredients with tobacco to create a distinctive sweet smell that doesn't linger long. I smelled hints of it in Nostrand's office."

"Sounds a bit refined for Nostrand's indulgences. So someone must be hiding in the museum, but we searched everywhere."

"Not the darkroom, I'd wager."

"What do you mean? We found no darkroom,"

"Neither did I, but what sort of photograph museum would be without a darkroom?"

Lestrade grimaced at this oversight, then snapped his fingers. "As a smuggler, it'd make sense for Nostrand to have a priest hole. Making it a darkroom kills two birds with one stone."

I didn't disagree.

"Whoever is hiding in there probably knows what happened to my missing men."

"Let's hope, but remember Holmes's precaution about theorizing before possessing all the facts."

"I remember all of Mr. Holmes's advice, but this is a leap to my liking. In any case, all we have to do is wait for our kretek smoker to show himself to find out."

We didn't wait long.

After approximately fifteen minutes a larger than average man came out of the museum. We were too far away to perceive him clearly, but I could tell he was dressed as a gentleman. We watched him shut the door, tack something to it, and walk away.

"That's it, then!" Lestrade ordered the driver to remain parked under the trees as he and I returned to the museum. Our quarry was a brisk walker and around a street corner by the time we reached The Photogravure, where Lestrade motioned me to look at what was tacked to the door while he continued the chase. I found a folded piece of note paper, opened it, and saw it was blank, but in the act I pushed the door ajar. Curious why the stranger left the museum unlocked I went inside, and it occurred to me he might have caught on to my gambit when I spotted a dim light emanating from Nostrand's office. Following the beacon I found the concealed door to the museum's darkroom standing open. A candle glimmered inside the darkroom, which was empty except for a stone statue carved in what I guessed was an Indonesian style and about the size of a young child. Before I could examine it, Lestrade shouted for me and followed my voice to the darkroom. "Come with me, Doctor! I found them!"

"You nabbed him?"

"No, but I found Ernest and Pratt! They were dropped in a doorway!"

"Your detectives? Are they all right?"

"They're unconscious, but just look knocked about a bit."

"I'll see. Better take this along, just to be safe." I lifted the statue with a grunt and more of an effort than I anticipated.

"What is that ruddy thing?"

I gave the statue a second look and made my best guess. "A rat, I think. Not my taste, I'm afraid."

Lestrade's diagnosis of the condition of his comrades was correct. Their injuries amounted to little more than the cuts and lacerations typical to a street brawl. As for how they arrived in the doorway, the last thing either could recall was overhearing a row in the museum's office and when they intervened they found themselves overpowered by a brutally large man. Lestrade set the detectives to writing this down to include in his official report mere moments before a government messenger arrived with instructions for us from Mr. Mycroft Holmes.

My first encounter with my late friend's older brother took place in the Stranger's Room of the Diogenes Club[17], the only chamber inside that oddest of London's clubs where anyone is permitted to speak, and it

---

[17] See "The Adventure of the Greek Interpreter."

was there Lestrade and I were to deliver the statue without delay. Mycroft was staring out the small chamber's bow-window overlooking Pall Mall when we entered. The elder Holmes seemed to have changed very little, still tall and portly, his deep-set grey eyes as alert as I remembered under his masterful brow, but there was none of the subtle play of expression in his face and his characteristically firm lips were tense.

"Good morning, Doctor Watson. Inspector Lestrade." Mycroft shook our hands warmly before gratefully patting the head of the statue, which I had placed on a table. "Thank you for recovering this. You may yet rescue our country and many others from the direst circumstances. To that end, I must beg a favor of you and ask you to call upon an acquaintance of mine named Ivanhoe ffriend."

"Who would that be, sir?" asked Lestrade, sounding understandably confused.

"The owner of this statue. If I am correct he should be able to answer any questions you still have regarding the events of last night." Mycroft presented Lestrade with an official envelope. "His address is in here on a letter that I pray you read before giving to him. Under no circumstances are you ever to discuss its contents with anyone except ffriend and myself, and anything he confides to you is to be brought back to me under the same confidence. I would also appreciate it, Doctor Watson, if you would apprise me regarding the condition of his health. I give you my word that there is a good reason for such secrecy, which shall be made clear when next we meet."

The address was in Chelsea. Lestrade and I could have walked there in a reasonable time but we hired a cab so we could read Mycroft's letter in privacy. Much of it made little sense, but to say one part of the letter upset Lestrade would be an understatement.

ffriend's house and the man himself were remarkable in different ways. Every available space of the wondrous abode was shelved with a library of books in a dozen different languages or decorated with at least one artifact or piece of artwork from what seemed like every tribe and culture on the globe, whereas the homeowner, with the exception of being somewhat bigger than what is common, was rather plain. His speech and dress were those of an educated American gentleman. He was neither ugly nor handsome. His age could have been late thirties or early fifties, and he appeared to be impassive except for his bruised knuckles and the cut on his right ear. His left arm also appeared to be mildly sprained, judging by the manner in which he held it while opening the envelope and removing Mycroft's letter. After reading it ffriend said, "This appears to be in order. Understand that up until now your government asked me to keep information regarding the statue confidential."

"Well, like the letter says, Doctor Watson and I are here on an unofficial visit."

"That sounds like an extension of immunity."

"It is. Nothing said here will appear in any official police report, but Mr. Holmes feels it's essential we tie up some loose ends regarding our recovery of your statue."

I added, "He is also concerned about you."

"I suppose that's compassionate, but I've always had trouble comprehending such things." ffriend paused to ruminate, during which time his expression barely changed. "All right. Sit down if you wish. Would you like some brandy? Or something else?" We declined. "Then, dispensing with pretense, I was at Damon Nostrand's museum last night. I was invited to bring the statue there by three of his men who arrived here around nine."

"'Invited'?"

"That was their word, Inspector, but one man fiddled with a straight razor, the second brandished a loaded bludgeon, while the third let his bulk do his intimidating. I saw no harm going with them so long as the statue remained in my possession."

"Was Nostrand there?"

"No, but a man claiming to be Damon's assistant was there in his absence. Mr. St. Clair was his name. As soon as we arrived I was escorted into Damon's office. The only people in the gallery were two Scotland Yarders in plain clothes, but I kept my face turned so they couldn't see it. It's a habit of mine. St. Clair thanked me for coming and our conversation proceeded as follows. You can write this down for Mr. Holmes, Doctor. I have a reliable memory and this will be accurate word for word. St. Clair appraised the statue before telling me, 'Like most tribal art, it's not a very pretty thing.'

"'There's more to art than beauty.'

"'Her Majesty's Government told you about its history?'

"'I was informed it belongs to Teuku Umar, leader of a guerilla campaign against the Dutch in the Sumatran sultanate of Aceh.'

"'And that it was stolen from Umar?'

"'In 1883 by a Dutch officer.'

"'Such a silly thing to do in a fit of pique. The officer was frustrated in his efforts to convince Umar to help the Dutch rescue the British ship *Nisero*, which had been captured in a part of southern Sumatra outside Dutch control. Umar had the last laugh, I suppose, when the Dutch rescue raid failed. Now all these years later the Dutch want the ugly thing returned to Umar as a gesture of reconciliation. The ebb and flow of politics, eh? But I guess it is a favorite of his. By the way, how did you come by the statue?'

"I have no intention of telling you that, Mr. St. Clair.'

"'Oh? Well, it doesn't matter, so long as we have it.'

"'And I have no intention of selling it to you.'

"'We don't intend to buy it.'

"'That's irrelevant. The statue belongs to me until the British government takes possession and returns it to Umar. I've given them my oath.'

"'And you have my oath that this statue will never be returned to Teuku Umar. We are employed by a powerful party that insists upon that. Because of your neutral reputation Mr. Nostrand believed that stealing the statue would be unnecessary once this was explained to you. He respects you as a client and a collector and wishes no harm come to you, but my instructions are quite clear regarding what to do failing your cooperation.'

"We had reached an impasse, so Mr. St. Clair and the three men attempted to take the statue. They failed."

"'Failed'?" I asked.

"Immunity or not, all I'll say is they're in no position to attempt anything like that again. There was some commotion and those two policemen tried to step in, but the bulky man overpowered them before I could reach him."

"Mr. ffriend," Lestrade started to ask, "are you trying to say …?"

"I'm not trying to say anything. You wanted me to explain about the statue and I have. If you doubt me I am sure the doctor can validate I am suffering from a few minor injuries consistent with close combat."

"I can see that for myself."

"Before I could attend to Damon's underlings, you and other policemen arrived and started searching the museum. I had no choice but to wait with the lot and the statue in the darkroom. After you left and I put St. Clair and his crew in their proper place, I carried your two men around the corner where you eventually found them, then returned for the statue. That's when you two arrived. I'm familiar with the doctor's stories as well as many of the late Mr. Sherlock Holmes's monographs, and I noticed the ship's manifest on Nostrand's desk earlier, so I tossed the manifest in the corner and smoked one of my kreteks to get you out of the museum long enough to get away."

"After all that, why did you leave the statue?"

"It was the simplest course of action. The doctor's reputation as a loyal servant of the Queen is common knowledge, and I was confident Mr. Holmes would contact you, Inspector, when word about it reached him."

This is the report we returned to Mycroft Holmes, who seemed to be only a little less amazed by it as Lestrade and I. We asked if he believed it and he told us, "I have no reason not to."

"Then what should we do, sir? Even if it was self-defense, ffriend all but admitted to killing four men."

"Four Moriarity men," I pointed out.

Mycroft said, "There's more to the matter, though. The Moriarities are defying the dismantling of the Professor's organization by wreaking as much havoc as possible."

"And preventing the statue's return to Umar furthers that cause?"

"Quite possibly, but the scheme goes much deeper. As we speak Damon Nostrand is on his way to Sumatra. He aims to tell its ruler Sultan Alauddin Mahmud Da'ud Syah II about our plan to return the statue. Nostrand is also going to show the Sultan stolen official Dutch articles detailing how to end the war in Aceh." Mycroft paused. "These articles minimize the Sultan's importance and recommend the Dutch government concentrate its recruiting efforts with the *Ulee Balang*, Sumatra's hereditary chiefs and nobles, rather than the *ulema*, Sumatra's religious leaders, while at least one article recommends be assassinated."

"My word."

Lestrade did not seem as horrified as he said, "Bad as that may be, I don't see the reason for all this worry and secrecy. What does any of it have to do with England, sir?"

"Moriarty's organization is well aware that the world sits upon a precarious point in its history. Events in one part of the globe can cause horrible conflicts to arise in another. The war in Aceh started in 1873 because of discussions in Singapore about a possible treaty between Aceh and the United States. The Dutch claim this violated an 1871 treaty they made with Great Britain, and since then they have frequently requested our aid in the war. Meanwhile the Sultan of Sumatra has solicited aid from nations like Italy, France, and Turkey. So far our nations have rejected these pleas, but doing so is becoming increasingly difficult. If it ever becomes impossible, this awful, little war on an Indonesian island could spark a multi-national conflict. That is why Nostrand is going to Sumatra and why we are currently doing our best to intercept him."

III. *The Adventure of the* Matilda Briggs

There my account ends.

Holmes asked, "Is there more you should add to your notes?"

"I've shared all I know."

Holmes returned the pages then leaned back, stretched out his long legs, and pressed the fingertips of both hands together. "Thank you, Watson."

"I presume ffriend's statue is the giant rat of Sumatra."

"It is." A smile quivered over Holmes's lip. "You and Lestrade are to be commended. I should never have suspected anything clandestine between you two and Mycroft, even though I have occasionally wondered why my brother brought Lestrade in tow to Baker Street when the disappearance of the Bruce-Partington Plans similarly threatened international peace only three years later.[18] A murder like Cadogan West's necessitated Scotland Yard be brought in, but after winning Mycroft's trust with ffriend I believe Lestrade would have been the professional he called in regardless. And you, Watson?"

"I?"

"How you let me prattle on that fog-shrouded day, bragging up Mycroft's role with the government. Truly, I was the one in a fog."

"I am sorry, old man, but what else could I do? I had my duty. Besides I felt you were proud to speak of your brother and his accomplishments."

"I'd never expect anything less from you, and, yes, while Germany had its Holstein,[19] I think history will show even he wasn't Mycroft's equal." A mischievous twinkle kindled in his eyes. "Time now to uphold my end of our bargain. Perhaps I should begin by telling you that Nostrand never talked to the Sultan."

"I guessed that when Mycroft's fears for Sumatra never materialized." Without warning I suddenly remembered my first

---

[18] See "The Adventure of the Bruce-Partington Plans."

[19] Friedrich August Karl Ferdinand Julius von Holstein (1837 – 1909). Civil servant in the German Foreign Office from 1876 to 1909. Holstein appears to have been an *éminence grise* and the most influential foreign policymaker under Kaiser Wilhelm II after possibly playing a part in the dismissal of Chancellor Otto von Bismarck in 1890.

conversation with Sherlock Holmes after his resurrection. "You told me once you remained in contact with Mycroft after Reichenbach, two years of which were spent traveling in Tibet."

"I've said it before, Watson. I'll never get your limits. Age seems only to sharpen your faculties while it incessantly dulls mine. You are correct, although my travels had carried me to neighboring Nepal by the time an agent from Mycroft's office requested my aid in finding Nostrand, who narrowly escaped being netted in Kathmandu. With the hounds at his heels it seemed most likely Nostrand would head for Patna, the nearest city where a vessel to Sumatra could be chartered from Morrison, Morrison, and Dodd, the shipping firm he did business with in London. We traveled fast but missed our quarry by two hours. The shipping clerk wired his office in Kolkata with instructions to seize Nostrand and his charter, the *Matilda Briggs*, when it arrived. The clerk also placed their fastest steamship at our disposal."

"What did you do with Nostrand after you reached Kolkata?"

"I've never been to Kolkata and we never did lay hands on Nostrand."

That seemed impossible. "You must have. If not, then what happened next?"

"While Kolkata lies upon the most expedient course from Patna to the Bay of Bengal and then Sumatra, I gave Nostrand more credit than to follow so obvious a path. By that time the *Matilda Briggs* would have already passed Farakka, south of which the Ganges splits into the Padma tributary. Taking this tributary is nearly twice the distance and far more perilous, but there are no cities along the way and the tributary offers several mouths into which to enter the Bay. As our presence in Kolkata would make no difference in Nostrand's capture if he went there, I had our steamship follow the Padma tributary." Here Holmes's face took on a faraway expression. "You and your Army revolver were never missed more than that day. Nostrand began firing at our steamship as soon as the *Matilda Briggs* came into sight. Her crew was unarmed and we hadn't thought to bring along firearms, but fortunately our quarry was no Colonel Moran when it came to marksmanship. Mycroft's agent would have jumped aboard with a kukri machete once we drew near enough, but her captain took matters into his own hands and ordered his crew to abandon ship and swim for shore, leaving the *Matilda Briggs* to the mercy of the current. A moment later we rounded a bend and a waterfall came into view."

"Good Lord."

"It was rather drastic, but our captain was not so willing to see the *Matilda Briggs* sacrificed. He ordered his crew to snare it with grappling hooks while there was a chance to haul the ship to safety. This they did even as Nostrand continued firing. When his supply of ammunition was depleted and it became clear the *Matilda Briggs* would be rescued, Nostrand flung himself into the water rather than face the penalty for failing the Professor's executors."

Holmes said nothing more. Considering his experience at the Reichenbach Falls it was natural the memory of Nostrand's suicide haunted him, but eventually he inhaled deeply, sat bolt straight, and pronounced, "And there you have it."

IV. *The Mark of a Man*

"You can't be finished," I protested. "Were the Dutch articles recovered? Was the statue returned to its rightful owner?"

"Ah! I warned you of my dimming faculties. My only defense is that lapses are to be expected whenever a man strays from his field of expertise. You are the gifted teller of tales while I shall never be more than a tyro. Mycroft's agent destroyed the damning articles as per his instructions and Umar's statue was returned. Have I forgotten anything more?"

"I don't think so, except perhaps the real reason for your visit today."

Holmes barely blinked. "What do you mean?"

"There's more going on here then you're letting on."

"How could you know that, Doctor?"

"I know you, Holmes. Everything about the business of the giant rat has more to do with Mycroft's field of national policy then the art of detection, so why would you even consider including it in your book? There are also your comments regarding man's destiny and God's will. Can you blame me for suspecting that your visit to The Diogenes Club's columbarium set you pondering about mortality as much as it did morality? After all, the latter isn't possible without the former, and man's destiny since Adam has also been to return to the ground, which means even the best of men—including Mycroft—are mortal."

There was no reaction from Holmes until he finally permitted his shoulders to sag. "Mycroft was good for me, as you are. I like to think I am a wise man, and a mark of a wise man is that he always keeps better persons than himself within his circle of acquaintances." He paused. "Think back on the glimpse Lestrade and you received that day of Mycroft's role in the government. A war was delayed. Unlike the Inspector, you surely came away appreciating the gravity of my brother's duties."

"I did, but I don't believe you're being fair to Lestrade."

Holmes tilted his head as he reconsidered. "Perhaps I am doing Lestrade some injustice. I have rarely met a more courageous or tenacious man, or one so proficient within his element yet so lacking whenever the problem called for more than the workmanlike skills of the professionals. So what effect did Mycroft's concerns regarding the delicate balance of world events have upon Lestrade? Certainly you must have discussed it afterwards."

"No. We might have if not for ffriend."

"So there is more than you wrote in your proceedings?"

"Only that ffriend perplexed me. I don't think it merits inclusion, but I did mention it to Lestrade."

"How did ffriend perplex you?"

"He reminded me of a wasp."

Holmes perked up. "An unusual statement."

"Lestrade commented how ffriend struck him as cold, but I suspected it was more than that. I still do. Once when I was a boy I was pulling weeds for my mother when I poked my face under a bench where some wasps had built their nest. The next thing I knew a swarm was buzzing all around me. I was at their mercy but not even one stung me. I had meant no harm and I think the wasps knew that because they let me be."

"Bees are more my flavor, but, based upon my limited experiences with the genus *Vespula*, I cannot deny there is some evidence to support your theory."

"Lestrade said I was lucky."

"There is some evidence that supports his theory as well."

"ffriend behaved like that swarm. Nostrand's men made threats but until they were actually going to harm him ffriend let them be, in which case they shared some of the blame for their fate."

"An intriguing hypothesis. What was Lestrade's opinion?"

"He permitted that men like Moriarty and St. Clair were evil, and it was his experience that history deals with evil men in one of two ways. In the first a villain confronts someone on the side of justice who refuses to acquiesce until the evil man is defeated or both men are dead."

Holmes slowly nodded.

"In the second the villain comes across what Lestrade called the wrong man. 'No matter how smart or big or cruel you are, there's someone who's smarter, bigger, or crueler.' That's what Lestrade believed happened to St. Clair and his men. They crossed paths with the wrong gentleman."

Holmes sat quietly, weighing my words, then stood, lit a cigarette, and paced. "It seems the journey from my brother's urn has only brought me round again to that perennial problem that perpetually confounds all human reason. I asked you once what object is served by this circle of misery, violence, and fear."[20]

"Which is what we've been discussing: God's will and mankind's destiny. 'What is the object?' In other words, 'What is our purpose?' When a man has a purpose and makes a difference in the world, isn't that proof of a greater underlying purpose at work? How can the universe be ruled by chance when our efforts—rather they are for good or ill—have some sort of outcome? There is misery, violence, and fear, but even the thorniest path has flowers, and as you observed once to a decent man at his nadir, we have much to hope from the flowers."[21]

Holmes halted and drew long on his cigarette. "A reasonable observation but one predicated upon hope. You have no more proof than the skeptic, who can just as reasonably declare there is no meaning to be gleaned from the historical process."

"I cannot deny that, nor shall I deny there are times when I 'faintly trust the larger hope.'[22] That said, no skeptic can refute my belief that

---

[20] See "The Adventure of the Cardboard Box."
[21] See "The Adventure of the Naval Treaty."
[22] From Alfred, Lord Tennyson's poem "In Memoriam A.H.H. CANTO 55" (1850):

I stretch lame hands of faith and grope
And gather dust and chaff, and call

our living and dying has a purpose, and it is that purpose that gives us what a wiser person than I calls 'point and direction to the life of man.'[23] A moment ago you said Mycroft delayed a war, but I say you're wrong."

"Surely not. There was no war."

"Precisely. He prevented a war that day, as I am sure he prevented a war a good many days he served the government, so it can't be a coincidence the Great War started soon after Mycroft's death. Who else was there to fill his role? If you're right then man's morality made the War inevitable, but I suspect Mycroft believed man's destiny is never unavoidable. How else could he dedicate his life to giving mankind time to choose a different path? That was his purpose. His mark, if you will."

"A mark very few men will ever know about and in the end proved futile."

"What does that matter? Not everyone can be a police inspector or an army doctor or the first consulting detective, and even the best of men have their limits, but within our limits lies so much potential. That is not hope. That is a fact. All God has ever asked of mankind is that it do what is best for itself and that has always been enough for me. I pray it may be enough for you, Holmes."

Holmes finished his cigarette and sat down. He leaned back in the chair and closed his eyes. "Perhaps it is, so long as there are men like

---

To what I feel is Lord of all,
And faintly trust the larger hope.

[23] As of this writing I have been unable to locate the source of this quote.

Mycroft and you to go with the ffriends and St. Clairs. No, Watson, I'll never get your limits. I pray I never shall."

THE THIRD ADVENTURE:
THE CASE OF THE UNPARALLELD ADVENTURES

Excerpt from Mycroft Holmes's Notebook

October 23, 1893 – Minutes of Meeting with Gladstone[24]

I.   Postmortem of defeat of Second Home Rule Bill.[25]

II.   IMRO, Thessaloniki.[26]

III.   Communications from Walter Simonson.
    A. Letter delivered by G. Lestrade being deciphered. Coded dispatch delivered via Queen's Messenger confirms Khalifa agrees to speak with our agents.
    B. Review of events preceding dispatch.
       1. W.S. and *zenko* tracked the Moriaritiess' 2nd Lieut. from Amol and Mecca to the Sudan.
       2. W.S. and *zenko* arrived in Khartoum last week after Maghrib prayer.
    C. P.M. concerned about Khalifa's insistence on meeting agents in Khartoum, not new capital Omdurman.
       1. P.M: "Khartoum must never become an embarrassment again!"
       2. P.M.: "Could use your brother's help. His death must not be in vein."
       3. Concurred.

IV.   Notified P.M. of a possible and equally embarrassing situation involving Moriarities.
    A. "Hammersmith"
    B. Jack the Ripper

---

[24] William Ewart Gladstone (1809 – 1898). British Prime Minister for a total of twelve years spread out over four terms from 1868 to 1894.

[25] Also known as the Government of Ireland Bill 1893. This was Gladstone's second attempt to enact a system of home rule for Ireland.

[26] The Internal Macedonia Revolutionary Organization was founded in 1893 in Thessaloniki, Greece, by Macedonian-Bulgarian revolutionaries seeking to gain autonomy for a large portion of Macedonia from the Ottoman Empire.

From the Unpublished Personal Reminiscences of John H. Watson, M.D.

I. *Dorsett Street*

The Streets of London have always been haunted. By ghosts. Monsters. And memories.

It was October of 1893 and my wife Mary was ill. Her health had grown tenuous since the onset of autumn and the dread of what winter would bring festered my thoughts. By this time I was all but completely devoting myself to her care, so when I received a request from a journalist with *The London Illustrated News* named Daniel Kingdom to speak with myself and Inspector Lestrade that evening concerning a matter involving Sherlock Holmes, I had every intention of declining, but Mary insisted I accept. "Ignoring yourself benefits neither of us, James.[27] You should go, to satisfy your own curiosity if for no other reason."

I was curious, as was Lestrade, who was preparing to contact me when I telephoned. He was familiar with Kingdom and felt certain this was no prank or gyp, even though he had no inkling as to what the journalist wanted to ask us.

The Inspector and I had not seen each other since early summer, and I was most grateful for his company and the revolver I knew he

---

[27] Mary Watson also refers to her husband as James in "The Man with the Twisted Lip." reason why is never given in The Canon, but William S. Baring-Gould provides several theories suggested by Sherlockians in the chapter "Good Old Watson!" in *The Annotated Sherlock Holmes*. Perhaps the most popular is by Dorothy L. Sayers (1893 – 1957), creator of Lord Peter Wimsey, who speculated that Mary was referring to her husband by his middle name, whose initial we learn is "H" in "The Last Bow." Sayers proposes the "H" stands for "Hamish," the Scottish Gaelic equivalent of "James."

always carried in his hip-pocket when we arrived on Dorsett Street at the requested hour. "Why meet here?" I wondered as I regarded the low, sloped, dilapidated Huguenot houses that huddled on each side of the dreary lane. "It appears the cleanup of the slums has not yet reached this bleak spot."[28]

"You think this is bleak? Go down that alley to the right and walk through Miller's Court. That's bleak. There are advantages to allowing your worst criminals to cluster in one rookery like we do, but such conveniences come with perils. Constables were patrolling in pairs here even before I was a peeler. I doubt there's a fouler part of London."

An instant later we were joined by Kingdom, a slim young man, slightly tainted in the Oxford manner, with an inquisitive, clean-shaven face and alert demeanor. Speaking in an unabashed tone, he pronounced, "And no spot is more notorious than Thirteen Miller's Court, where Mary Kelly was eviscerated by Jack the Ripper before he was nibbed."

"What are you about? We never arrested The Whitechapel Murderer."

"I disagree, Inspector. I have it from a source that the Ripper died of Hempen fever in Newgate Prison nearly five years ago."

"What source would that be?"

"Confidential but reliable. Still, I was hoping you gentlemen would help me verify this information."

"You mind telling me how?"

---

[28] See "The Tragedy of the Petty Curses."

"You were with the CID in November 1888?"

"I was. Not H Division, though, and this is their district."

Kingdom looked at me and cocked his head with the air of a solicitor already acquainted with the answers to his queries. "Did Mr. Holmes lend his assistance to Scotland Yard with the murders?"

I answered, "No."

"Did the police ever consult him?"

"No."

"Did anyone besides the police ask for his help?"

"Yes. George Lusk of the Whitechapel Vigilance Committee approached Holmes a week after Miss Kelly's murder, but he assured Lusk he was more than satisfied with Scotland Yard's efforts. There were no more killings after that, thank God."

"Are you sure? Some insist there were, and not just after Mary Kelly but before Mary Ann Nichols."

Lestrade snorted. "Those opinions are the merest moonshine and nothing more."

"And are you sure, Inspector?"

"Dr. Bond[29] assured the head of the CID[30] there were only five killings. He has an excellent reputation with A Division, so that's enough for me."

---

[29] Thomas Bond (1841 – 1901). British surgeon and consulting railway surgeon for the Great Western Railway and Great Eastern Railway.
[30] Sir Robert Anderson (1841 – 1918). Assistant Commissioner of the London Metropolitan Police from 1881to 1901.

Kingdom cocked his head again before asking me, "Was Mr. Holmes working on any cases at the time of the Whitechapel murders?"

"He was, but nothing in relation to them."

"Did he work on any cases immediately after Mary Kelly's murder?"

"None that I can recall."

"May I ask what you were doing during this time?"

"I was in Dartmoor near the end of September and for a good deal of October at Mr. Holmes's request.[31] After that I was preoccupied with my wedding and setting up a new home and practice."

"I see." Kingdom smirked. "Inspector, did you consult Mr. Holmes on a murder investigation in Hammersmith that November?"

It seems unlikely that Lestrade could ever look more confounded. "A murder? In Hammersmith?" Then he laughed in a most unpleasant manner.

Kingdom shot him an angry glance. "What's so funny?"

"The Hammersmith Ghost Murder was ninety years ago![32] A bit before even my time."

Giving Kingdom the benefit of the doubt, I said, "Surely he is referring to something more recent."

"Then he can surely tottle over to west London and poke bogey with the Hammersmith Police."

---

[31] See *The Hound of the Baskervilles*.
[32] In 1804 a plasterer named Thomas Millwood was fatally shot by a man named Francis Smith, who mistook Millwood's white greatcoat for a specter that had reportedly been haunting the Hammersmith district.

Kingdom was not about to be dismissed. "Did you consult Mr. Holmes on any murders that November?"

"I can't say that I did."

"Think again, Inspector. You must have."

Whatever patience Lestrade still possessed at this point evaporated. "Look, I don't know who put this bee in your bonnet, but you can come to the Yard and check the official files from the Factory[33] if you want."

"I do."

"You're funeral." The Inspector asked me, "Coming, Doctor?"

My own patience as well as my curiosity had likewise been depleted. "No. I have more pressing matters waiting at home."

A somber mein overshadowed Lestrade's irritation. "Of course. My best to Mrs. Watson."

"Thank you." I bid Kingdom good night as politely as I could and departed.

II. *George Lusk's Visit to Baker Street*

The hour was late by the time Mary dropped asleep and the nurse took over her care so I could retire, however I could not put away Kingdom's allegation. Like the rest of London I spent the autumn of 1888 absorbed and repulsed by the Whitechapel Murders, and I had read and reread George Hutchinson's statement in *The Illustrated Police News* about what he claimed to have witnessed during the night of Miss

---

[33] Lestrade appears to be referring to Scotland Yard's original headquarters, which was damaged in a bombing on May 30, 1884. The Metropolitan Police moved into New Scotland Yard in 1890.

Kelly's murder. I recalled the accompanying illustration of an opulently dressed man Hutchinson described having seen accompany Miss Kelly inside Thirteen Miller's Court no more than three hours prior to her death. I also could not stop reimagining the landlord's agent Thomas Bowyer going to collect Kelly's rent the following morning, only to commemorate Lord Mayor's Day by discovering her mutilated corpse.

I pulled out my notebook for the year 1888 and located my transcript of Holmes's meeting with Lusk. My friend had had no intention of intruding without invite into a matter that was becoming a whetstone of public ridicule towards Scotland Yard. There were radical elements using the Whitechapel Murders to sharpen their arguments that the police were mismanaged and maladroit. By talking with Lusk, Holmes hoped he might pacify one of the Yard's critics. As I scanned my notes I was surprised to see that I had forgotten Lusk had brought along another member of the Committee, a young tinsmith named Minor Barnes:

HOLMES: I applaud your committee's sense of civic obligation in patrolling the Whitechapel district, Mr. Lusk. Not being trained as sentries or detectives, however, I fear your efforts may prove to be of little benefit.

LUSK: We're also petitioning the government to offer a reward for information about this monster. And we've hired other unofficial detectives to interview any witnesses.

BARNES:	But there must be more we can do. The newspapers are right. The police are nothing but stumbling fools.
LUSK:	Minor! Keep a civil tongue or out with you! I'm sorry, Mr. Holmes.
HOLMES:	Not necessary. I share your frustration that the murderer has so far escaped justice, Mister ... ?
BARNES:	Barnes, sir. Minor Barnes.
HOLMES:	Mister Barnes. What more would you have the police do?
BARNES:	Follow your methods.
HOLMES:	Which I can assure you they are. By all accounts they have done an exemplary job collecting and examining all the pertinent evidence. I also have every confidence in Dr. Thomas Bond and concur with his findings and opinions. A thorough search of Whitechapel has also been conducted by dozens of policemen, who have interviewed over two thousand people and investigated over three hundred suspects.
LUSK:	But Mr. Holmes, this brute kills on or near a weekend at the end of the month or soon after, and each killing has been more savage than the last. If we don't find him ... if he isn't stopped ... I dread to think what will happen when the calendar nears December.

67

Lusk's dread was justified but never realized. The murders seemed to stop as abruptly as they began, but if Kingdom were correct that was because the vilest villain this side of Professor Moriarty was in prison.

Only how?

Why?

And who was he?

Apparently my curiosity was not as spent as I supposed.

* * * *

I managed to nod off sometime soon after this and it was past dawn when I woke. Mary had already managed to eat a little breakfast and my meal was waiting along with the first batch of morning mail. One envelope immediately attracted my attention. There was no return address but there were four backstamps on the rear of the envelope along with a message scribbled in Latin:

Mea gloria fides.

My friend Walter Simonson had said this to me before departing England in June of 1891. I had heard nothing from him since and my fingers trembled from anticipation and apprehension as I opened the envelope, but all it contained was another envelope addressed to "I.G.L." This could only mean Inspector G. Lestrade, Simonson's liaison with Scotland Yard.

I went to Lestrade's office to deliver the envelope but was informed that he was not in, so I left word for him to call at my house. "Tell the Inspector I wouldn't ask if it weren't urgent." Stepping outside I realized I had not read any morning newspapers yet, so I purchased a *Morning*

Herald for the cab ride home. I did not peruse it long before coming across news that Daniel Kingdom had been shot on Great George Street by a hansom driver who fled the scene and remained at large.

III. *A Distinct Touch*

It was nearly time for lunch when Lestrade arrived. The man looked done in so I instructed the maid to bring him some food as I led the Inspector into my consulting room, where I offered him a seat and some brandy.

Lestrade took a judicious sip. "Very much obliged, Doctor. Much as I hate to admit it, working all night uses me up more than it once did."

"We all get older. You haven't been home at all since we left Spitalfields?"

He shook his head before taking a second small sip. "Have you told anyone about last night?"

"Only my wife."

"I see."

"This is yours, I believe." I presented Simonson's envelope to Lestrade, who tucked it into a pocket.

"Aren't you going to open it?"

"Not for my eyes, and I have to ask you and Mrs. Watson not to discuss anything about last night with anyone. This request does not come from me, mind you, but the Prime Minister and Her Majesty."

"Of course, but does this mean Kingdom was right?"

Lestrade nodded with a weary frown. "What I am about to tell you must stay a secret between you and me, like that Sumatra business a few months ago. Even Leather Apron was never informed we knew who he was, although I suspect he guessed we might."

"How is that possible?"

"Chalk it up to good fortune or luck. I think they call it kismet in India. If the Moriarities get their way it'll all be undone, and the government and the throne will be the worse for it. Those curs are still up to their anarchist tricks, and not just in England, but our friend is on to them." Lestrade patted the pocket with the envelope. "That's all I can go into now, but Walter ought to have some tales to tell us whenever he returns."

The maid arrived with cold beef and beer, and I waited for Lestrade to eat. Reinvigorated, he continued, "After that Dartmoor business, Mr. Holmes and I didn't cross paths again until near the end of November."

"Did he know about the Ripper?

"He did. So does his brother."

"And Kingdom, of course. And the Moriarities you say?"

"One of them must have been Kingdom's reliable source."

"How is it they know? Was that cab driver one of them?"

"All good questions, Doctor. I took Kingdom to the Yard to look at the old files, but nothing was ever put there to find so he left. I shadowed after him to see where he went, hoping to find out how he knew to mention 'Hammersmith.'"

"So there was a Hammersmith murder five years ago?"

"No. Kingdom likely misunderstood that part. It was midnight when we reached Great George Street and that hansom pulled up along the curb. I couldn't see the driver and when we tracked the cab down by its number it turned out to be stolen. No one else was near enough to overhear the driver ask, 'Need a cab, Mr. Kingdom?' Daniel asked how the cabbie knew his name. 'Wouldn't that Yarder tailing you like to know!'" Mortified rage blotted Lestrade's features. "He plugged Kingdom twice and was off before I could even shout. By the time I could search Kingdom's rooms any notes he kept about the Ripper were gone. Whoever beat me to them left this." He removed a scrap of paper from another pocket and handed it to me. "Sound familiar?"

I read: "'Dear me, Inspector! Dear me!'"

"The Birlstone Murder may have been MacDonald's[34] case, but there's not a jack who doesn't know about the note the Professor had put in your letter-box after the Moriarities caught up with that Pinkerton agent."

"'Dear me, Mr. Holmes! Dear me!'" I recited. "Holmes might have called this 'a distinct touch.'"

"Very much so, in this case."

"Why is that? I don't understand what the Moriarities gained by killing Kingdom?"

"It's always been their way. 'Dead men don't bite.'"

"I'm sorry but you're going to have to be more specific."

---

[34] Scotland Yard Inspector Alec MacDonald, often referred to as "Mr. Mac" and "friend MacDonald" by Holmes.

71

"I suppose I do. This goes back to November 26 in 1888. I might be getting older, but I'll never forget that date much less anything about it. A bobby found two men fighting near Saint Katherine Docks. Each swore the other had let some daylight into a dead sailor named Thomas Corder lying a few feet away. One man, Richard Parsons, was a tailor, and the other, Minor Barnes, was a tinsmith. Corder was just back from South Africa and hadn't been in England since he signed on with the *Palmyra* in January."

Hearing Barnes's name intrigued me, but hearing the ship's name was startling. "You're sure it was the *Palmyra*?"

"The same ship Birdy Edwards went overboard?[35] I'm sure. I wasted no time informing Mr. Holmes and he wasted no time talking to Parsons and Barnes. Parsons was a lousy duffer with a couple of murders in his past, although we could never prove that, while Barnes insisted that he found Corder and Parsons fighting and that he had tried to help the sailor. I was inclined to believe Barnes since he had never even been arrested before."

"While Parsons sounds like just the sort who could have killed Edwards."

"Oh, he did, just like he killed Corder. The Pinkertons had never stopped searching for Edwards's killer so we contacted them. It turns out one of their best operatives, Governor Winters, had just missed garnishing Corder in Cape Town. Corder probably came back to London to beg the Professor for sanctuary."

---

[35] See *The Valley of Fear*.

"Only dead men tell no tales."

"You think Parsons would have known that. Anyway, with the Professor being involved, we weren't about to settle for half-measures, so Mr. Holmes and I took a look about both men's residences." The hardy man's face pinched with disgust. "We found things in Barnes's rooms."

"Uhm … what --?"

"One of the things we found was a clasp knife. It was straight, about six inches long with a strong, sharp blade pointed at the top and an inch thick. We compared it against the five women's wounds and …well … Barnes was the Whitechapel Murderer all right."

"My word." Several moments passed before the shock of learning the truth and how it was uncovered withered sufficiently to ask, "You never arrested Barnes?"

"Not for what he did to Kelly and the others. How could we without explaining why we searched his room? We had no proof against Professor Moriarty, whose name was bound to come up."

"So what did you do?"

"All we could do was take the matter to Mr. Holmes's brother…who took it to Gladstone…who took it to Her Majesty, whereupon I was ordered to arrest Barnes for Corder's murder…release Parsons…and file everything about the investigation with Mycroft Holmes under the cryptonym 'Hammersmith' after the old murder case."

"Why use that?"

"I can't claim to understand the ways of government, but the irony serves as a caveat to me of what we did." Such introspection from the Inspector was unexpected. In the Hammersmith case King George III had commuted the guilty man's sentence from hanging to one year's hard labor, but here the King's granddaughter condemned Barnes by changing his sentence from innocent to guilty.

"I understand the dilemma, but I can also sympathize how this solution doesn't seem proper, especially with Parsons going free."

"You needn't fret about that. The hope was that the Professor would attend to Parsons and from all accounts he did, but Mr. Holmes liked no part of the plan. He also warned that the Professor might figure out about 'Hammersmith,' and it looks as though Mr. Holmes was right. The way it seems to me is the Moriarities slipped word about Barnes to Kingdom expecting he would just print it. It probably never crossed their minds he'd want to dig up more about it first."

"So following his journalist's nature alerted you ... which made Kingdom a liability to them ... so they silenced him. But surely the Moriarities will try to expose 'Hammersmith' again."

"I don't know why they wouldn't, but they've tipped their hand so the powers that be will keep sharp. It's just one more reason why the sooner the Moriarity gang is finished the better."

"That's easier said than done, as Holmes knew too well."

Lestrade gave a long sigh of melancholy. "Poor Mr. Holmes. I think he knew too much about some things."

"Why do you say that?"

"Jacks like me can do our job because we know this city. I grew up on London's streets and I've been with the Yard over half my life. Now Mr. Holmes knew London but he wasn't raised here, and he grew up studying crime the way schoolboys do history. We were both doing all right for ourselves in our own ways, but then along comes Leather Apron. I've seen some brutal murders but nothing like those. Neither had Mr. Holmes, but he knew about some like them from the past. Some that was even worse." Lestrade stood and patted the pocket with the envelope again. "I'd best deliver this. Thank you for the food and drink. And, again, my best to Mrs. Watson."

IV. *Sherlock Holmes's Appraisal of the Matter*

By myself once more, my mind was awhirl from all I had discovered during the last twenty-four hours. As the minutes passed I found myself fixating more and more upon Lestrade's observations regarding Holmes, which eventually led to my recalling a rumination Holmes made shortly before the tragic events at Reichenbach regarding the likes of Moriarty.

"One of the burdens of my unique profession is my familiarity with the worst of mankind. Professor Moriarty is in some ways unprecedented as a tyrant-monster, but that has as much to do with the opportunities afforded him by this current era as his personality. There have been clever criminal bosses like Worth,[36] Grady,[37] and Mandelbaum,[38] but they tended to be intolerant of violence. Not so

---

[36] Adam Worth (1844 – 1902).
[37] John D. "Traveling Mike" Grady (? – 1880).
[38] Fredericka "Marm" Mandelbaum (1825 - 1895).

much Richard Lines,[39] proprietor of the Red Lion Tavern, who might be considered an actual forerunner to the Professor. At the other extreme are rivals to Moriarity's brutality but not his intellect. Gilles de Rais[40] and Jonathan Wild[41] fall into this camp. Perhaps worse than any of these, even Moriarity, are creatures like the unidentified brute who recently butchered eight women in Austin, Texas, over a period of two years. More often than not he employed an ax.[42] About this same time in the Netherlands Maria Swanenburg[43] definitively poisoned at least twenty-seven people to collect their insurance or inheritance, but I am far from the only person who suspects the actual count to be above ninety. Keeping such knowledge in my brain-attic is necessary, but being aware such persons exist can be a curse. Except for those rare instances where Providence intervenes, humanity is powerless to prevent the havoc wrecked by these bestial beings. All we can do is remain vigilant, and, if the time comes, act to put an end to their disasters at whatever cost."

Walter Simonson's Journal

17 October, 1893 – Governor-General's Palace, Khartoum.

It was well past sunset, closer to Isha than Maghrib,[44] and there was still no sign of the Khalifa.[45]

---

[39] See *The Old House on West Street*.
[40] ? – 1440. French knight and serial child murderer.
[41] 1682 or 1683 – 1725. Crime fighter and criminal boss.
[42] 1839 -1915.
[43] What was called at the time The Servant Girl Murders took place between 1884 and 1885.
[44] "When should a Muslim pray? Five times daily—upon rising, at noon, in mid-afternoon, after sunset, and before retiring. The schedule is not absolutely binding." So writes Huston Smith in

Had he changed his mind?

If so, what did that mean for our plans? Or us?

As more time passed the tranquility of the courtyard seemed to grow more circumscribed than the surrounding tiers of shadowy archways and lattice-work.

I noticed that Mr. Sherlock appeared pensive as he gazed at some stairs leading from the ground level to the west wing's first floor, so I asked what was on his mind.

"I was imagining what General Gordon[46] might have been thinking that last morning. Possibly standing right there. Had he erred ignoring orders to abandon the Sudan? Or was he more convinced than ever that he had done the proper if not the wisest thing?"

"Or maybe he's still wondering, like President Lincoln's ghost wandering the White House corridors." Our voices carried in the stillness, but I decided to risk it after noticing a silhouette in an archway. "Some insist that a merchant saw Gordon standing on those steps later that day, all dressed in white and just staring into the darkness."

"I've heard that, too. It would seem Khartoum, like London, has its ghosts."

The Religion of Man (p. 219). Salat times (prayer times) are Fajr (dawn), Dhuhr (after midday), Asr (afternoon), Maghrib (sunset), and Isha (nighttime).
[45] Abdallahi ibn-Muhammad (1846 – 1899). Successor to the self-proclaimed Mahdi Muhammad Ahmad (1844 – 1885).
[46] Major-General Charles George "Chinese" Gordon (1833 – 1885). Gordon arrived in Khartoum in February of 1884 with orders to evacuate soldiers and loyal civilians in light of several raids in the Sudan by the Mahdi, but Gordon remained in Khartoum, determined to smash up the Mahdi. A siege ensued and Khartoum fell to the Mahdist on January 26, 1885, two days before the arrival of a British relief expedition.

"I wouldn't know why not." I lowered my voice. "Although I doubt that's Gordon's spirit watching us." I had assumed Mr. Sherlock was already aware of the silhouette and judging by his blasé reaction I was correct.

He whispered, "Unlikely. I suggest you ready your revolver."

My hand was already upon the grip of my Webley and I drew and cocked it as I barked, "You in the shadows! Come out where we can see you!" The stranger unhesitatingly stepped into the moonlight and I just as swiftly lowered my weapon. "The Khalifa! Please forgive me!"

The reply: "No, Mr. Sigerson. Or should I say Mr. Simonson? I cannot claim to be the Khalifa. I am only here at his behest." A spry, lean stranger smiled as he approached.

Keeping the Webley cocked, I asked: "Where is he?"

"Across the Nile in Omdurman." The stranger beamed at Mr. Sherlock. "Is it possible you are Sherlock Holmes of whom I have heard so much?"

I said, "Sherlock Holmes is dead. This is my guide Haj."

"And what a wonderful guise it is. Sir Richard Burton's could not have been better when he made his celebrated *Hajj*."[47]

Mr. Sherlock ended all pretense of our charade with a shrug. "Well, perhaps no better than Achilles's in the court of King Lycomedes. Simonson, if I'm not mistaken, this gentleman is a *daroga*."

"A police chief?"

---

[47] (1821 – 1890). British scholar, soldier, and explorer. Burton made his *Hajj* (pilgrimage to Mecca and Medina) disguised as a Muslim in 1853.

"From Māzandarān,[48] where, until recently, he spent some years in jail."

The *daroga* was impressed but even more delighted. "Oh, your eyes and ears would be the envy of a soothsayer! I am Nadir Khan, just pardoned for most heinous crimes."

I asked: "What sort of crimes?"

"Chiefly for not killing a man as ordered by the Shah-in-Shah. Now, please, allow me to show you why the Khalifa did not come himself." From somewhere on his person Nadir drew a long single-edged gilt steel knife with a Persian recurve blade tapered to a needle-like point. "This was found stabbed beside the Khalifa's bed the morning before he received your request regarding the *majrim*[49] you are hunting."

Mr. Sherlock asked to examine the knife and Nadir gratefully presented it. "A *pesh-kabz*?"

"Correct. An innovation of the Safavid dynasty.[50] Its reinforced tip is designed to spread the links of an opponent's coat of mail apart so the blade may penetrate the armor."

I mentioned how leaving a knife as a present in this way was an old assassin tactic to intimidate enemies into submission, and Mr. Sherlock never paused in his inspection as he commented, "I believe the term is *hashashin* and they always included a threatening note."

---

[48] Region bordering the Caspian Sea and Elburz Mountains. Its climate is subtropical with extremely hot summers.
[49] "Criminal"
[50] The ruling Persian dynasty from 1501 to 1736.

79

Nadir applauded twice. "Both of you are correct! However the Khalifa found only the *pesh-kabz* and the *hashashin*—or Nizari Islaimis—were all defeated by the Mongols in 1256. Some insist that a few *hashashin* do still exist, plying their trade for personal rather than political purposes."

"You are an absolute font, Nadir. Is your expertise of the *hashashin* the reason for your pardon?"

"In part, yes, although I like to think I still possess some small police skills."

"I would wager you possess considerably more than that." Mr. Sherlock handed back the knife. "Do you believe this belonged to a *hashashin*?"

"The Khalifa believes it's possible. That is all that matters."

I asked, "Can't you verify if it belonged to someone skilled in murder?"

"This knife is too pristine to display any tendencies of its owner."

Mr. Sherlock said, "Which does not eliminate that a mercenary *hashashin* is behind this. Leaving a new *pesh-kabz* might have been preferable to relinquishing an accustomed knife. Still, there is no note, leaving us to ponder who else might wish to threaten the Khalifa and why. The Ashraf, perhaps?" [51]

"The Khalifa has survived several Ashraf attacks since succeeding the Mahdi, but they wish him defeated, not cowed."

---

[51] The Ashraf are the descendants of Muhammad, the founder of Islam, by way of his daughter Fatimah. The Khalifa was an Ansar or disciple of the Mahdi, and in the end was unable to overcome tribal dissension in his attempts to unify the Sudan as part of a military caliphate.

I added, "It's also been two years since the last Ashraf attack."

"Correct, although during that time many tribal disputes have intensified to a point where the Khalifa has had to hire Egyptians as administrators."

"So what's the motive? You don't risk your life leaving a knife in the Khalifa's bedroom without a reason."

"Whatever the motive it has resulted in the Khalfia being even more cautious than usual. It is no secret he fears assassination. Not so much by infidels as potential rivals, supporters, even his family. Do you think this man you seek capable of such a feat?"

"I'd say he is. Whatever Connor Newcomb lacks in skill he makes up for in daring and he's no dullard. He is even more adept at learning customs and languages than I. He might have gone far in any number of professions, but he enlisted with the Coldstream Guards,[52] was part of the Camel Corps at the Battle of Abu Klea,[53] and was never quite right after that. Still, if it was Newcomb that left this knife, why not slay the Khalifa right then?"

A wry smile played over Mr. Sherlock's lip. "I once overlooked what should have been the simple explanation to an investigation when I failed to recognize its similarities to one of the exploits of King David.[54] Somehow, though, I suspect that will not turn out to be the case here."

---

[52] The oldest, continuously serving, regular regiment in the British Army.
[53] Battle fought January 16-18, 1885 between Mahdist forces and one of the British columns sent to the Sudan to aid Gordon.
[54] See "The Adventure of the Crooked Man." The exploit here is "the small affair of Uriah and Bathsheba" in 2 Samuel 11: 1-26, but in 1 Samuel 24:4 David spares Saul while the king is sleeping, choosing instead to cut off only a corner from Saul's robe.

His expression grew more thoughtful. "Sergeant Newcomb is the third most dangerous man of what remains of the late Professor James Moriarty's criminal empire, which intends to inflict as much hardship upon the world as it can with its death throes. Just imagine the chaos they could ignite throughout northern Africa if news got out the Khalifa had been assassinated by Newcomb. Imagine the humiliation that would rain down upon Great Britain, whose citizens have barely forgiven the Prime Minister for the fall of Khartoum."[55]

Nadir paled. "Such horror for what sounds like futile nonsense!"

"True, but nothing compared to what they want to attempt next."

I injected, "After what I've seen, I wouldn't be surprised to find out the Moriarities were behind the Mayerling Incident."[56]

As usual, however, Mr. Sherlock drove my point home better than I could: "I'm afraid men are rarely reasonable when their passion for power or lust for retribution is on the boil."

* * * *

---

[55] The ten-month siege and fall of Khartoum occurred during Gladstone's second term. The public believed Gladstone purposely delayed sending relief and Queen Victoria sent a letter of rebuke to Gladstone which found its way into the press. Gladstone resigned as Prime Minister in June 1885.

[56] On January 30, 1889, the bodies of Rudolph, Crown Prince of Austria, and his mistress Baroness Mary Vetsera were discovered in the Imperial hunting lodge in Mayerling. The deaths may have been a murder-suicide or a double murder, but Rudolph, the heir-apparent of the Austro-Hungarian Empire, died without sons, leaving Rudolph's uncle, Archduke Karl Ludwig, and Ludwig's son, Archduke Franz Ferdinand, next in succession. This disrupted the delicate security of the Habsburg dynastic direct line of succession, which endangered what at the time was a growing reconciliation between the Austrian and Hungarian factions of the empire. Developments arising from the Mayerling Incident worsened each year, a destabilization that would eventually lead to the start of World War I after the assassination of Ferdinand and his wife Sophie in 1914.

Nadir informed us that the Khalifa had invited us to bivouac in his palace, and Mr. Sherlock and I gratefully accepted, seeing as we were in no position to demur.

The "palace" turned out to be one of five unimposing brick buildings situated around the Mahdi's tomb and Great Mosque in an unpaved compound encircled by a formidable stone wall. Omdurman had been a large village of mud hovels and straw-walled huts at the time of Gordon's death, and the Mahdi had intended it to be a temporary capital before his own untimely demise. His plan was to establish a permanent capital for a pan-Arabian empire in Cairo or Damascus, but the caliphate never materialized and since then several desert tribes have been relocated to Omdurman by the Khalifa's centralization decrees, their numbers engorging dingy slums which had once been home to only some fishermen and the infrequent bandit.

Our expedition to the Sudan must have been more exacting than Mr. Sherlock and I realized. We slept later than we intended, but there was still time for us to formulate before Nadir visited us. The sun was on the verge of turning orange when Mr. Sherlock greeted him: "I see you've changed clothes since arriving. Does this mean you have spoken with the Khalifa?"

"I have and he has agreed to all the recommendations you suggested."

Mr. Sherlock suspected this would be the case, but it still struck me as impressive. "No wonder you've been gone so long. Nadir, you're a miracle worker!"

"I'm Persian. I know how to barter. Even as we speak the number of palace guards is being increased and a review of all Egyptian administrators shall commence within the hour. Naturally the Khalifa's personal bodyguards were informed as to the reason for all this, but these men were culled from his own Taiasha tribe and if the Khalifa trusts anyone, it is they. After the incident with the *pesh-kabz* they also know whose heads will pay the penalty if word leaks out."

Mr. Sherlock commented, "I dare say the Khalifa could teach our government a thing or two about efficiency and decisive action."

I added, "And motivation," before excusing myself. "I had a bit too much coffee with my beef stew." Out of habit I paused outside the room to eavesdrop and heard Nadir say, "I like your companion."

"As do I. His intuitiveness and courage remind me of my friend, John Watson."

"Another man I should like to meet. I pray your mission here will be over quickly so you can see him again."

"Thank you, but I'm afraid our reunion is still some time off."

"Why? Won't your task end once you have intercepted Newcomb?"

"There remain other tasks, not the least of which is the problem posed by Newcomb's commander. He is a wily tiger prowling in plain sight with nothing linking him to the Professor, and until I can prove otherwise returning to London would be as foolish as it would be fatal for Simonson and myself."

Later. –

Isha prayer came and went by the time a servant baring a goblet approached the ante-chamber to the Khalifa's bedroom and connecting harem. Inside the harem a regiment of eunuchs attended to some four hundred wives, while a dozen bodyguards stood sentry in the ante-chamber where anyone seeking an audience with the Khalfia was required to relinquish his sword and knife. No one—not even dignitaries such as the Mahdi's one-time heir apparent Ali Wad Helu and the emir Osman Digna of the Hadendoa—could approach their leader unless he disarmed first. As he did each night at this hour, the servant told the chief bodyguard: "I bring the Khalifa's *doogh*."[57] And like he did each night the chief bodyguard replied, "Enter," but tonight added, "The Khalifa is in a temper. Just leave the drink and go."

"I taste all his food for poison. What if --?"

"If you have to come back to taste it, so be it. Do as you're told."

The servant acquiesced and went in.

The Khalifa's bedroom was furnished like most chambers in the palace with carpets and several pillows, but it was also the only room in Omdurman with a brass bed. Not even the Khalifa's somewhat disobedient son Osman Sheikh el Din, who lived in a far more lavish house with its own garden, could boast of such a jewel. The Khalifa's

---

[57] A cold drink of water and curdled milk seasoned with mint.

back was to the room as he stared out a northern window towards the Kerreri hills as the servant said, "Your *doogh*, Khalifa. May I --?"

"Put it down and leave."

"Of course, Khalifa." The goblet was set on the floor near a pillow propped against the foot of the bed. With his free hand the servant surreptitiously reached beneath the mattress to extract an arm dagger. "So be it." Approaching the Khalifa on tiptoe, the servant drew the dagger from its scabbard before shouting in English, "For Gordon!"

The Khalifa turned around.

Only it wasn't the Khalifa and the imposter wielded the *pesh-kabz*. "*Masá alkhayr*,[58] Sergeant Newcomb," Nadir greeted the servant.

Newcomb paused.

Mr. Sherlock and I stepped out from hiding as I aimed my Webley. "Drop the chiv or I'll fire."

Newcomb did an about-face to look our way.

Mr. Sherlock instructed, "Do as he says, Sergeant Newcomb."

Newcomb squinted, peering through Mr. Sherlock's guide costume. "So that's where you've been hiding! Out of twig as a native, eh? No wonder the Colonel couldn't track you down."

"Moran and I shall find each other at the proper time."

"Oh, no doubt. He might prefer card clubs to staking out trees and watering holes these days, but that old *shikari*[59] will never stop lying for

---

[58] "Good evening"
[59] "Hunter"

you." Newcomb glowered at me. "I've wanted to ask if you turned nose on us or were you always working for Holmes?"

"Oh, I've always worked for Mr. Holmes. Now you might as well drop that chiv. No one else is coming."

This rattled Newcomb, who suddenly realized that the bedroom had not been overrun. "What's going on?"

Nadir explained: "We have no intention of permitting you to sully England's Empire at our expense."

I added: "You got careless in Amol and Mecca. We tumbled to your plan and warned the Khalifa."

Mr. Sherlock provided specifics: "Leaving the *pesh-kabz* without a note beside the Khalifa's bed was inspired. A feint worthy of Moriarity. Slaying the Khalifa late at night when he was sleeping might not create the necessary spectacle to humiliate the Empire after it was discovered you are British, but striking him down when his bodyguards and his wives and their attendants are awake would be more than ample. And leaving no note with the *pesh-kabz* not only enticed people to leap to wrong conclusions, but pre-occupied them so they failed to search the bedroom for another knife that might be employed at a later time."

Newcomb sneered, "*Omne ignotum pro magnifico*. You said so yourself."[60]

"To accomplish this you almost certainly had to have positioned yourself within the palace. Posing as a guard would be too prominent. Better a servant. They are often taken for granted and therefore invisible.

---

[60] "Everything unknown is taken as grand." See "The Adventure of the Red-Headed League."

87

But how to flush you out? Increasing the palace guards and reviewing the administrators would suggest that the Khalifa harbored suspicions against someone inside the palace, leaving you little choice but to act before he got around to the servants."

"I see. A neat little trap you set. But --"

I cocked the Webley. "'But' nothing. Last warning."

"My presence here can still disgrace Her Majesty's Government. All I have to do is kick up a ruckus --"

"Try it and I'll gut-shoot you, drag you into the desert, and leave you on some lonely anthill. Give up your weapon and I'll see to it you die quick and easy."

Several seconds passed before Nadir gingerly took the dagger from the reluctant Newcomb. "Take it from one who once faced a similar decision, Sergeant, this is the best choice."

19 *October – Governor-General's Palace*

The Khalifa requested we set out for Upper River after Maghrib, so with his permission Mr. Sherlock and I bided our time in Khartoum until Nadir joined us after sunset. "Thank you so much for waiting." Nadir wore traveling clothes and carried all his worldly possessions in a ruck sack that he strapped to the saddle of the camel we brought for him.

I told him, "It's the least we could do. Besides, we wanted to see Gordon's palace again. We may never have another opportunity."

"True, but a pariah, even a grateful one such as myself, can be a risky travel companion."

"A risk we cheerfully accept."

Mr. Sherlock scowled. "Now that we are all across the Nile and free to speak, exiling you seems unduly harsh considering the risk you took for the Khalifa."

"I gratefully accepted the risk to have my sentence commuted. Better to die a free man."

I could not argue with the sentiment, but, "He used you as bait!"

"To catch a wily tiger. Mr. Holmes can appreciate that." Nadir winked.

Mr. Sherlock quietly said, "*Touché.*"

"In any case my exile is a consideration from the Shah-in-Shah, who only agreed to release me from prison because he thought I would probably perish impersonating the Khalifa. He has also agreed to a recompense of a small monthly pension that I shall receive as a member of the royal house. By the way, the Khalifa was most impressed that you … how do you say it? 'Tumbled?' That you two tumbled to his employing me as his decoy. May I ask when you first deduced this?"

I said: "Right here, when I mistook you for the Khalifa."

Mr. Sherlock provided specifics: "Why pardon even so qualified a prisoner as yourself to hunt a *hashashin*? Abdullah Ibn-Mohammed Al–Khalifa is a slim man, and it is not hard to see that your normally stocky physique was whittled down in prison. Taking advantage of the resultant resemblance to lure the *hashashin* into the open seemed a more suitable reason."

"And let's not forget that you changed your clothes before you came to tell us the Khalfia had agreed to Mr. Sherlock's entire plan."

"You would have seen the Khalfia in camera, not in audience, so the condition of your wardrobe should not have mattered. On the other hand if the Khalifa were in hiding in Omdurman whenever you were supposed to be in Khartoum to assure his safety, then you would have had to wash and then change clothes or we would have seen the dust from your journey."

Nadir chuckled. "Mr. Holmes, you always make me feel like a man who doesn't know he is playing with marked cards. And, Walter, the Khalifa assured me Sergeant Newcomb has been attended to."

"May I ask how?"

"In the same manner that the Mahdi would have ordered: decapitation. The Khalifa's chief bodyguard performed the execution and delivered Newcomb's head to him. Newcomb's death was mercifully swift and anonymous."

"I see. Well, it was the best thing for everyone."

Mr. Sherlock was hesitant to agree. "But was it the proper course? Certainly it was the most prudent, but as more and more years pass I find myself pondering more and more what terrible costs decisions based upon doing what is best over what is right shall reap."

* * * *

Excerpt from Mycroft Holmes's Notebook

October 24, 1893 – Review of W.S.'s Letter with Gladstone

The P.M. thanked me and asked me to thank "our loyal agents."

"I'll tell Simonson and Lestrade, Prime Minister."

"Tell me, Mycroft, do you see an end to this conflict with the Moriarities? Each battle is worse and threatens more of the world than the last."

"History teaches us that the bloodiest conflicts occur at the end of wars. We might take some solace in that."

"Perhaps, but these last two strikes cut especially deep. They resurrected memories I prayed would never haunt England again. Perhaps I'm getting too old."

"We all dread the turning of the calendar page and what it inexorably brings to everything we hold dear. There is nothing we can do about that, but thanks to Providence and acting upon the best of our abilities we have helped to keep England on her proper course."

"We have, but at what cost, Mycroft? At what cost?"

"Only time can tell, Prime Minister. Only time will tell."

THE FINAL ADVENTURE

I. THE WHETSTONE

The Notebook of Dr. John H. Watson, Late Indian Army

8 December, 1893. – Mary died today.

10 December. – Mary is to be buried this morning. The service shall be private, since neither of us has kith nor kin in England.

Later. – I returned home around two o'clock in the afternoon. Memories of Mary are everywhere. I cannot escape her ghost even as I long for her spirit. To make matters worse, part of the homily haunts me:

> No man can find out the work that God maketh from the beginning to the end. [61]

I have never believed myself to be susceptible to impressions, but like Poe's lighthouse keeper I find myself pondering what may happen to a man all alone as I am.[62]

Later. – I left the house and walked without direction or purpose and eventually found myself at Wellington Street late in the afternoon. I imagine I allowed my grief to draw me like a lodestone towards the Lyceum Theater, where foot traffic streamed around me as I stared at the grand portico.

Specifically the third pillar from the left.

---

[61] Ecclesiastes 3:11: "He hath made everything beautiful in its time; also he hath set the world in their heart, so that no man can find out the work that God maketh from the beginning to the end."

[62] "The Light-House" is the uncompleted last written work by Edgar Allan Poe (1809 - 1849).

Today was temperate with clear skies, but all I could feel was the drizzly fog from that dreary September evening when Thaddeus Sholto's instructions brought Mary, myself, and Holmes here, and all I could see was the three of us being whisked away mere moments after we arrived upon an expedition that changed our lives.[63]

Glancing towards the Strand I spied the Lyceum's private entrance. It brought to mind last summer when I glimpsed Irving[64] and Stoker[65] hurrying through it towards a cab on who knows what adventure. Perhaps to make arrangements for their current American tour? I remember fancying how people must look upon Holmes and me in much the same way as the billow-haired doyen and his ginger-bearded Trojan. Irving is a genius and trailblazer in his calling while Stoker is an accomplished man in his own trade as well as a competent writer, yet Stoker is most often identified as the Baruch to Irving's Jeremiah. It might be interesting to ask Stoker if he has ever entertained similar thoughts, although I am not Beefsteak Club[66] material so the opportunity shall probably never present itself.

From the West End I meandered northward, passing former haunts and revisiting familiar sights while drifting to Marylebone and Baker Street where I stopped in front of Camden House, which currently

---

[63] See *The Sign of Four*.

[64] Henry Irving, born John Henry Bodribb (1838 – 1905). Actor-manager of the Lyceum Theatre. In 1905 became first actor to receive a British knighthood.

[65] Abraham "Bram" Stoker (1847 – 1912). The author of *Dracula*, Stoker was best known during his lifetime as Irving's loyal personal assistant and the Lyceum's business manager.

[66] Between the eighteenth and twentieth centuries several men's dining clubs in Great Britain and Australia were called The Beefsteak Club. Watson is referring to the one hosted in the Lyceum's dining room from 1878 to 1905 and whose membership included some of the greatest names of Victorian literature.

stands empty across from 221B. This was my first visit here since I put our old rooms in order after Moriarty's attempt to set them on fire,[67] and looking through one of our old windows I could picture Holmes examining Sholto's letter to Mary. I had nearly convinced myself to go speak with Mrs. Hudson, who was always very kind to Mary, but was interrupted by a peddler who put his Jew's harp down upon recognizing me and plied me about Holmes until my endurance failed and I hailed a cab. Now I am home dreading this hollow night and the prospect of so many more to come.

Walter Simonson's Journal

7 January, 1894 – Montpellier

Mr. Sherlock returned from Paris today, having concluded his investigations into the French and Russian negotiations, at least for now.[68]

---

[67] See "The Tragedy of the Petty Curses."

[68] This would seem to be a reference to the Russo-French military-political alliance formalized through an exchange of letters between the ministers of foreign affairs of France and Russia between December 27, 1893 and January 4, 1894. The Russo-French Alliance was triggered in the late 1880s when rumors of attempts to have Great Britain join the Triple Alliance military agreement between Germany, Austria-Hungry, and Italy began to spread. Although Great Britain would never join the Triple Alliance there were many in Russian diplomatic circles who suspected differently; meanwhile France perceived the Triple Alliance as a military threat they could not afford to ignore. Considering Europe's precarious state of affairs in the late nineteenth century, Great Britain would have naturally been interested in learning as much as it could about the Russo-French Alliance. "The whole of Europe is an armed camp," the illustrious Lord Bellinger, twice Premier of Britain, tells Holmes and Watson in "The Adventure of the Second Stain," which appears to occur during the autumn of 1886. Bellinger adds, "There is a double league which makes a fair balance of military power. Great Britain holds the scales. If Britain were driven into war with one confederacy, it would assure the supremacy of the other confederacy, whether they joined in the war or not." The Russo-French Alliance meant there were now two hostile military blocs in Europe.

I can only hazard how chock-a-block Mr. Mycroft's schedule has been since Christmas, yet he somehow finds time to work wonders, not the least of which has been arranging Mr. Sherlock's invitation to become a distinguished visiting professor at the *Université de Montpellier* under the guise of Felix Benet, D.Sci. Chem., recently returned from the Kāla Valley in Tibet with his orderly Brictwen and specimens of the rare night-blooming *marifasa* flower. I am told we have my childhood friend Sven Hedin to thank for them,[69] and they have made Benet a *célébrité universitaire* with the medicinal plants section of the *jardin des plantes de Montpellier* as well as some of the garden's more fetching young *habitués*, who I suspect are not only impressed with Benet's academic acumen but his explorer's complexion, black door-knocker, and penetrating grey eyes.

Before leaving Paris Mr. Sherlock visited Nadir. "Our friend has settled into a little flat on the rue de Rivoli with a servant named Darius." I told Mr. Sherlock it was good of him to call on Nadir. "Yes. An exile's life is not an easy one. I think we can both sympathize with that."

* * * *

[69] Sven Anders Hedin (1865 – 1952). Swedish explorer, writer, and illustrator of his own works. I do not know why Simonson would attempt to mislead in his own journal, but it is doubtful that Hedin could have provided anyone these samples since the first of his three celebrated expeditions to Central Asia (which included Chinese Turkestan [Xinjiang] and Tibet) began in 1894.

11 *January*

Mr. Sherlock is in a foul temper again.

Being away from England for nearly three years is increasingly frustrating him, and it didn't help when the Foreign Office informed us about a Moriarty lookout spotting John Watson near Baker Street after his wife's funeral. It should have been obvious that John was making a nostalgic visit born from melancholy, and I reminded Mr. Sherlock, "The Colonel has his faults, but going off half-cocked isn't one of them. The Professor had good reasons for making Moran his chief of staff for a time."

"True, Moran is no fool. It's doubtful he'd risk calling down the wrath of Scotland Yard unless he were absolutely certain Watson had an ulterior purpose for visiting Baker Street." Mr. Sherlock was making my case for me, although he seemed to be speaking more to himself than me.

Today I hoped I might take his mind off his problems by reporting how my visit to the offices of *Les Petit Marseilles* had uncovered a contemporary newspaper article about the *Kettleness* shipwreck. It ran in this way:

TRAGEDY AND MYSTERY IN TINY COASTAL VILLAGE
24 FEBRUARY, 1860

From a Correspondent.

One of the greatest and suddenest storms ever experienced along the Provence coast has brought strange and unique results to the tiny village of Providence, where a shipwreck and the disappearance of a local fisherman have all transpired within the span of twenty-four hours.

The shipwreck of the British merchant ship *Kettelness* took place just before nightfall on 22 February outside Providence Bay and was witnessed by several locals. The *Kettleness* was sailing from Varna to the Port of London with a crew of eight men and seven passengers. There were no survivors.

On the following morning the disappearance of a Providence fisherman named Massallo was reported by his wife and daughter. Massallo had been among a party of mariners that vainly searched for survivors from the *Kettelness*, and he was the last of this group to remain at Providence Bay after his companions returned home. According to the mariner's family, Massallo was a native of Corsica and was himself the sole survivor of a shipwreck seventeen years ago.

Meanwhile, the Gendarmerie Maritime have cordoned off the bay and the area of the shipwreck to prevent scavenging before salvage operations can be executed. The Minister of Commerce and Industry is working out details with the British Board of Trades and the ship's owners, De Chiel & Albemarle of London.

Mr. Sherlock read this and asked, "You located no other articles?"

"None."

"This one is remarkable in its lack of relevant details."

"I'll keep looking, but newspapers weren't as commonplace here back then as they were in southeastern England. In fact that article's publisher shuttered his doors soon after and there were no newspapers in this area again until 1868."

"Try expanding your search to more metropolitan areas."

"I will, but even there is a problem. Shipwrecks in the Mediterranean Sea may not be commonplace but they are hardly rare, so they generally receive little more than one or two comments in city newspapers unless there is something outré about them."

"It is worth a try nonetheless." Mr. Sherlock stared at the cutting and stroked his whiskers. "This Massallo was the last to forsake the search, perhaps out of empathy, but who is to say what happened after his comrades departed? He might have searched without interruption and left, after which he could have been waylaid or chose to abandon Providence for who knows what reason. He might have been murdered as soon as he was alone and his body cast into the bay. He could have even drowned himself. The suppositions are endless without details. I must have facts." He rose from his seat and stood very erect. "I shall see how Mycroft's investigations into the Board of Trades, Minister of Commerce, and De Chiel and Albemarle are coming, but an expedition to Providence might be necessary before too long."

14 *January*

Mlle. de Galais rapped upon our door around half past ten.

It is the third time in the past seven days that she has extended Benet an invitation for to join her father Vernon de Galais, chair of the mathematical department, for lunch at their home in the Quartier Les Arceaux. On this occasion she was dressed in a peridot walking suit with shirtwaist and rainy daisy that complimented her golden hair and superb figure, and like each time before she sulked but did not protest when I informed her that my master was incommunicado.

I have come to enjoy her visits in spite of myself. Mlle. de Galais possesses the most amazing face. When her head is tilted one way she is a classical beauty with wide smoky quartz eyes, but when she cocks it another way she reveals the delightful visage of a scamp with a broad nose and crooked smile. Janus has nothing on her. It is no wonder the men of Montpellier find her the most tantalizing woman in their town. I don't think I could ever tire of watching this fetching metamorphosis, and I have to keep reminding myself that her father is one of the few men to have called Professor Moriarty a friend.

The Notebook of Dr. John H. Watson

7 February, 1894. – I visited Mary for the first time since her funeral.

January's intense frost and a malaise evoked by the monotonous rains that followed were enough to keep me homebound, but today the weather improved enough to brave the venture. After all, Mary and I agreed upon Brompton Cemetery over the other Magnificent Seven[70] because of its proximity.

The clement air felt almost balmy and I doffed my overcoat as I rounded the cemetery's modest domed chapel and proceeded down the main avenue until I veered towards my wife's grave. The groundskeeper

---

[70] Seven large private cemeteries established outside central London during the nineteenth century to alleviate overcrowding in the city's small parish churchyards. The Magnificent Seven are (in order of when the cemetery was opened): Kensal Green Cemetery, West Norwood Cemetery, Highgate Cemetery, Abney Park Cemetery, Brompton Cemetery, Nunhead Cemetery, and Tower Hamlets Cemetery.

is waiting until spring to lay sod on her mound and the tumulus was a bit worse for wear. I stood there an indefinite time and might be there still if not for Inspector Lestrade, who insists he called my name several times before attracting my attention. "I wasn't sure there if you were coming back to us."

"I must have been deeper in thought that I realized."

"Lost in thought, seems more like it. I apologize for not presenting my condolences sooner and for this intrusion. I would never have come if it weren't important."

Several moments passed before I was functioning properly. I felt a discoordination between brain and body in the manner of a person roused from the deepest slumber. Lestrade waited patiently until I was ready to ask the reason for his visit.

"I bring a message from a mutual friend." Lestrade lowered his voice even though no one was near. "'*Mea gloria fides.*'"

Walter Simonson! "Is he well?"

"He's in full fighting trim, but is asking for assistance."

"He's returned to England?"

"I am afraid not, but Mr. Mycroft Holmes would consider it a favor if you would discuss the matter with him."

Part of me snapped to attention, the veteran slipping into harness, even as another part rebelled, blistered with shame at my response in light of Mary's passing.

Lestrade not only espied my conflict but understood. "It's been my experience to trust your first reaction. I'm not sure Mr. Sherlock Holmes would agree, but it's right and it's no use saying it ain't. There's no better antidote for grief than plain old hard work. So if you feel up to it there's a hansom waiting on Old Brompton Road to take you to the Foreign, India, Home, and Colonial Offices. If you'd rather not, I'll tip the cabbie and tell him to be about his business."

Within half an hour I was seated in Mycroft's office overlooking Whitehall. After expressing sympathy for Mary, he confided, "Walter is helping us attend to the remnants of Professor Moriarty's criminal empire outside of England. I dare say it's kept him nearly as active as you and the Inspector these past few months."

"I stand ready to be of service, even if I am just an old solider with a war wound."

"'Old?' Why you're in your prime! 'Soldier?' That you are. You're also a respected medical man and the preeminent student of my brother's methods. It is in the latter capacity that I've asked you here, although I make this request with some reservations. There is distinct danger, but Walter requires help. Now before you remind me which of us shares Sherlock's skills for deduction and observation, let me remind you which of us shares my brother's ambition and energy. Our one foray together also demonstrated just how incapable I am of working out an investigation's practical points.[71] So while neither of us is the ideal candidate, you are the most qualified. Naturally my talents as an armchair reasoner shall be at your disposal."

---

[71] See "The Adventure of the Greek Interpreter."

Intimidation does not begin to describe the wear I felt on my nerves. I am not sure if I had felt more nervous when I landed in Bombay. "Exactly how can I assist Walter?"

"He will explain when you arrive." Mycroft removed a folded itinerary from his breast-pocket and instructed me to memorize it, after which he put it to fire and ground the ashes with a makeshift pestle before opening a window to let a breeze carry away the powder. "*Momento, homo, quia pulvis es, et in pulverem reverteris.*"[72] He closed the window. "This campaign has taken a toll. Shall we end it, if we can, before it robs more from us?"

"I'd like nothing better." I stood to leave. "Unless you require anything further?"

"No. *Pax vobiscum*[73] and good hunting."

II. THE LODESTONE

The Notebook of Dr. John H. Watson

10 *February, 1894* – As far as the world is concerned I am going to Montpellier at the invitation of a friend, Felix Benet, who came under my professional care during the Afghan Wars and is currently a visiting professor at the University. When news of my wife reached Benet, he offered the use of his address as a retreat while he is away on a research trip.

---

[72] "Remember, man, that dust thou art, and unto dust thou shalt return."
[73] "Peace be with you."

When I departed England the weather was boisterous, but as I traveled south it moderated, and when I arrived in Montpellier it could almost be called mild. The night was very dark and a thin, tepid rain was falling when Simonson greeted me at the station in his identity as Benet's servant Brictwen. He remains unpresupposing and sinewy, but his hair is definitively whiter while his skin is brown as a nut and somewhat wind-worn. Arrangements were made for my luggage to be sent to Benet's home and then Simonson escorted me to a waiting tram occupied by a driver, conductor, and two weary passengers. We departed after Simonson selected seats near the rear exit and he spent the journey commenting on the city.

"Montpellier is a tot compared to her neighbors. Most cities in this part of France have some sort of Roman history, but the first known document that mentions Montpellier is dated 985 A.D. Up until then this area's most prominent settlement was Maguelone, but when it became a favorite target of pirates its residents decided to move further inland. A local feudal dynasty called the Guilhem cobbled Montpellier together by uniting two hamlets, building a castle, and surrounding all three with a defensive wall. In 1180 William VIII of Montpellier granted freedom for all to teach medicine in the city, but it was forty years before Cardinal Conrad of Urach founded the faculties of law and medicine. By the thirteenth century the city had prospered into an important trading center as well as a stop-off for pilgrims traveling the *Via Domitia*,[74] and

---

[74] The first Roman road built outside Italy. Constructed in 118 AD, it is one of the oldest of all Roman roads and links Rome with Spain and runs through modern-day southern France.

its status increased over the next few centuries despite a series of plagues that included the Black Death. The botanical gardens and many grand buildings were constructed during the sixteenth century, during which time the city developed its own style of architecture. For a while Montpellier became a key economic center after Cœur[75] established himself here in 1432."

The conductor commented, "You are extraordinarily familiar with our city's history."

Simonson scrutinized the man. "I acquaint myself with wherever I am visiting." He turned to me. "I'm afraid Dr. Benet's home isn't in one of the city's *hôtels*. He rented a house in the *Cèlanòva* neighborhood, which is congenial but hardly ostentatious." A few minutes later the tram stopped. "Here we are. The Avenue de Lodéve."

We stepped out onto a long, curving street graced by two-story and three-story terraced homes. Benet's home had white painted window frames and decorative fencing over its upper floor windows and on its roof, and once inside Simonson escorted me to my room before leaving me to join him when I was ready.

Later. – I found Simonson waiting in the front room with a modest but much appreciated dinner and strong *café noir*. As I ate, I asked, "Does this Benet work for the British government like you?"

---

[75] Jacques Cœur (1396 – 1456). Merchant and government financial official. His motto was, "To a valiant heart, nothing is impossible."

"No, but Benet stands ready to volunteer his services whenever they are needed. My orders are to watch over him as the Moriarities almost certainly know he's helping us. For the sake of general appearances I had to remain here to keep up the house, but a colleague is keeping an eye on Benet during his research trip." Simonson poured some coffee and took a gulp as I informed him of everything Mycroft Holmes had appraised me. "I see. You understand that duty proscribes me from discussing certain particulars of my mission, so please forgive any necessary vagueness as I tell you why I need your help. It has to do with a precious stone. Not precious in the normal sense. I mean it possesses no great value nor does it represent anything about the planets, sun, and moon like a gemstone. It is precious in the sense that it is not to be treated carelessly. That is why I have been instructed to locate and then destroy it." I asked why. "I shall get to that. This stone has a rather unique and sinister past, although you won't find it mentioned in many histories. That may be because it doesn't have a name like the Black Prince's Ruby or the Great Mogul. It has sometimes been referred to as the Ash Stone because it resembles a chunk of tuff except for its color and infinite hardness. The stone is said to be darker than the blackest patches of the Cup of the Ptolemies[76] and is reflectless."

"Where does it come from?"

---

[76] Also known as the Cup of Saint Denis. A cameo *kanthoras* (two-handled cup) with Dionysiac emblems and vignettes carved from onyx sometime during the period of Classical Antiquity.

"No one knows, but conjectures abound. It might be a by-product of investigations into the philosopher's stone by Zosimos of Panopolis[77] or it could have broken off the monolith at Stregoicavar.[78] There is even a legend that some addled worker got himself lost in the mines of Azakov[79] and recovered it from a stratum roofing the highest corner of Hades."

"That sounds more like Haggard[80] than history."

"Whatever its origin, the Ash Stone appears to have been introduced to modern civilization by two travelers who swore they had recovered some of King Shaddad's treasure in the lost city of Iram.[81] These two travelers somehow managed to stumble across a cave that led to an underground chamber in which they found a large dead man sitting in a golden throne surrounded by an assortment of riches. The giant's body was covered with jewels and dressed in silver and gold, and near its head lay a golden tablet engraved with a warning from Shaddad the Lesser, the King's son. Our wayward travelers packed up as much of their new found wealth as they could carry, but when they opened their packs

---

[77] Greek alchemist and Gnostic mystic born in Egypt and who lived near the end of the third and beginning of the fourth centuries. Author of *Cheirokmeta*, one of the oldest known books on alchemy.
[78] Known as the Black Stone, this monolith stands in the mountains of Hungary. The nearest village is Stregoicavar, which translates approximately into "Witch Town."
[79] Ancient iron ore, nickel, and copper mines near the Khibiny Mountains on the Kola Peninsula in northwest Russia.
[80] Sir Henry Rider Haggard (1856 – 1925). British author. Best known works include the Lost World novels *King Solomon's Mines* and *She*.
[81] The destruction of Iram is alluded to in Sura 89 of the Quran. According to some Islamic beliefs Allah wiped away Iram and the road leading to the city because its citizens turned to idolatry and the occult.

upon returning home they inexplicably found the Ash Stone amongst their booty. Tell me, have you heard of the Black Stone in Mecca?"

"I have, but it's been some time."

"It supposedly dates back to Adam and Eve and has been kept inside a silver frame mounted to the eastern corner of the Kabba[82] since the tenth century. The story goes that when Ismail I[83] heard about the Ash Stone he believed it might be a comparable relic and ordered it brought to Tabriz,[84] hoping its prestige could help legitimize his new capital. It was stored in the city's Blue Mosque but there is no historical account that the stone was ever mounted and displayed. No one knows why. The only clue it was ever truly stored in the Blue Mosque comes from an Ottoman manuscript.[85] When the Ottomans raided Tabriz after the Battle of Chaldiran[86] they looted the mosque but left behind what the manuscript describes as a 'noxious black volcanic stone.'"

"'Noxious' in what way?"

"I'm getting to that. Not long afterwards the Ottomans were repelled from Tabriz and the capital was eventually moved to Qazvin.[87] During these years a series of earthquakes damaged the Blue Mosque until it was beyond repair, so Tahmasp I[88] had the Ash Stone brought to Qazvin as the personal property of the Shah. Tahmasp supposedly

---

[82] The most sacred site in Islam, this cube-shaped building stands at the center of the *Masjid al-Haram* mosque in Mecca, Saudi Arabia.
[83] Shah Ismail I (1487 – 1524). Founder of the Safavid Dynasty. Ruled from 1501 to his death.
[84] Capital of East Azerbaijan Providence in northwestern Iran.
[85] As of this writing I have been unable to identify this manuscript.
[86] The Battle of Chaldiran was fought on August 23, 1514, after which the Ottoman Empire annexed Eastern Anatolia and northern Iraq.
[87] City in northwestern Iran and capital of the Safavid Dynasty from 1555 to 1598.
[88] Shah Tahmasp I (1514 – 1576). Ruled from 1524 to his death.

became so fascinated or bewitched by it that he had a fragment set into an ornate ring he kept near him whenever he wasn't wearing it, which was practically all the time.

"You may already know that Tahmasp fell gravely ill twice in 1574. Both times poison was suspected, as it was two years later when Tahmasp suddenly died. On those first two occasions he was nursed by his favorite and rather remarkable daughter Pari Khan Khanum.[89] Before Tahmasp's first bout of illness he fell into the habit of burning coal procured from Spain in his bedroom's brazier instead of the usual charcoal. It was normally the job of servants to maintain the brazier, but it seems on very cold nights Tahmasp must have found it more convenient to attend to it himself. Pari Khan Khanum did not recognize the coincidence until later, but her father began to recover after his servants began burning charcoal in the brazier again. Then, during an unnaturally frigid night in 1576, Tahmasp apparently ran low on charcoal and poured the leftover Spanish coal into his brazier. The next morning Tahmasp was found dead. The setting of his ring had also partially decomposed during the night."

"Are you suggesting the setting was hazardous?"

"It's a possibility. People have died after coming in contact with arsenopyrite or cinnabar, although it doesn't seem like the Ash Stone is lethal to touch. Anyway Tahmasp's son Ismail II[90] ascended to the throne with the assistance of his sister, only to die about a year later

---

[89] 1548 – 1578
[90] 1537 – 1577

under similar circumstances as his father. It is no secret that the new Shah was less than grateful for Pari Khan Khanum's assistance, and after her brother died, she regained a great deal of the authority she had enjoyed immediately after Tahmasp's death. According to legend Pari Khan Khanum had the Ash Stone stored inside a three-lock box and cast into the vaults of the Imperial treasury."

"I'm sorry, but what is a three-lock box?"

"A type of coffer the Muslims borrowed from the Spanish. A plate with three keyholes is set around the lock so three keys are needed to open the box. Only the owner of the box would have a master set of keys. If the box ever needed to be transported, two keys were sent ahead to the recipient and one key would be given to the courier. Anything meriting a three-lock box tended to be extremely valuable, terribly important, or awfully dangerous."

"I can understand protecting something of worth or significance, but why go to such extremes to guard something perilous?"

"Possessing something dangerous can sometimes be beneficial."

A horrible possibility suddenly swirled my imagination. "Tobernite and coloradoite release noxious gases when heated."

"Now you're getting it. What if the Ash Stone does the same thing when it comes into contact with coal fumes?"

My heart seized as I thought about London—where coal burns in nearly every hearth—having its yellow and green fog transubstantiated into a poison belt. "The Moriarities would do something so monstrous?"

"I'd call it vindictive."

"But the princess's three-lock box is in Persia?"

Simonson turned pale and sad-faced. "I don't think so. I think it went down with a British merchant ship called the *Kettleness* that sank near a Provenance fishing village in 1860."

"How did the property of a Shah come to be on an English vessel?"

"I have been to many places since we last met, and during my travels I discovered that Pari Khan Khanum's three-lock box was nicked over thirty years ago by the friend of a *bon homme*[91] I met in the Sudan. Great Britain and Persia owe much to this *bon homme*, but his friend...well...while an extraordinary person in many ways, he was merciless in as many others."

"Can you share any details about him?"

"He was a French expatriate. He was born deformed. To put it bluntly, the gentleman was hideous. He ran away at an early age and picked up with some Gypsies touring the European fairs. The boy possessed an angelic singing voice and by the time he was a young man had become supremely skilled in magic and the arts. Asian caravans carried news of his performances back to Persia, where the Shah-in-Shah ordered the *bon homme* to invite this amazing fellow to Mazandaran[92] to entertain the sultana, but it wasn't long before the magician was aiding in the Shah's war against the Emir of Afghanistan. As a political assassin the magician had no equal and I cannot overstate the authority he came to wield; however, as can happen in even in the most civilized halls of

---

[91] "Good man"
[92] Province along the southern coast of the Caspian Sea.

110

power, the magician became so indispensable that the Shah came to view him as a threat. The Shah ordered the magician's execution and it fell upon the *bon homme* to carry it out, but he let his friend escape. The *bon homme's* treachery was never proven, but he nearly lost his head when it was discovered that the magician had made off with some of the Shah's possessions, including a three-lock box. The *bon homme* was reprieved when news of a corpse dressed in the magician's clothes had washed up on the island of Vulf in the Caspian Sea, but over time he lost his imperial favor, his property, and finally was tossed into prison without a trial before being banished after performing his service to Great Britain and Persia."

"So who was it that washed up on Vulf?"

"I doubt we'll ever know, except that it wasn't the magician. The *bon homme* has been able to piece together that his friend traveled to Asia Minor on the way to Constantinople where he offered his services to the Sultan, which eventually led to the bounder escaping another execution with some of his patron's possessions. A few months later a masked stranger boarded the *Kettleness* at the Port of Varna with a crate he insisted be stored in his compartment. The stranger paid a good deal to keep the crate's contents as well as his identity a secret, but the *bon homme* is convinced this mysterious passenger was his friend and the crate contained the magician's swag from Persia and Constantinople. The *Kettleness* was bound for the Port of London, however the stranger was scheduled to disembark at the *Grand port maritime de Marseille*. Unfortunately the *Kettleness* sailed into the worst storm to strike the

Mediterranean in nearly twenty years and sank off the village of Providence."

A line by William Clark Russell[93] came to mind: "'...there arose such a violent storm that they were all shipwreckt, but happily in sight of land, to which by timely assistance they all got safe.'"[94]

"Timely assistance was waiting. A group of fisherman kept watch as the *Kettleness* smashed into the rocks off Providence Bay, but there was nothing they could do to help. According the Gendarmerie Maritime everyone and everything aboard the *Kettleness* went down with the ship. One strange thing, though. The last fisherman to keep watch was a Corsican who barely survived a shipwreck in the same spot almost twenty years earlier. His name was Massallo and he never returned home that night or was ever seen again."

"There was an investigation?"

"Yes, by the nearest representative of the gendarmerie, a fellow named d'Armilly. A charitable man might call his efforts perfunctory. Perhaps less than earnest. After one day d'Armilly was unable to find any trace of Massallo, who was by all accounts a dedicated husband and father, so he concluded this old man of the sea must have been swept up in a rogue wave generated by the storm. I suppose it's possible."

"Now who's being charitable?"

Simonson shrugged. "As for the Gendarmerie Maritime, they recovered no bodies and precious little cargo, none of which resembled

---

[93] 1844 – 1911. British sailor, reformer, journalist, and author.
[94] From "Mysterious Disappearances" in *A Book for the Hammock* (1887).

anything that might have come from Persia or the Ottoman Empire. They also found no evidence of scavengers getting at the *Kettleness* prior to their diving on the wreckage."

"So it seems the magician and his ill-gotten gains—including the Ash Stone—lay in the dim green depths of the Mediterranean Sea."

"Perhaps, but for several nights after the shipwreck villagers reported seeing a corpse walking around the bay during low tide. That's their description, not mine. The villagers presumed it might be the restless ghost of one of the *Kettleness* dead or maybe even Massallo's spirit, but each witness described the nightwalker in similar terms: dressed in black…tall and gaunt…with a death's head for a face. A few tried to follow the corpse, but it always disappeared."

"You think it was the magician? That he survived the wreck?"

"The description matches his deformity. And it makes sense. Neither the Sultan nor the Shah will stop sending assassins if they suspected the magician is alive. If his trail stopped at a shipwreck with no survivors, however, the magician is a free man. Or as free as someone with a face like his can be. On the other hand, if Massallo rescued him, then he would be forever beholden to some stranger to keep his secret."

"Unless he killed Massallo. But why remain in Providence after that?"

"How is he to live without calling attention to himself? The poor man would have had two hopes. The first is the Gendarmerie Maritime salvages at least some of his booty, which he can steal back. Risky, but, again, what choice does he have? His second hope is that some of his swag will wash ashore as flotsam."

"I suppose that is possible."

"Now who's being charitable?"

I shrugged.

"John, we must know if the magician somehow recovered the Ash Stone. You would not only be doing me but our government a service if you go to Providence to try to find out. I cannot abandon my post here. Even if I could the Moriarities know me, and it's possible they have already dispatched an agent to Providence to search for the stone."

"I'm known to the Moriarities, too, Walter."

"Not as an antagonist. At least not until your visit to Baker Street after Mrs. Watson's funeral."

"How do you know about that? And why should that make a difference to them?"

"You remember a peddler with a Jew's harp? He wouldn't stop pestering you?"

I remembered

"His name is Parker and the Moriarities have been paying him and other peddlers to keep an eye on 221B since before Mr. Sherlock's death. The gang is curious why Mr. Mycroft insists on keeping up the rooms."

"That is ridiculous. Having Mycroft maintain our old rooms was in Holmes's disposition of property.[95] That is public record. As for the reason, Holmes was very fond of Mrs. Hudson, a widow who is getting on in years. This situation provides her with security since she doesn't have to worry about new tenants."

"They know that. Nevertheless that visit made them edgy, and you visiting Providence right now will test the limits of their credulity. On the other hand if Fred Porlock shows up, they will know I am up to something. If I remain in Montpellier then any agent they have in Providence may lower his guard, but any way you look at it, you will be taking a great risk if you accept."

I did not answer right away, but I have no doubts Simonson knew what my decision would be before I told him.

11 *February* – Simonson and I discussed the details of my reconnaissance well into the night, leaving little opportunity for sleep before I had to board an early Midi to the train station nearest Providence. It was late in the morning when I disembarked with ten miles remaining to my destination, but Brictwen had packed me a light meal and lent me a Victor Flyer he used when running errands. The safety bicycle's pneumatic tires traveled more smoothly over the country roads than I expected, and I enjoyed an agreeable ride through the sweet, simple Gallic landscape of umbrella pines, evergreen shrubs, and a few scattered buildings dotting the scenery. Eventually I veered onto a

---

[95] See "The Final Problem."

side road dominated by Aleppo pines and hart's tongue ferns, and over the next two miles the banks on either side of the lane rose dramatically deeper until the road emptied onto a beach that extended for several miles along the base of a rugged cliffline facing the Mediterranean Sea. The only interruption in either direction was the fishing village, Providence Bay, and a granite chateau overlooking both from a dominant position upon one of the looming crags.

I walked the Flyer to the village hostel and secured a room. Simonson and I had discussed rather I should register under an assumed name but judged it to be too suspicious, even though I could have always explained I was traveling incognito. So as not to appear too eager to any vigilant eyes, I am resting for a few hours before venturing from my room.

Later. – The last red streaks of sunlight were fading and fishermen were beaching their boats when I asked the innkeeper where I might have dinner. He recommended a café where the cassoulet was more than tolerable, and as I waited for my meal I realized it had not taken long for news of my arrival to spread amongst the villagers. They had heard of Sherlock Holmes even here. As men gathered to drink, eat, and congregate, they took the opportunity to make my acquaintance. They were so patient with my passable French and sympathetic to my recent losses that I paid no mind when they plied me with the same questions I have been asked a hundred times. When one young mariner pointed out that Provence boasted many sprightlier villages than Providence, an older fisherman glanced my way with sympathy and said, "Aye, but none as secluded." In return I asked them about their trade and lives upon the sea, and after a splendid evening of conversation I excused myself to take a stroll before returning to the hostel.

I walked to the bay and watched long green waves burst in a shower of spray against the rocks that had splintered the *Kettleness* thirty years earlier. I could not imagine anyone traversing this gauntlet in calm weather without being dashed and broken much less when the water and wind were in a frenzy. I gazed up towards the somber chateau and wondered what it had witnessed on that tempestuous night or the nights that followed when a corpse supposedly prowled this stretch. If only the mansion would speak, but it frowned and kept its secrets.

I lowered my sights and spotted some sort of shadow moving towards the cliff base beneath the chateau. The shade could have been a man, possibly tall if stooped and maybe wearing some sort of cloak or duster, but it was too distant to be sure of details. I shouted but the shape either could not or pretended not to hear. It maintained a lead ahead of a beam of moonlight that pierced some gathering clouds and was slicing across the beach, but when the shadow reached the cliff base it vanished before the beam exposed it.

I scuttled to the base and found a rather tortuous path leading to a road running along the top of the crag. Unable to locate any tracks or evidence that anyone had recently passed this way, I decided the best course was to return after sunrise when my eyes and mind would be fresh. Nothing more was to be gained by continuing tonight.

III. THE GEMSTONE

The Notebook of Dr. John H. Watson

12 *February* – Clouds continued to gather throughout the night until they blanketed the sky. Shortly before dawn the Levant turned the grey day foggy with a cool drizzle. The fog not only dampened my spirit but sent a tremble through me, serving as it did as a constant reminder of why I am in Providence. During the past three years I have found myself missing Holmes on several occasions, but I have never missed my friend more terribly than this morning when the threat of the Moriarities seems so great and I feel so out of my depth.

Later. – I walked to the café for breakfast to find a swarm of fishermen passing time until the fog lifted. I took a seat at the last empty table and ordered socca, and the mariner who had commented on Providence's seclusion asked if he could join me. "My name is Herrera." I could not help feeling cautious, but it was obvious by the way the other fishermen treated him that Herrera was one of them and therefore an unlikely recruit of the Professor's organization. I asked him to sit and told him I was sorry about the weather.

"Aye, we might as well be landlocked, thick as it is over the water." Herrera recommended that I spread some tapenade on my crepe, which turned out to be quite good. "How long will you be here, Doctor? I don't mean any offense. We're honored to have you. We just don't get many visitors in February."

"No offense taken. I shall be here a few days I suspect. Even this weather is more tolerable than late winter in London. By the way, I saw something strange near the bay last night."

"Not a ghost?"

"Why do you ask that?"

"A friend of mine went missing in the bay after a storm several years ago, and ever since people have seen what might be him walking along the beach."

"I don't think I saw ghost. What I saw was more like a shadow."

Herrera smiled patiently. "The night is made of shadows."

"So it is. Perhaps I let my imagination get the better of me. I had been looking at the chateau when I noticed what I thought was the figure of a man walking towards the cliffs. I called out but he kept walking until he reached the base and I lost sight of him. I followed and found a steep trail leading to the top of the cliff."

"You didn't go up the trail at night?"

"I did. It probably wasn't wise. When I reached the top no one was there."

"What did this shadow man look like?"

"He was tall with rounded shoulders. I think he was wearing a long coat or cloak."

Herrera chuckled. "That sounds like the Beadle."

"'Beetle?'"

"'Beadle.' Like your Richard Plunkett,[96] only this man is a vagabond. A lot of English tramps pass through here during the winter. The weather is nicer, like you said, and your workhouses are crowded. Most vagrants keep out of sight except when they're begging, but this fellow patrols the bay like a night-constable."

"How long has he been here?"

"A few days that we know of. He was probably making his way to the Châteaux de Pelfrey. It's abandoned so vagrants take advantage. That trail is the shortest path between it and the bay. Otherwise you have to go all the way round the cliffs, a good six kilometers."

"Where are the chateau's owners?"

"The Pelfreys? They moved to New Orleans in 1804. Things got less to their liking under Bonaparte. The chateau has been empty since. Being where it is, no one besides a tramp would want it."

"It's hard to believe someone would abandon such a fine-looking house."

Herrera laughed. "Not if you knew the Pelfreys!" A few fishermen joined in on the laugh. "Some call the Pelfreys an old and exalted family and that is true. So is calling them wild and reckless, although they were hardly the only *sauvages* among *la noblesse*."

A mariner barked, "'The fiend strike me blue!' That should have been the Pelfreys's motto!" All the café laughed.

---

[96] 1788 – 1832. Beadles were in charge of the watchmen for a district or parish and were the forerunners of London's modern police force. Plunkett served as the Whitechapel beadle from 1817 to 1826.

"They were untitled nobility, Doctor. They had no use for *titres de courtoisie* even though they were *noblesse chevaleresque*.[97] More than that, they were *noblesse d'épée*, the French knightly class. Perhaps that is why the family never lost its nobility although they were threatened many times with *dérogeance*."[98]

"Why?"

"It was frowned upon for nobles to take part in certain commercial or manual activities like smuggling."

"They were contrabandists?"

"Not out of any noble sense of retribution like Louis Mandrin.[99] They simply had less use for taxes than titles. *Henri le Grand*[100] granted Henri Pelfrey the land atop the cliffs in 1601. Why? Perhaps because Pelfrey fought beside him as early as the War of the Three Henries.[101] Perhaps because Pelfrey supported his conversion to Catholicism even though Pelfrey was a Huguenot. Or perhaps because they were likeminded men who ruled with a sword in hand and arse in the saddle. They were also incorrigible *coureur de jupons*.[102] Most likely all of that played a part, but none of it changes the fact that the land granted to the Pelfreys is dismal. The forests are dark and its ravines and grottos are

---

[97] French nobles sometimes made distinctions based upon the age of their status. *Noblesse chevaleresque* or "old nobility" inherited their title prior to 1400.

[98] Loss of some the privileges of nobility but not full revocation.

[99] 1725 – 1755. "The Robin Hood of France," Mandrin took to smuggling after declaring a personal war against the *Ferme générale*, the tax collecting agency for the royal government.

[100] Henry IV (1553 – 1610). King of France (1589 – 1610).

[101] The eighth and final French civil war known as the Wars of Religion (1562 – 1589), the War of the Three Henries was fought from 1587 – 1589.

[102] "Skirt-chaser"

wild and rugged. Why present anyone with such a *seigneurie*[103] if not because such lands and the cliff serve as excellent concealment for the smuggling of contraband? It would be just the sort of exemption to the *taille* those two foxes would have appreciated, as did Henri Pelfrey's descendants for nearly two centuries."

Later. – Having already traversed the steep trail from the bay, I decided to explore the lengthier path to the chateau to see what it might reveal. Once again I waited to set out, but I underestimated how long the trek would require. The dull, foggy day was giving way to gloaming by the time I reached the lands above the cliffs, where I followed an often winding road that took me past the top of the steep trail. Judging by its width and ruts the road had once been well-traveled, but now it was nearly overgrown with shrubs and noxious weeds. These thinned out as the road narrowed and swept round a curve that cut through a rock before coming out on the plateau upon which stood the great grey stone Châteaux de Pelfrey.

The quoins were blemished with chips. The chimneys projecting through the high-pitched hipped roof leaned. Mullioned windows loomed like dark, shapeless blurs, while the chilly, moist sea air and the reverberations of waves breaking against the rocks below accentuated a pervading sense that this was a place shut out from the world. Inside the reek of age and decay permeated every room as a lantern I had borrowed from the hostel cast great shadows on walls dense and wooly with dust.

---

[103] "Lordship"

The uneven floors were likewise carpeted except for where there were footsteps. These tracks along with fresh ashes in the fireplaces and rubbish strewn without care verified vagrants used this as a refuge, but at present the only occupants were rodents in the walls. I paid little attention to their scurrying until I noticed there were no such low, distinct noises coming behind an outstanding angle in the inner hall. I examined the angle and uncovered a concealed latch. When held in a horizontal position the latch permitted me to push aside the wall and expose a cavity, within which was a rough staircase excavated from the rock. This led to a small cavern dimly lighted by a few faults in the rock which had been fashioned with iron shutters. The ceaseless reverberation of waves was muffled but definitely louder here, emanating through a corroded grating set flush in the floor. Looking through its bars I could make out stone steps tapering into blackness from which streamed brisk sea air.

This must be the passage the Pelfreys used to transport contraband to and from the bay!

I threaded my muffler through a large ring welded to the grating's frame, pulled, but could barely budge it. I would have to approach the matter from the other end. Peering through one of the faults I memorized landmarks in the crags before fastening my lantern to the rope of one of the shutters. After making sure its light shone through the fault outside I started to leave, but what first struck me as pile of deadfall in the opposite corner caught my eye. On second glance it turned out to be the skeletons of two adult men. What remnants of clothing remained were sparse and unrecognizable, but the rusting blade of a knife with a whalebone handle was jammed between one skeleton's third and fourth ribs. I had seen such knives during my travels to Australia and India. They were popular with sailors and I wondered if one of these skeletons belonged to Herrera's missing friend. I examined the second skeleton and saw its hyoid bone was crushed, suggesting this man had been strangled by a strong pair of hands.

Leaving the cavern and shutting the angled wall behind me, I descended the steep trail and walked along the cliff base until I spotted the lantern light through the fault. Even with the mist and clouds I could see the landmarks I had memorized, which pointed me towards a promontory. Ebb tide was still receding where this cliff jutted into the bay, leaving me nothing to do except wait. Feeling a bit like William Legrand,[104] I passed the minutes pondering the puzzle of the skeletons.

Who were they?

Who killed whom?

How did they come to be in the cavern?

They might have been smugglers who had a falling out, killed each other, and their bodies left to rot. If one of the dead men was Massallo, however, was the other one the magician or an assassin sent to kill the magician? It seemed to me that the *bon homme's* disfigured friend would have more reason to cache a body than an assassin, but how would he have known about the cavern? It is possible the magician could have come across the seaside entrance I was searching for while combing the

---

[104] Protagonist of Poe's "The Gold Bug" (1843).

beach? As for the second skeleton, an assassin tracking the magician could have been waiting on the shore like Massallo. Or the assassin could have followed the magician aboard the *Kettleness* and likewise survived the shipwreck. In either case the magician could have dispatched Massallo with the sailor's own knife and strangled the assassin, after which he hid himself and his victims in the cavern while waiting to hopefully recover at least some of his lost booty.

The tide eventually retreated enough that I could slog around the base of the promontory. As best as I could tell the tide never receded completely at this spot, a natural impediment to curious eyes or casual onlookers. Squaring my sights on the lamplight and landmarks I succeeded in locating an obscured crevice of such a size that a single man could just fit through by stooping, and I clambered up into a littoral cave where the water was only ankle-deep. After several minutes of stubborn exploration I located a flight of dripping, puddled stone steps littered with marine debris leading up a niter-encrusted passage.

"*Heúrēka!*"

I climbed the steps and in due time spotted a square patch of light ahead. My hope had been that pushing the grate from below would prove more successful than trying to pull it up, but as I drew nearer I saw no bars crisscrossing the opening. A moment later a voice said, "That's far enough."

I halted.

A broad-shouldered ginger-haired man of medium height dressed in white flannel stepped into the patch of light. The lantern light behind him left the stranger's face in shadows, but judging by the timbre of his voice and his posture he was a Scotsman of early middle age. He held a Baldock knife in one hand and I cautiously slid my fingers into my coat pocket as I asked, "Who goes there?"

"Sergeant Connor Newcomb, formerly of the Coldstream Guards. If I'm not mistaken you are Dr. John H. Watson, formerly of the 5th Northumberland Fusiliers."

"I am John Watson, but I've not heard of you. What is it you want?"

"That's what I was going to ask you. After all, if you're here, can Sherlock Holmes be far behind?"

Another man's voice shouted, "Sergeant!" and Newcomb turned around. I caught a glimpse of his grim, virile face before he bolted out of sight and the grate crashed down into its place. Desperate sounds of struggle ensued commingled with what might have been a third man's voice. I could see nothing through the bars so I put my shoulders to the grate and pushed until I thought my legs would give out or my spine snap, but the obstruction barely budged, leaving me no choice but to return the way I came. When I reached the cave the tide had turned and water was surging through the crevice, sweeping in detritus that clung to my clothes and wedged in my boots. Getting outside was a near thing and I was exhausted when I reached the beach, so I am not sure if I heard Herrera calling my name right away. When I did I saw him and several other fishermen congregating at the base of the rocky wall near the trail as Herrera pointed towards the chateau. "We think he fell from there!"

"Who fell?" I trudged towards the fishermen as they stepped aside to reveal a man's body sprawled on the sand, his head cocked in a frightful angle. For some reason I shuddered, thinking it might be Holmes. Perhaps it was the circumstances or the location or because Holmes and the dead man were similar in height, weight, and hair color. This poor fellow's features were nowhere near as determined or intelligent, though they did not lack such qualities.

"It's the Beadle."

"Good Lord. What happened?"

A pale young mariner said, "I heard him. I was checking my nets when I heard a wail like a frightened loon. Then it just stopped."

Herrera explained, "Baptistin came running into the village to tell us and we got here a few moments ago."

"Does your village have a doctor?"

"He is coming." Herrera held up the knife with the whalebone handle, blood smeared on its corroded blade. "We found this near him. It looks like one that friend I told you about owned." He stared at my wet clothes. "What's going on, Doctor?"

"I'm not sure but I'll show you what I can."

Herrera motioned three of his companions to follow and I led the way up the trail then to the chateau. Inside we found the angle wall open. The fishermen were curious but quiet as I took out my revolver and cautiously stepped into the cavity, but it and the cavern were empty. I unfastened the lantern and brought it into the center of the chamber, where we found a sparse trail of blood leading back to the house.

Herrera spotted the skeletons. "What is this?" As I described how I found them earlier he stared at the bones, straining to recognize if either could be Massallo.

I handed the lantern to Herrera and the other fishermen and I tracked the droplets outside, where we picked up three fresh sets of footprints that went around the chateau to the edge of the cliff, where we looked down.

One sailor said, "It looks like the doctor has arrived."

Two sets of footprints and the occasional blood droplet led away from the edge, but the tracks and blood vanished after the road turned hard as its passed through the cutting and try as we might we failed to pick up another trail.

13 *February* – The village doctor is Édouard Morrel, a pleasant and competent fellow of around sixty. I assisted the fishermen with moving the Beadle to Morrel's cottage, where he and I waited for d'Armilly, a tall, horsey-faced man with crisp and curling black hair who was exceedingly curious regarding my presence in Providence. I repeated the reason for my holiday before explaining how I had seen the Beadle the previous night, had decided to explore the chateau after Herrera shared its history with me, and how I chanced across the smuggler's cavern.

"Impressive. An observation worthy of Sherlock Holmes."

I do not know how sincere d'Armilly was but I thanked him. "When I couldn't open the grating I decided to see if I could find a way into the cavern from the bay. I did but couldn't open the grating from below so I decided to return to the chateau. By then the tide was coming in and when I finally reached the beach I saw Herrera and the other fishermen around the body."

"So whose blood is in the cavern and around the chateau?"

"I can't say. There was no blood in the cavern when I found it and I thought I was alone in the chateau at the time."

"Dr. Morrel? Are you certain there are no lacerations on the body?"

The doctor answered, "All the injuries are consistent with what I would expect to find on a man who struggled for his life before succumbing to a lengthy fall."

"Did you examine the body, Dr. Watson? Do you concur?"

"I have and I do."

"Dr. Morrel? Has anyone suffering anything resembling a knife wound visited you tonight?"

"No. I would have told you."

"Don't you think that's odd?"

I answered, "Dr. Morrel hasn't had an opportunity to see the blood trail. The small diameter of the drops and the spacing between them suggests it's possible the wounded man could have tended to the cut himself or bound it long enough to seek attention elsewhere."

"That doesn't change the fact that the blood had to have come from at least one of the men this poor fellow fought," d'Armilly brusquely replied; then with a smile, "That explains everything."

"It does?"

"Finding that secret door must have attracted some vagrants squatting in the Châteaux de Pelfrey. They investigated…there was some sort of falling out…a fight ensued that concluded with two men tossing a third off the cliff."

"What sort of falling out?"

"Perhaps over the whale-bone knife. Does the reason really matter?"

Similar suppositions by Athelney Jones and Tobias Gregson[105] echoed in my memory, but it served my purpose to agree with the gendarme. When d'Armilly left I asked Morrel if he would send me word if anyone with a knife wound visited him.

"Of course. You know there could be another explanation for the blood drops. Perhaps no one was wounded. I have read your accounts of M. Holmes and know you've encountered such a situation."

"If you're referring to *A Study in Scarlet*, the blood drops here do not suggest anything like aortic aneurysm."

"Perhaps something else then, like hematidrosis. As for the blood on the knife…well…blood can be wiped on a blade as easily as it can run there from a laceration."

I agreed, but added, "Considering the corroded condition of the knife, whatever caused the man to bleed may be the least of his worries."

"That is so. I shall inform you and M. d'Armilly of any case of tetanus that comes my way."

---

[105] Scotland Yard inspectors. Jones appears in *The Sign of Four* and possibly "The Adventure of the Red-Headed League" as Peter Jones, while Gregson appears in *A Study in Scarlet*, "The Adventure of the Greek Interpreter," "The Adventure of Wisteria Lodge," and "The Adventure of the Red Circle."

I left Morrel and was returning to the hostel when I noticed someone standing near the cliff where the Beadle had fallen. Curious who this might be I made my way to the bay, but whoever it was was gone by the time I reached the spot, and I could not help imagining the bay's old ghost had found a new companion. I looked up to where the struggle had occurred as I listened to the dashing waves behind me, and before long found myself conjecturing the personal contest between Holmes and Moriarty. I am not sure how long I stood there before a rustling interrupted and I snatched my revolver. The sound had come from the steep trail and I spotted a tatterdemalion standing behind some foliage. At first I thought the tramp was an older boy or smaller man, but it turned out to be a young woman with most of her blonde hair tucked under a tweed cap. "Dr. Watson?" She kept her voice hushed.

I instinctively did the same. "Who are you?"

"Mycroft Holmes says you should leave Providence." She spoke excellent English with a slight upper class Montpellier accent. "He also said to tell you, *'mea gloria fides.'*"

Perhaps I should have remained suspicious, but I said, "I can't leave. A man was murdered tonight."

The woman struggled to find her voice. "Two men are lying in wait for you in the village. If we travel fast we might reach the train station before they realize you have taken flight." If this was true I could not allow this stranger to risk her life for me. I started to explain how my war wound would slow us down, but she ignored my protests and started up the trail.

Swept up in the circumstances I pursued.

Upon reaching the top we rushed past the chateau towards the rock cutting where a horseless carriage sat parked. The contraption had no roof and its only protection against weather or road debris was a semi-circular shield like a Roman chariot situated above the front wheels. A round lamp was attached to the shield. The coach was painted a robin's egg blue, all four spoked wheels were painted bright red, and an upholstered leather box seat was perched atop the motor housing.[106] The woman climbed onto the seat, engaged the motor, and grabbed what appeared to be the vehicle's tiller. "Get in."

"Is this yours?"

"It belonged to a friend."

Sitting to her left, I reflexively asked, "Should you be steering?"

"Do you know how?"

"No."

"Then I'll have to." And we were off.

Except for a low humming from the electric motor and the crunching of road beneath the wheels the horseless carriage traveled as quietly as a skiff upon the water.

"We should arrive at the station in about half an hour," the woman said. "That gives us time to catch the next train, which is going to Avignon. From there we go to Paris."

"Why not Montpellier? Am I being recalled to London?"

---

[106] Based upon Watson's description this horseless carriage appears to be an 1893 Jeantaud.

"I really do not know. I doubt we'll even reach the station if those men catch on to what we're doing and they can find fast horses within the next twenty minutes."

I turned to keep watch. "If they do, they won't find us easy prey." I glanced the woman's way. She was shivering and not from the night air. "What's your name?"

"Call me Geat."

An uncommon *nom de guerre*, though not as uncommon as her face, the features of which alternated from exquisite maturity to guileless prepubescence like the facets of a gem. "Why did Mycroft send you instead of Brictwen to fetch me?"

"I was not supposed to fetch you. I was supposed to tell the minder watching you to bring you to Paris. This is his automobile."

A Barachiel had been watching over me? "Do you mean the Beadle?"

Geat scrunched her face, confused. "Who?"

"The murdered man. The people in Providence call him the Beadle."

A sorrowful grin purled Geat's lip. "He would have liked that."

"What was his name?"

Her grin faded but not the sadness. "The Beadle will do for now."

"All right, but I still don't understand why Mycroft sent you. Simply delivering this message put you in great danger and you're obviously unaccustomed to such adventures."

"Why do say that?" she asked, a trifle huffed.

"Your bearing and accent suggest you belong to the *haute bourgeoisie*."[107]

"Why should my class matter? Look at Lady Stanhope!"[108]

"I doubt she or even Jeanne Baret[109] were ever as nervous as you are right now. Perhaps I'm wrong."

There came no immediate reply and eventually I wondered if Geat would talk again. Finally she said, "You flatter me. I am *petite brougeoisie*."[110]

"I stand corrected."

"I couldn't abandon you. I'm trying to carry out my instructions to the best of my ability regardless of my station."

"You're right, of course."

We traveled the rest of the way in silence. When we reached the station Geat sent a telegram before boarding the train. I pray for her sake we encounter no obstacles while switching trains in Avignon or upon our journey to Paris.

* * * *

---

[107] "Upper middle class"
[108] Lady Hester Lucy Stanhope (1776 – 1839). Adventuress, antiquarian, aristocrat, and traveler.
[109] Jeanne Baret (1740 - 1807). Believed to be the first woman to circumnavigate the globe. Baret pretended to be a man so she could serve as valet and assistant to naturalist Philibert Commerçon (1727 - 1773). In 1785 Baret was granted an annual pension from the Ministry of Marine for sharing Commerçon's labors and dangers with great courage and exemplary behavior.
[110] "Lower middle class"

IV. THE TOUCHSTONE

Walter Simonson's Journal

13 *February* –

A telegram arrived a few minutes ago.

Mr. Sherlock read it with a frown, handed it to me, and wrote a response on a cable form while the messenger waited. The telegram read:

> Pandora's Box. L'Enfer.
> "HERBERT DE LERNAC"

"What's all this?" I asked after the messenger had departed.

Mr. Sherlock rubbed his face as if he were tired, in the process wiping away his worried expression the way an actor did greasepaint. "What do you make of the mixture of English and French? *'Le boite de Pandore'* would have only cost a trifle more to send than 'Pandora's box,' but M. de Lernac has a reputation for dotting his i's. You've heard of him?"

"I met him."

Mr. Sherlock's eyes sparkled. "Have you now?"

"Yes. He was consulting Professor Moriarty about a local job Lernac needed help with. The Professor assigned another agent to assist him so I was never briefed on the particulars."

"I see. What do you know about Lernac?"

"Not as much as you, I'm sure."

I thought for a moment Mr. Sherlock might blush. "To call Lernac an arch-criminal would not be a disservice, but he is no Gallic Moriarity. He is rather like a Loki where the Professor was an Odin. Lernac and I have never crossed swords, but his file with the Sûreté bares testament that he is clever, resourceful, ruthless, and not the least bit humble. Lernac shares many qualities with Vidocq,[111] although I doubt he possesses even the seed of redemption." Mr. Sherlock leveled his eyes upon me. "Do you think Lernac would remember you?"

"I couldn't say. He saw me that one time. It was only for a minute and there were others in the room."

"It's best not to underestimate. You wore your mustache then?"

"Yes."

"Would you mind shaving it? Did you part your hair the same way then?"

"Yes. Change it?"

"Down the middle would be best. Trim the sides so it appears natural. I can help with that, but we must be ready to leave within the hour. That will give me time to send a cipher telegram to Mycroft on the way to the station. My reply to Lernac was that I shall meet him at noon tomorrow, so if all goes well we should be back in Montpellier before Mycroft can notify Watson's guardian angel in Providence of our absence. Nevertheless I'm taking no chances."

---

[111] Eugène François Vidocq (1775-1857). French soldier, criminal, and privateer. Became an informer while in prison and later established the *Brigade de la Sûreté* (Security Brigade). Opened the first private detective agency and is considered the father of modern criminology. The Vidocq Society, a members-only club made up of forensic professionals offering their services in solving cold cases, is named in his honor.

"Where are we going?"

"Montmartre."

Lernac's telegram now made sense. "He knows about the Ash Stone."

"I will be surprised if 'Pandora's box' refers to anything else."

"What's it to him? I have to believe he is helping the Moriarities lay a trap. Violence does not go unnoticed in Montpellier, but that isn't always the case in Paris."

"Our thoughts travel parallel lines. Therefore I suggest you bring your Webley as well as anything else you think may prove useful and I shall do the same."

14 *February* –

We arrived at the *Cabaret l'Enfer* on the Boulevard de Clichy at the appointed time.

The establishment and its neighbor the *Cabaret du Diel* are crude yet spectacular, delivering Dante's *Divine Comedy* to the *flâneurs*[112] frequenting the foot of the Montmartre hill. The façade of the *Cabaret l'Enfer* is particularly menacing: a red and black stucco of demons roasting beautiful nudes surrounding an entrance resembling the gargantuan face of Leviathan, the Devourer of Those Accursed.

---

[112] Can mean "loafer," "saunterer," "lounger," or "stroller." Sometimes used to refer to a man of leisure.

"A bit tawdry," I mumbled before passing through the satanic jaws, feeling a little like Robert Blair's school boy whistling past the churchyard.[113]

"It is certainly theatrical, but *de gustibus non est disputandum.*"[114]

We entered a cramped cavernesque dining room, its sculpted walls an eruption of papier-mâché outstretched devils and writhing doomed. The room appeared to be vacant except for Herbert de Lernac, who sat at a table reading *Le Matin* as casually as if he were sitting at a café along the Champ-Élysées. He was average height, average weight, neither pale nor tanned, with brown eyes and short, trim chestnut hair and mustache. Lernac wore round eyeglasses and a brown sack suit with pinstripes. A bowler lay atop the table. He appeared nondescript by design, but there were telltales of Lernac's personality if one knew what to look for, one example being his posture, which was indefatigably confident. This man was nonplussed in the contronym use of the word: unfazed, unperturbed, and unimpressed. Lernac folded his newspaper before placing it on the table and nonchalantly slipping a corner beneath the bowler's brim. "Please sit down. Would you like something to drink after your journey?"

Mr. Sherlock answered for us. "Thank you, no."

I took the liberty of sitting across from our host and waited for Mr. Sherlock to take a seat, which he eventually did.

Lernac said to Mr. Sherlock, "You know who I am."

---

[113] A reference to Blair's poem "The Grave" (1743).
[114] "Taste, there is no dispute."

"If you sent the telegram then you are Herbert de Lernac."

"There can be no other. According to *Université de Montpellier* you are Dr. Felix Benet."

"Yes. This is my man, Brictwen."

Lernac smiled at me. "Certainly not." He tapped his newspaper a few times. "*Le Matin* has been publishing the remarkable explorations of a Norwegian explorer named Sigerson. Or is he Swedish? It can be hard to differentiate between the two. There are those who have the same trouble with French and Belgians. Nevertheless it does not become men such as us to deny pride or abhor boasting unless there is a good reason." He stared at Mr. Sherlock. "Don't you agree?"

I asked, "What did you mean by 'Pandora's box'?"

"I thought it an adroit analogy for a box containing contents best kept locked inside three times."

A new voice added, "A box you and we want very much to find."

Two brutes arrived behind us to block the way back out of Leviathan's mouth. Three more thugs stepped out from a recess meant for musicians at the front of the dining room. All five carried a knife or cudgel. I recognized one. "Hello, Brunel."

"Porlock. I always was peery about you."

"Fair enough. I always thought your idea-pot was cracked."

"Give the red rag a holiday and toss that Webley of yours on the table. Same with any other barking-irons you've tucked away. Be careful about it. In the meantime Sergeant Newcomb asked me to pass along his regards."

Mr. Sherlock looked as calm as if he were sipping tea. "I doubt that."

"You mean because he has no manners? That may be right. If you mean because he's dead, then you're wrong."

I said, "He certainly isn't alive."

"Sure he is. You two are a pair of goosecaps. Didn't you think Newcomb might make friends in Omdurman same as you? That wasn't his head that got shown to the Khalifa. That one came off some British scout. The Khalifa never saw the sergeant so he had no way of knowing when he was told different."

I cursed myself for overlooking this but said, "Quite a yarn."

"You'll see for yourself when he gets back from Daisyville."

"What is he supposedly doing in the countryside?"

"He had business with your friend Dr. John Watson." Brunel smirked, sensing he had struck a nerve. "Where's your enthuzimuzzy now?" He told Lernac, "You can be on your way. We'll let Newcomb know you played your part down the line."

Lernac started to stand as he pinched the closest end of the newspaper towards him with one hand and reached for the bowler with the other. He genuinely looked like he intended to leave, so Brunel and his men were unready when Lernac flipped the hat aside to snatch a Lebel revolver concealed underneath. In the same moment some of the papier-mâché devils split open and four men stepped out from concealment to aim Lebel rifles at Brunel and his pals.

Brunel fidgeted and snarled like a caged beast. "What's all this?"

"Don't be poked up, M. Brunel. All I ask is you divest yourself of your weapons. After that my comrades will see that you and your comrades return to England."

"We're not going anywhere before getting what we came for."

"I am afraid you are. I have no desire to injure you, but that is not the same as being unwilling." Lernac casually cocked his revolver.

Brunel and his men wisely relinquished their weapons.

Lernac guided them towards a bar that resembled a cauldron. He grasped the bar and swung it away from the wall to reveal a lath-and-plaster gangway running between the cafés. "My comrades will escort you to the rue des Martyrs and then make sure you are safely on your way."

"Newcomb isn't going to like this. Depend on it."

A look of uncommon pique blotched Lernac's face. He uncocked his revolver and whipped its barrel across Brunel's skull. Brunel's legs buckled and he crumpled to the floor. "You can tell Newcomb I like what he has done even less." Lernac glowered at Brunel's companions. "Carry him." They did as told and Lernac shoved the cauldron back in place. By the time he returned to our table so had his equanimity. "My apologies."

Mr. Sherlock still might have been sipping tea. "Do not think me ungrateful, but the Moriarities will not be in a forgiving mood if you had an arrangement to turn us over to them."

"The only arrangement I have is with M. Mycroft Holmes, who would like me tell you he sends his regards."

Neither Mr. Sherlock nor I reacted.

"I am also to extend regards to M. John Reeves with hopes that Caprice is well."

Mr. Sherlock peeked my way and nodded.

Lernac noticed. "We understand each other now?"

I confessed that there was much I did not understand, starting with why Mr. Mycroft would make any sort of arrangement with him.

"He required an inventive, resolute, adaptive man who is at his most masterful when anyone else would be appalled. Who else is there in all of France, M. Sigerson? Or may I call you M. Porlock? I regret now we did not have the opportunity to work together. By the way, how is M. Moore?"

"You mean Horace Moore?"

"Yes, the man who assisted me four years ago. He was tall. Broad chested. No ear lobes. Octopus tattoo on his left forearm." Lernac smiled at Mr. Sherlock but said to me, "Shall I go on?"

"No need. That's him. He worked his way up to be the Professor's chief of staff. The last I heard he has eluded capture."

"I would have expected no less. His brain is one of the acutest in England and he has a considerable future before him."

"Unless some complaint of the throat catches up to him before his time."

Lernac waggled a finger. "Before I go further let me say that your friend John Watson is well and on his way here."

Mr. Sherlock stiffened. "Why is he coming to Paris?"

"Remaining in Providence became too hazardous."

"There was supposed to be a man posted in the area for protection."

"Yes, I know. Mycroft Holmes asked me to select your friend's guardian. Too many agents with the Sûreté are familiar to the French authorities, many of whom in turn are beholden to the Moriarities."

I said, "I'm still confused about why you're helping the British government?"

"It is simplicity. I am indebted to Mycroft Holmes and Herbert de Lernac honors his debts."

"How are you indebted?"

Lernac waggled his finger once more.

Mr. Sherlock: "If Watson is on his way to Paris, is your guardian accompanying him?"

Deep lines serrated Lernac's brow. "No. My man died yesterday in the performance of his duties."

Lernac buffaloing Brunel now made sense. "How did it happen?"

"I am told Connor Newcomb made it a point to confront John Watson, so my man made it a point to ensure theirs was a brief encounter. The doctor escaped baffled but in excellent health. As for those responsible for my man's death, they will face justice or retribution. I prefer the latter, but one or the other shall be carried out."

Mr. Sherlock weighed all this in his mind before telling Lernac, "Please consider myself in your debt."

Lernac genuinely smiled. "I would say this wipes our slates clean. I've been told how you risked your reputation for me at Mycroft Holmes's request."

I asked Mr. Sherlock when he did this, but our host changed the subject. "Getting back to the reason I asked you here." Lernac strolled to one wall where he twisted the head off a particularly atrocious demon and reached into its neck to withdraw an alligator Gladstone bag. Carrying the bag to our table, he unpacked a small grey metal chest with Arabesque scrollwork and an inlaid lock fashioned with three keyholes. "Messieurs, from the jaws of the Devil himself, I present Pandora's box."

I instantly asked, "Have you opened it?"

"Not I."

"Someone else has?"

"Yes, its current owner. We are silent partners in this business."

We waited to hear more.

"As far as the world is concerned, Antonin Alexander is the sole owner and mastermind behind the *Cabaret l'Enfer* and the *Cabaret du Diel*. These establishments were his idea, but he lacked the full financial and creative resources to make his fantasy a reality. Even acquiring a lease along the Boulevard de Clichy proved more of a problem than he anticipated, but I am fortunate enough to count Antonin among my acquaintances and was happy to provide my assistance."

Mr. Sherlock: "Especially since a base in the Place de Clichy could prove beneficial to an inventive, resolute, and adaptive man."

"Antonin made much the same point. This building is serviceable, though we hope to relocate down the street soon."

"Should I assume the owner of this box provided the creative resources?"

"An extraordinary Renaissance man. I don't know if anyone can call him a friend, but I respect him and I think he respects me."

"May I ask his name?"

"The gentleman insists on anonymity. These days he prefers the wings to the limelight."

I asked, "Do you know if he ever lived abroad? Say in Russia? Or Persia?"

"I am not a man to betray confidences, but I don't think he would mind if I told you he has been making his living as a contractor in France for several years."

"A Renaissance contractor?"

"Some of the greatest Renaissance artists were also architects. These days he wants nothing more than to be like every other man, but it is hard to deny your passions, so he indulges in the odd theatrical job. These cabarets are neither sublime nor refined, but that is not their purpose. Antonin's aim is to entertain, not enlighten, although I suspect our contractor's secret panels and tunnels would be the envy of smugglers like your Hawkhurst Gang."[115]

Mr. Sherlock: "Do you know the contents of the box?"

---

[115] Violent group of smugglers who operated throughout southeast England from 1735 to 1749. Legends about the gang tell how it employed a network of tunnels originating from their headquarters at the Oak and Ivy Inn in Hawkhurst.

"An Arabic ring missing its setting and a curious black stone." Lernac reached into a jacket pocket and withdrew a sealed vial containing a sliver of what looked like dried coal tar pitch. "This sample of that rock is yours."

Mr. Sherlock studied the vial's contents like a lapidary.

"My partner is aware of the stone's history and has no quarrel if you wish to destroy it, so long as you can verify it is the same stone your government is searching for. Until then the box and its contents must remain in my safekeeping. I should mention that John Watson will be brought here once his train arrives in a few minutes, so Dr. Benet might wish to return to Montpellier with his gift."

"Sound advice." Mr. Sherlock stood, eager to depart.

"Might I suggest that M. Porlock remain?"

I had been ready to make the same suggestion. "Dr. Watson might be more at ease if he finds a familiar face here. Afterwards I can accompany him back to Montpellier."

Lernac asked, "Are you sure you want to take him there?"

"What choice do we have now?"

"Won't his presence be an impediment to Dr. Benet's research? Besides, with the death of my man, it falls squarely upon my shoulders to make certain John Watson is protected until it is time for him to return to London. I can do that much more effectively if he were to remain in Paris."

I looked to Mr. Sherlock, who agreed with Lernac.

"Excellent! If you wouldn't mind, M. Porlock, when you do return to Montpellier you could do me a great favor by accompanying Mlle. de Galais home. She is bringing the doctor here."

"How --?"

"Her story is not mine to tell. You will have to ask her."

Mr. Sherlock slipped the vial beneath his glove and pointed to the bar. "May I use your egress?"

"Permit me to open it for you. By the time you reach the street I shall have a cab waiting to take you to your station."

"I appreciate that. In the meantime, take care with my companions." Mr. Sherlock vanished into the passage.

Lernac momentarily left the café to make arrangements for the cab. When he returned he was grinning like a Cheshire cat. "How shall we pass the time until your friend arrives? Écarté? Faro? Or shall we share what secrets we know about the Holmes brothers?"

The Notebook of Dr. John H. Watson

14 *February, afternoon* – We arrived in Paris shortly before one o'clock and took an omnibus from the Gare de Lyon to the Boulevard de Clichy.

Our destination was bizarre in every sense of the word.

I am familiar with restaurants such as the *Café du Bagne* and *Château d'If* with their prison motif and *L'Abbaye de Thélème* where the servers dress as medieval monks and nuns, but none of those compare with the *Cabaret l'Enfer*.

"It is like walking into one of Dore's cartoons for the *Inferno*," Geat commented. She had slept intermittently on the trains and was exhausted, though she did her best not to show it.

"To each his own." I followed Geat through a doorway shaped like a monster's maw and passed into a kitsch interpretation of Bosch's *Hell* that served as the cabaret's dining room. Simonson sat waiting at a table with an unremarkable-looking man who introduced himself as Herbert de Lernac. I asked if there were anywhere Geat could rest, but she insisted, "Please don't fuss about me." She took a chair next to Simonson and appeared to be familiar with Lernac as she said, "This is a pretty thing."

He replied, "I imagine the first woman might have said something like that." This all sounded like stuff and nonsense until I spotted the object of their attention was an ornate metal box with a trio of keyholes. I asked Simonson, "Is that it?"

"Yes. I'm sorry, Doctor, it turns out I sent you on a bootless errand."

"Where did you find it?"

"I'll explain later. First I need you to tell me what happened in Providence. You can talk in front of M. Lernac. He has the confidence of Mycroft Holmes."

I told Simonson all that I had discovered and that had transpired. "From what Geat tells me --"

"'Geat'?" Simonson chuckled when I pointed at the young woman. "This is Jacinth de Galais, the daughter of Professor Vernon de Galais."

The young woman blushed as if ashamed as I asked, "M. de Galais is helping you like Dr. Benet?"

Lernac laughed. "No."

"But Professor de Galais knows what his daughter is doing?"

The mademoiselle bristled. "I can make up my own mind."

"He is your father."

"My father would prefer I help the Moriarities." The young woman frowned as she decided what to say next. "He met James Moriarty when they were at university. They had no peers when it came to mathematics. Father reviewed Moriarty's treatise on the Binomial Theorem and Moriarity later reviewed Father's monographs on celestial mechanics that introduced the Galais recurrence theorem."

"I see."

"Do you? Do you see that my father has been ambivalent at best and disinterested at worst when it comes to Moriarty's criminal proclivities? Father was instrumental in securing Moriarty a position after gossip lost the man his mathematics chair, and now he thinks I should assist the Moriarities in finding out how Dr. Benet is assisting the British government." The mademoiselle leveled her gaze at Simonson. "I was to flirt and ply whatever I could. It didn't seem to matter that Dr. Benet is notorious for being the antithesis of a libertine. Father was adamant I try."

Simonson did not seem surprised to hear this as I said, "Now that it seems the stone has been found, I suspect the British government wants it destroyed."

Lernac interjected, "So long as the stone inside the box is the Ash Stone."

"Yes, we have to make sure of that, so a sample has been given to Dr. Benet to analyze."

"I see," I said. "It appears I am no longer needed."

Lernac said, "I had hoped you would be my guest in Paris for a few days."

Simonson added, "Or at least until we know what the Moriarities think about you going to Providence."

"Isn't that obvious? They were going to waylay me."

"To kill you or to question you? We don't know which."

"I told you what that man Newcomb said. Even though he is dead Sherlock Holmes remains a palpable threat to the gang, and now they view me the same way."

"Newcomb is not Sebastian Moran, and the Colonel's opinion is what counts in London. We just don't know if Moran has changed his mind about you, but if he has then I've put your life in as much in peril as my own."

"I have never been one to shrink from danger." An angry resolve settled into my chest as I recalled what Mycroft Holmes said about the toll of this campaign. "I will do anything it if it means bringing an end to the organization Holmes sacrificed himself to destroy."

Lernac interjected again: "You shall be safe so long as you remain in Paris."

I asked Simonson if that is what Mycroft Holmes wanted.

"I still need to inform him what you've told me, but I believe he will agree with M. Lernac."

I suddenly found myself in a worse situation than being out of my depth. I felt helpless and useless as I accepted Lernac's offer. "What other choice do I have, at least for the moment?"

V. THE RAGSTONE

Walter Simonson's Journal

15 *February* –

I accompanied Mlle. de Galais as Lernac requested. She was quiet during most of the journey, but when we were a few minutes from the Gare de Montpellier she said, "Dr. Watson is a man of action." It was a comment, not an appraisal.

"He is, among other things."

"He resents being forsaken in Paris." The young woman gazed my way with no glimmer of immaturity.

"It is not his style, but he is a solider so he follows orders."

"You are a man of action. Wouldn't you feel the same way?"

"I have felt the same way."

"Because you follow orders." She turned towards the window and her kaleidoscopic profile exposed a few childlike aspects. "So did Benajah."

It felt inappropriate to say anything, so I left the choice of continuing to her.

"That's the Beadle's name. Benajah Place." Pleasant memories brushed the childlike highlights away until only the satisfied expression of a young woman remained. "You and Dr. Watson wonder why I agreed to help Lernac but refused the Moriarities."

"I can't claim to be privy to Dr. Watson's thoughts."

"You wonder."

"I do."

"I am no adventuress. Dr. Watson saw that and said so to me. I resented that. My pride. The truth is I can barely pass for a modern woman, but M. Lernac has always been courteous to me and is honorable in his own way. More than that Benajah trusted him, so when he asked this favor I agreed."

"May I ask how you knew M. Place?"

"He had…business…at the university a few months ago." She smiled quietly to herself. "You might call him a scoundrel and you'd be right. I called Benajah a rascal and was not wrong." That was all she was going to say regarding the Beadle, so our conversation ended there.

I escorted Mlle. de Galais from the station to the Quartier Les Arceaux, but at her request she walked the last few steps alone. Once she was inside I took the tram to the Avenue de Lodéve. I presumed correctly that Mr. Sherlock would be deep in his analysis, but he heard me and asked, "How is Watson?" I entered the tiny vestibule to Mr. Sherlock's bedroom, now converted into a laboratory, and found him wearing his dressing gown and stooping over a table covered helter-skelter with chemicals, test-tubes, beakers, retorts, and Bunsen burners. I answered, "He is in excellent health but feeling put-out."

"I shouldn't wonder, but a little rest can do no harm. I wish to hear everything he reported to you as soon as I'm finished and have sent my results to Mycroft."

"That sounds encouraging."

"Let us see." Mr. Sherlock picked up a two-liter measure that had been collecting distilled drops condensing from a large curved retort that boiled over a Bunsen burner. A portion of the sample from the vial floated inside the clear contents, and as Mr. Sherlock sprinkled some black powder into the retort the condensation instantly turned a miry color even as a white dust precipitated to the bottom of the glass.

"Well?"

"That was my third trial. Each result has been the same."

"What does it mean?"

For the first and only time that I can recall Sherlock Holmes appeared dumbfounded. "This sliver came from the Ash Stone. We've found it."

Later. –

It was more than two hours before we boarded the tram to the telegraph office. The telegraphist may be a confidential agent with the Sûreté, but I suspect Mr. Sherlock sent the most prudently composed cipher telegram of his career to his brother. While I waited to depart I took the opportunity to transcribe all that John had told me as well as update my journal.

After the telegraph office Mr. Sherlock suggested we walk home. "A stretch of the legs will do our bodies and minds." I agreed and we fell into our own thoughts as our stroll led us to the gloomy rue d'Auseil vicinity and down a long dirty street bordered by brick warehouses. Neither of us had spoken for at least fifteen minutes when we reached a ponderous dark stone bridge spanning an odorous river. As we crossed Mr. Sherlock said, "I know you were fond of your Victor Flyer, but Watson had no choice but to leave it behind."

Mr. Sherlock had not yet read the transcript, but I have gotten used to his making ratiocinations without warning, so instead of asking how he had reasoned out what I was thinking, I told him, "You're right, we should be prepared to move when Mr. Mycroft replies."

Mr. Sherlock grinned. "It is a pleasant thing when a companion applies my methods against me."

"I can't accept undeserved praise. You employed observation and deduction, but I only used common sense. What else would you be thinking about right now?"

"Common sense is a necessary component of deduction. You do yourself a disservice, which, if you forgive me, is a fault you share with Watson. I have never been one to rank modesty as a virtue. Underestimating one's self is as much a departure from the truth as exaggerating one's abilities. Neither you nor Watson does the latter, but you'd benefit more by abandoning the former."

I thanked Mr. Sherlock without mentioning that Mr. Mycroft has given me comparable advice over the years, although I couldn't help wondering if Mr. Sherlock didn't already know that. He said nothing more until we reached Écusson, where he muttered, "I almost wonder if the Ash Stone was some alchemist's early attempt to create a phenolic coal tar derivative. Perhaps an analgesic or anesthetic."

"I thought alchemist were just about turning lead into gold."

"Chrysopoeia was one aim of alchemy. So was creating panaceas. Alchemists also discovered the elements of arsenic, antimony, and bismuth...they created new alloys...they may have also invented the process of distillation. Even their failure to transmute base metals into noble metals eventually had its practical applications. Alchemists were inspired by their understanding of the nature of metals and our ability to manipulate their structure, an important stepping stone towards the purification of metals. Many natural philosophers gnash their teeth when they hear this, but modern chemistry owes much to Albertus Magnus,[116] Paracelsus,[117] and their brethren, which includes Newton and Robert Boyle[118]. It is inconceivable to me that the dedicated pursuits of any knowledgeable group of men, even if erroneously directed, can fail to one day lead to solid advantages for mankind."

"I don't see where the Ash Stone is beneficial."

---

[116] Saint Albert the Great (c. 1200 – 1280). Alchemist, astronomer, Dominican friar, philosopher, and bishop.

[117] Philippus Aureolus Theophrastus Bombastus von Honenheim (c. 1493 – 1541). Swiss alchemist, physician, lay theologian, and philosopher.

[118] 1627 – 1691. Regarded as the first modern chemist. Best known for Boyle's law. Author of *The Skeptical Chymist* (1661).

"Almost anything meant for good can be used for evil, but focus on the empirical applications of the Ash Stone. Coal tar contains no arsenic, unlike coal, which contains small amounts. This derivative exponentially intensifies the toxicity of any arsenic it comes in contact with by a manner which my analysis has yet to reveal. I suspect the small portion of the Ash Stone that was set into Tahmasp's ring must have intensified the arsenic contained within the ring's metal. The toxic effect was minimized by the setting's size and the almost insignificant amount of arsenic in the metal, but gradually that arsenic was absorbed through Tahmasp's skin. The effect was much more dramatic whenever the portion came into contact with coal fumes."

We had reached the *Cèlanòva* neighborhood and were walking down our street. "I'm not sure we'll ever be able to prove that's what happened."

"It is not necessary that we do. Not right now. Conjecturing on the song the Sirens sang to Odysseus is a chronos pastime, but it feels like everything we have accomplished is leading to a fast approaching kairos moment. Yes, we would be best served making preparations." He stared at me with mischievous eyes. "It is only common sense."

The Notebook of Dr. John H. Watson

15 *February* – I spent the morning in *La Librairie Hantée*, an obscure bookshop on the rue Montmartre where I purchased a volume of

Reade's *The Martyrdom of Man*[119] to pass the evening hours. Although I was by myself I sensed I was never alone, which left me feeling as safe and confined as a foundling in a nursery.

From the bookshop I strolled down the rue de Richelieu to find a café before visiting the *Bibliothèque nationale de France*, but instead found Lernac waiting for me at the corner of the rue de Montpensier. In spite of the grey clouds and wafting snow he stood arms akimbo and remarked on it being a lovely day before waving to a waiting cabman. Inside the hansom Lernac removed a folded piece of paper from the inside pocket of his mouse-colored greatcoat. "One of your Queen's Messengers just delivered two communiqués from M. Holmes. Here is yours." It ran in this way:

> Stone identified. Eradication essential. Will old soldier deliver to FO?

"Rather cursory," I grumbled.

"My instructions to accompany you to London are nearly as brisk. I will have it no other way, naturally, but such a journey seems foolhardy when there may be those in England who wish you harm."

"Does it really matter? If it turns out the Moriarities have a vendetta against me then what's to prevent them from coming here?"

"Me, monsieur. Me and my comrades in the underworld. Like your young Irregulars we go everywhere, see everything, but we also defend

---

[119] William Winwood Reede (1838 – 1876). British explorer, historian, and philosopher. Holmes recommends *The Martyrdom of Man* to Watson in *The Sign of Four*.

each other. Even the Société des Mines de Lorraine thinks twice before threatening anyone under our protection."

Simonson had filled me in on Lernac's biography before returning to Montpellier, but I find it difficult to believe this unostentatious-looking man is not frequently braggadocious. Nevertheless, I asked, "Why should a mining company threaten anyone?"

"The Société is merely a prime example. If the Moriarities have a rival in France it is they."

"This company is a criminal organization?"

"The Société is a different animal from the Moriarities. It may be even more dangerous. The Société des Mines de Lorraine is owned by a ruthless dynasty whose goal is to become France's largest employer. Few doubt they shall succeed. The Société wields considerable influence in my country, like Krupp[120] does in Germany, and their interests extend into shipbuilding, foundries, and armaments. One day the European powder keg will explode and when it does the Société is well-positioned to become rich beyond the dreams of avarice, and woe to anyone who attempts to impede them."

"But not you?"

---

[120] Arndt Kruipe emigrated from the Netherlands to Essen, Germany around 1587 and became a successful merchant. In 1810 Frederich Krupp (1787 – 1826) planted the seeds of the Krupp dynasty when he built a cast steel foundry, but it was his son Alfred (1812 – 1877) who developed a way to produce seamless, no-weld railroad carriage wheels that found a considerable market in Europe and North America. Alfred parlayed this into even more enormous successes during the nineteenth century through a savvy combination of innovation, research, marketing, philanthropy, and a persistent goal of long-term gains over short-term maximization. Krupp also offered special training, subsidized housing, and health and retirement benefits as incentives to the top ten percent of its employees. By the beginning of the twentieth century Krupp was Europe's largest corporation, but by 1999 significant financial losses led to it merging with Thyssen AG to form the conglomerate ThyssenKrupp AG.

"I have no wish to impede them. Our paths rarely intersect, although the Société did hire me once to perform a deed for them. It was at a moment when it and several of its most powerful associates were uncharacteristically vulnerable.[121] My swift and sure actions rescued them and we have had an understanding since then. They do what they do and I do what I do. Now returning to M. Holmes's communiqués, why do you think he does not assign this errand to M. Porlock? Such a task seems more in his line of work."

"I suppose for the same reason Porlock asked me to go to Providence. Porlock is tasked with protecting Dr. Benet and nothing has happened to change that."

Lernac's scowl suggested he found flaws in my logic, but he said, "M. Holmes makes no mention in his communiqués on how we should travel to London."

"What good is an itinerary if it is intercepted? I am sure Mycroft trusts you to attend to that. Isn't this your bailiwick?"

Lernac seemed to find this logic acceptable. "It is."

"Have you told the owner of the three-lock box that the stone is genuine?"

"He shall know by tonight."

"Then how soon can we be on our way?"

"A day. No more than two. In any event you should be prepared to leave at a moment's notice."

* * * *

---

[121] See "The Lost Special."

Walter Simonson's Journal

15 *February* –

Mr. Sherlock and I spent a restive night and even more restive day anticipating Mr. Mycroft's reply. Our provision of patience was nearly played out when a Queen's Messenger knocked on Dr. Benet's door. The young fellow looked weary and I asked, "Are you all right?"

"May I sit? I haven't slept since bidding London adieu."

"Of course," I told him as Mr. Sherlock asked, "You weren't followed?"

"A couple of Moriarty men picked up my scent after I left Whitehall. My orders were to let M. Lernac's crew attend to anyone dogging me, which they did as soon as I reached Paris." I asked if he had seen John Watson. "No. Only M. Lernac." The messenger withdrew a small packet wrapped in brown paper from his traveling cloak and handed it to me. "My instructions are to present you with this. M. Lernac also said I should tell you it is with the compliments of Mlle. Pandora." I exchanged cautious glances with Mr. Sherlock as I unwrapped a cardboard box. Tucked inside a large wad of cotton was a black cast-iron bit key. The messenger explained, "You are to deliver that to Sangatte[122] at four o'clock tomorrow. Go alone. Another Queen's Messenger will be waiting on Cap Blanc-Nez to take it to London."

Mr. Sherlock scratched an eyebrow. "From Paris to Montpellier to Calais to London? A curiously byzantine route."

---

[122] A commune on the northern coast of France on the English Channel.

"It's meandering, all right."

"This key could be in London now if you had been allowed to return straight back to England."

The messenger rose to his feet and buttoned his cloak. "'Ours not to reason why.'[123] I must be going."

"Surely you should rest first. It is nearly ten o'clock. Have some dinner. Catch your breath."

"It's a kind offer, Doctor, but duty first. Good evening, gentlemen."

After the messenger had gone I confessed, "I wonder why there was no message for you."

"Mycroft's missives can say as much if not more indirectly than directly. What do you make of being given only one key to deliver?"

"Mr. Mycroft is doing what you're supposed to do with a three-lock box: dispatching its keys separately. What I'm not so sure about is why it's new."

Mr. Sherlock scratched an eyebrow again. "I noticed that, but new keys can fit old locks."

"Except bit keys are designed for modern locks, and Pari Khan Khanum's sixteenth-century box should have pin tumbler locks or possibly ward locks."

"You know I abhor guessing, but with no facts to work with I must presume the original locks have been replaced. Perhaps Lernac's silent

---

[123] From Alfred, Lord Tennyson's poem "The Charge of the Light Brigade" (1854):

Theirs not to make reply
Theirs not to reason why
Theirs but to do or die

partner damaged the original locks when he opened the box. Or perhaps Mycroft instructed the locks be replaced as a precaution before transporting the box to England."

"Or this key is just a decoy."

"That is just as possible, further demonstrating how guessing erodes the logical faculty. Nothing reasonable can be eliminated, which leaves us in a purgatory of suppositions. Let us say you are holding a decoy. Don't you think Mycroft would have fashioned it to resemble the original keys? The Moriarities are not fools."

"Then perhaps so obvious a decoy was meant as an indirect message to us."

"How so?"

"You tell me. He's your brother. I'm only applying common sense."

Mr. Sherlock nodded. "*Touché*. Let me offer this *riposte*. Do you believe that Mycroft would send you on such a goose chase?"

"If it benefited England? Without a doubt he would."

"I agree. I only wish I knew for certain if that is what he's doing now."

This was getting us nowhere. "To paraphrase a better man than I, what choice do I have?"

"Let us consider this. You have been told to go to Sangatte alone, which equates to me waiting here alone. You are to pass off the key at a location where you may see England on the horizon. I believe my brother is telling us that we are to continue our exile. That returning now could upset his immediate plans to eliminate the stone and the gang coveting it."

"Even though no one understands the situation better than us?"

"Like the messenger said, ours not to reason why. He captured the sentiment in spite of misquoting Tennyson, frustrating as it is." On the word "frustrating" Mr. Sherlock clapped his hands before thrusting them into his pockets. "You better make ready if you are not going to be late for your appointment tomorrow."

VI. THE COAL-TAR DERIVATIVE

Walter Simonson's Journal

16 *February* –

Luck favored me and I succeeded in procuring a berth in a sleeping car on a train to Boulogne through Paris. From there I rented a bicycle and with some dedicated peddling arrived at the highpoint of the chalk ridge of Cap Blanc-Nez by four o'clock. The day was clear and Dover's snowy bluffs were visible along the azure skyline. A solitary four-in-hand was parked on a road towards the bottom of the ridge and the only person in view was a young woman with golden hair and a superb figure wearing a peridot walking suit seated on a bench overlooking the channel. As I approached the bench I glanced around from habit to make certain we were alone, and then asked, "What are you doing here, Mlle. de Galais?"

"Waiting to begin my stage of our relay, M. Brictwen." Her expression was guileless.

"'Relay?'"

"*Exactement. Mea gloria fides.*"

"I see. But you're not a Queen's Messenger."

"*Au contraire*, I have been pressed into service of the silver greyhound."[124]

"By whom?"

"M. Mycroft Holmes."

I suddenly had a pretty good idea where the Queen's Messenger went to after leaving Benet's home. "Doctor Watson was wrong. There is more to you than meets the eye."

"He was not wrong, and neither are you if you think I have no business being involved. Be that as it may, I could not live with myself if I permitted the Moriarities to get away with murdering Benajah."

"I see." Feeling as uncertain as I can remember, I sat on the bench and glanced at the Pas de Calais. "Be that as it may, I think I shall go to London in your stead."

A shiver rattled her body as her face paled. "You can't."

"I can."

"No. I couldn't live with myself if anything were to happen to you." Suddenly no trace of the girl remained, only the mien of a frightened yet determined woman.

"Then I shall go with you."

"You mustn't. M. Holmes informed me that it's not safe for you in England."

---

[124] Symbol of the Queen's Messengers.

164

"And you think you'll be any safer after I give you this?" I took the packet with the key from my coat pocket.

Mlle. de Galais gingerly accepted it. As she did she leaned in a way that I saw only her face and nothing of the cape or the hill below. "M. Holmes assumes the Moriarities will not attempt to hamper me."

"M. Holmes is full of opinions."

"Once I cross *La Manche* I am to take the boat train to London and deliver this to Whitehall."

"Will M. Holmes have agents watching you just in case?"

Jacinth glanced at her purse as she tucked the packet away. "I shall not be alone. You have my word, M. Brictwen."

We sat in stillness for several moments. Finally I asked, "Would it be too forward to ask you to call me Walter?"

This seemed to please her as she appeared to study my face. "Would it be too forward if I said you look very handsome without your mustache?" She smiled. "You remind me of Benajah in some ways. You are much more serious, of course."

"I suppose that comes from being on different sides of the law."

"Perhaps not as much as you think. I should like to tell you about him later." She stood.

"Will you at least do me the favor of being very careful, Mlle. de Galais?"

"If you do the same, Walter." She made her way to the four-in-hand and looked my way before entering the carriage.

I remained seated until it rode out of sight.

The Notebook of Dr. John H. Watson

16 *February* – Late in the afternoon of the 15th of February, the superintendent of the Chemins de fer du Nord,[125] received a cable from the Principal Librarian of the British Museum requesting a special be reserved from the Paris du Nord to Calais for phytologist Professor Sir Christopher Saxton, who was arriving the following morning with his personal secretary and general dogsbody Captain Peter Wells after a lengthy expedition in and around China's Yarkand River Valley and Kunlun Mountains. Many of the specimens Saxton was bringing back were being kept frozen for their preservation, so the timing in transporting them from Paris to London was critical.

Shortly before noon on the 16th a strongly built, middle-aged Englishman with a square jaw and thick neck arrived at the office of M. Fade, the superintendent, and introduced himself as Captain Wells. Fade informed Wells that a special consisting of a French class 120 steam engine (No. 721 on the Nord company's register) attached to a tender, luggage car, passenger car, and guard van[126] was waiting. The guard[127]

---

[125] French rail transport company that operated from 1845 to 1937, when it and several other railroad companies were nationalized into the French National Railway Company or SNCF (Société nationale des chemins de fer français).
[126] Also known as a brake van in the United Kingdom, Australia, and India. The American equivalent is a caboose.
[127] The American equivalent is a conductor.

was Jacob Michael, the engineer was Henri Comte, and the stoker was Etienne Roulet, all of whom had been with the company for more than ten years. The lighter had the fire in the boiler ready and the traffic manager would have the line cleared in one hour. Wells informed Fade that Professor Saxton would supervise the loading of the specimens onto the luggage car, and within forty minutes Saxton and his attaché were seated and waiting in the passenger car.

Just before the appointed hour a singular coincidence occurred when Fade approached Saxton and Wells with a request. A Mr. Gabriel Chase of Perivale[128] had just been escorted into Fade's office. Mr. Chase's only son had suffered a serious accident and it was imperative that not an instant be lost in the father reaching his family, so the desperate man was inquiring if he might be permitted to join the Saxton special if he shared the expenses. Wells expressed sympathy for Mr. Chase's misfortunate, but since the British Museum had commissioned the special only they had the authority to grant the request. As far as taking the time to contact the Principal Librarian, Wells insisted the fragile state of the frozen specimens necessitated that the special depart immediately, which it did.

* * * *

Lernac dropped into a nap almost as soon as the special departed on its northbound odyssey, so I passed the time reading *Martyrdom of Man* and had nearly finished the fourth chapter when he awoke. Lernac glanced out the window and asked for the time. I looked at my watch. It

---

[128] A small suburb of London.

was three minutes after one o'clock. We were scheduled to reach Amiens around two and the Gare de Ville in Calais a little more than an hour after that. As I put my watch away my eyes lingered on the initials H.W. engraved on its back and I marveled how much had happened since I showed it to Holmes only a few years earlier.[129] Lernac noticed and inquired, "An heirloom, Doctor?"

"My father gave it to my brother, who passed it on to me."

Lernac indulged a wistful smile. "Heirlooms are touchstones to our past. Guard and protect any you own. The only such treasure I possess is a bauble that belonged to my father."

"It's the sentiment of the object that matters, not its value."

"We are of one mind in that. As a boy my mother filled my head with my father's exploits as a Hussar. I never knew the man. Like Zacharias my father had me quite late in life. He died before I was born."

"What about your mother?"

Lernac beamed. "She was no Elizabeth." He chuckled. "She was rather a Gascon Moll Cutpurse."[130]

"And you followed in her footsteps."

Lernac beamed brighter. "Like M. Reade, I see no purpose in genteel-sentiment or the vanity of birth. My father was a hero many times over on and off the battlefield and in her manner my mother was just as daring. If either had been a scintilla different I would not be here

---

[129] See *The Sign of Four*.
[130] Born Mary Frith (c. 1584 – 1659). English pickpocket, highwayman, and fence.

168

nor would I be who I am. I am proud to have their blood in my veins. I suppose in that regard I have two heirlooms. Perhaps if a Napoleon were emperor I could have taken up the sword, but Carnot is president and I am content with my chosen path. How many men can say the same?"

Before I could respond the door facing the luggage car opened and Connor Newcomb barged in. Instead of white flannel he was dressed in a neat suit of sober black and matching overcoat, and instead of the spear knife he brandished a revolver. I shouted, "How did you get on this train?"

"Doctor Watson? I can hardly recognize you without your mustache." Newcomb glowered at my companion. "Lernac."

My companion was less nonplussed than I. "Newcomb. Or should I call you Chase today?"

"I'd be careful about what comes out of your sauce-box right now. Not after the pounding you gave Pierre Brunel. He still isn't himself."

"His chances of recovering exceed those of the man you killed in Providence."

"Oh, right, I forgot about that." Newcomb's lip curled in a smirk. "I'll tell you what, I'll call barley on the condition you two disarm yourselves and give me the stone without any humming and hawing."

"I am afraid – "

Newcomb cocked his revolver.

"Your condition is agreeable."

All I could do was glare as Lernac confiscated my revolver, retrieved his portmanteau from beneath his seat, and packed our guns and his navaja. "You'll find the stone in here." Setting the bag in the aisle he used his foot to push it towards Newcomb, who warily peered into it before placing it on a seat. Taking out the three-lock box, Newcomb said, "Thank you. Now bring me the key."

"You need three keys to open that."

"A little bird told me the works have been refitted so it opens with one. If I've been sold a dog, we'll have the other keys soon enough. Now give me yours." Lernac shrugged and carried the key to Newcomb, who insisted Lernac unlock the box. "I hope you'll forgive me for thinking you may have taken precautions."

"Very prudent under the circumstances." Lernac inserted the key into the center keyhole, turned it, and the lid opened.

"Lift it up so I can see inside."

Lernac did.

"So that's the stone?"

"That's the stone."

"I don't see the Shah's ring."

"The gentleman who owns the box has a sentimental attachment to it and we had no use for it."

Newcomb grunted. "All right, pack it back up. You don't mind if I keep your bag, do you?"

"I have no sentimental attachment to luggage."

"Very prudent. Now if you two will make your way to the guard van." Newcomb left the portmanteau on the seat as he motioned us to precede him, and we heedfully traversed the frosty platforms swaying over bucking couplers, all the while bracing ourselves against frigid gust after frigid gust that seemed dedicated to blowing us overboard. After a brief but interminable time we invaded the guard van, where Jacob, a tall, spare figure with a dull, apathetic face and long, grizzled moustache frowned upon seeing us. For some reason Newcomb asked him, "Who are you?"

"I'm the guard," Jacob answered, speaking English with a Breton accent. "Are you Mr. Chase? M. Fade said you were supposed to stay in the luggage car."

Lernac started to laugh at Newcomb, who savagely raked the revolver's barrel across Lernac's frontal and parietal bones. Lernac crumbled and Newcomb retreated a few steps lest they collide, but Newcomb kept the revolver aimed my way to discourage me from bolting at him. I snarled, "What happened to barley?'"

"Did you see me cross my fingers? Now do your assistant surgeon duty and check if the blighter is breathing."

Lernac's skin was split near the coronal suture but there was no immediate bruising, however it had been a severe blow so a skull fracture or brain contusions were possibilities. "I suspect he's suffered a concussion. I can't be certain until he regains consciousness."

"I suppose he'll live then." To Jacob, "These gentlemen will stay with you for the rest of our journey."

"Passengers are not permitted in the guard van."

"Passengers aren't permitted in the luggage car, either, but M. Fade made an exception for me. Make one for them." Newcomb assessed the guard van. "I don't see where barricading you in here is doable, so remember this: if even one of you tries to rush the passenger car or tries to scale it I'll shoot all three of you." He pointed towards the van's veranda. "It's all right with me if you want to leap off the porch, though that's going to be risky so long as we're travelling fifty miles an hour. You might try slowing us down first with the hand brake, but M. Michael knows how long that takes. I'd have more than enough time to return and finish you three. Now be quiet and behave." With that Newcomb departed.

Jacob and I spent the next few minutes improvising a camp bed for Lernac, who started to rouse as we moved him to it. I had Jacob fetch an empty water bucket as I asked Lernac, "How do you feel?"

He responded almost at once: "What happened?"

"Newcomb pistol-whipped you."

"*Lâche!*"[131]

"Can you tell me your name?"

"Certainly. I am Herbert de Lernac."

I waved a hand back and forth before his eyes. "How is your vision?"

"A bit blurry, though not so bad as after a magnum of Bollinger."

I couldn't help grinning. "Have you a headache? Are you nauseous?"

---

[131] "Coward"

"Yes, but not so bad as after that magnum."

"Do you have any ringing in your ears?"

"I always have ringing in my ears, Doctor."

"Is it worse than usual?"

"I don't think so."

There was no slurring of speech, so I told him, "Let me know at once if any of these things worsen, but I think you will recover in a few days."

"Thank you. I am in your debt."

"You're just fortunate that your head is as hard as Mons Meg's cannonballs.[132] Newcomb lashed you with everything he had."

A dangerous expression disfigured my patient. "I shall return the favor one day." His expression intensified when he noticed Jacob. "So who are you? Really?"

"I am Jacob Michael, sir."

"What are you doing here?"

"I'm the guard."

"Giovani is supposed to be the guard. What happened to him?"

"Giovani Martini? He failed to show up this morning so I was assigned his duty."

"And why you, monsieur?"

"My name was first on the substitute list."

---

[132] Mons Meg is a bombard that was presented to James II, King of the Scots, as a gift from Philip the Good, Duke of Burgundy, in 1454. According to legend the name Mons Meg is a combination of the name of the lands gifted to the blacksmith who built the bombard and the blacksmith's wife.

I asked, "What is all this?"

Lernac struggled to sit up. "Newcomb obviously expected to find someone other than this man here. My guess is another Moriarty. So what happened to Giovani? Doctor, didn't M. Fade give you the names of the train crew this morning?"

"He did and Jacob was listed as the guard."

"Why didn't you tell me that?"

"It never occurred to me and you never asked."

Embarrassment and puzzlement seeped through Lernac's expression. "I didn't? I wonder why not."

"What does it matter?"

Fatigue overtook Lernac and he propped his back against the wall. "I cut a deal with the Société des Mines de Lorraine."

"Why?"

"Because this is France and I decided to take extra precautions. For all the good it's done." He stared at Jacob. "Were you given any instructions by anyone?"

"Only to assume Giovani's post as guard."

"Nothing more?"

"No, sir. I swear."

Lernac suddenly seemed to remember something important and forced himself to rise and peer out a window. "Where are we?"

"We should pass the Braches station in another minute."

Lernac blanched. "You must make the 'proceed' signal to Comte!"

"But we are proceeding."

"Agents from the Société are waiting for Giovanni to signal 'proceed' as we approach Braches, but they may still stand down if you signal them."

I asked, "What if they don't stand down?"

"Then they will use mercury fulminate to cripple the trusses of the bridge on the other side of the station to derail the train."

Jacob snatched a lantern and sprinted to the veranda. I joined Lernac at the window and watched Jacob swing himself out over the side of the van and pump the arm with the lantern straight up and down. "Your folly may not just kill us but thousands in London."

Lernac kept his own counsel as the Braches station barreled past and the Avre River began racing alongside the train. The water was unseasonably near to the tracks and for several seconds the world felt as if it was holding its breath. The air seemed frightfully still despite a clacking cacophony trooping through the open veranda door. Then I heard an explosion followed by a furious snapping of timbers and crumpling of metal as the special was bashed askew. I am almost certain I glimpsed Jacob twirling away from the train just before Lernac and I were catapulted about the guard van and I was knocked senseless. If I had been given the opportunity at that moment I would have estimated the odds to be very much in favor of my reuniting with Mary, but I woke to find myself lying on a bench inside the tiny Braches station. Lernac was stretched out on the other bench where the engineer was tending to him, and I started to sit up only to discover the stoker was watching me. "Careful now, Doctor."

"M. Roulet?"

"That's me and that's M. Comte. Everyone in the village has gone to look at the wreckage, but assistance is on the way from Paris and there's nothing to do but rest until it arrives."

"Are you two injured?"

"Nothing we couldn't attend to ourselves and we have."

"Where is Jacob?"

"You two were our concern. If the guard is all right the villagers will help him."

Comte said, "We'd know by now if he had survived."

My heart filled with anguish to think someone not involved in our venture had lost his life because of it. "What about Newcomb? And the stone?"

Lernac said in a soft voice, "The Société has attended to both."

Roulet spat. "Only fools ever trust the Société." To this Comte added, "The Société must have got Giovanni out of the way so the Moriarities could try to plant a man in our crew."

"I will see to it they make amends if what you say is true."

This pacified Lernac's comrades for the time being but not me. "How do you know the Société has attended to Newcomb and the stone?"

"Comte, Roulet, and I heard the explosion."

"You mean when the Société sabotaged the bridge?"

"After that. We heard a loud explosion on our way here."

Comte said, "It came from the north. Perhaps two or three miles away. Right, Etienne?"

"I never could estimate distances by sound, but I did see smoke rising from a line of trees towards that direction."

I asked, "And what is the significance of this second explosion?"

I would not have thought it possible, but Lernac blushed. "My apologies, John Watson. I haven't been forthcoming with you regarding all the details of our mission."

"Like enlisting your comrades and the Société or that the three-lock box can now be opened with one key?"

"Your government approved of my placing men I trust on the train crew, and it was they who insisted you be informed of that and the new locks only if it were necessary."

"Mycroft Holmes told you that?"

"His superiors did."

My emotions overwhelmed me for several moments. I am not even sure I can explain the concoction. Confusion? Certainly. Anger? Most likely. Betrayal? Distrust? Depression? Loss? None of this made sense but all I could do was press on. "What else don't I know?"

"Why it delighted me that it was Newcomb who came to fetch the box."

"Fetch it? You gave it to him!"

"I gave him a bomb."

I was stunned speechless.

"The Ash Stone could not fall into the hands of the Moriarities. We can all agree on that. At the same time Connor Newcomb could not be permitted to escape justice for the murder of my man in Providence. That is something on which I shall not be dissuaded."

"So you took it upon yourself to rig the box with an explosive?"

"Those instructions were also from your government."

"Why would they do that?"

"If the Moriarities did manage to seize the box, M. Holmes's superiors hoped it would be opened in the headquarters of the Moriarities. Opening the box triggers the bomb."

"But you opened it."

"Inserting one key into the center lock and turning counterclockwise opened the lid but only armed the bomb. If the box is opened again without using all three keys the bomb will go off. One of the three keys was delivered to your government before we left Paris. I had the second key while the third key is on route to England by one of your Queen's Messengers."

"Does anyone have a set of all three keys?"

"Of course, though I am not at liberty to say whom."

"Are you at liberty to tell me why Her Majesty's Government would risk an explosion going off in London where innocent persons could be killed?"

"They knew you would feel that way, which is why they insisted you be kept in the dark. Rest assured, my friend, I would never permit the Moriarities to take the box to England. That is why I arranged with the

Société to have teams made up of their men and mine posted at agreed-upon locations along the track. If Giovanni failed to signal a team at any of these checkpoints, that team was to derail the train and see to it that any Moriarity man aboard was eliminated and the stone destroyed."

Despite a plethora of remonstrations, I settled for telling Lernac, "All of us could have been killed."

"What is that to men like us? You were prepared to die carrying out this mission. So were we. Now Newcomb is dead, which hobbles the Moriarities further, and the stone has been obliterated. No innocent lives have been lost and neither has ours. Fortune favored us and things have worked out for the best."

"What about Jacob Michael?"

Lernac turned his face towards the ceiling and closed his eyes. "If M. Michael is a casualty then he died in a noble cause and I shall see to it that his family is compensated and his funeral costs settled."

VII. THE BLOODSTONE

Cable from Walter Simonson to Mycroft Holmes

16 February

Bringing you sharp sword and polished arrow.
"SIGERSON"

Walter Simonson's Journal

17 *February* –

Mr. Mycroft appeared neither disappointed nor delighted when I was ushered into his office soon after midnight, but he did nothing to

179

disguise his relief upon seeing Mlle. de Galais. The tall, portly man approached her without a trace of his characteristic inertia and pressed her to sit by the fire. "The hour is late and the Channel winds are bitter this time of year. Are you comfortable?"

She was.

"Have you the key?"

She did and gave it to him.

"Our Queen thanks you and our nation thanks you." He locked the package in a desk drawer. "I trust this b'hoy was at your disposal throughout the crossing and afterwards."

"This gentleman saved my life."

Mr. Mycroft sat in his desk chair. "This gentleman is my finest field hand, and I expected nothing less if the need arose."

I am not going to deny I was proud to hear this, but told him, "You knew I was going to disobey orders."

"You say that as if it's unprecedented. Mlle. de Galais, I assure you it is more the norm than an exception."

The young woman grinned and I could almost hear her thinking: "You remind me of Benajah in some ways." I told Mr. Mycroft, "You were counting on it."

"It is folly not to depend upon the inevitable. Under no circumstances were you going to permit Mlle. de Galais to journey to London unchaperoned, but I could not let the Moriarities know that."

"So you asked me indirectly instead of directly."

Something like mischief twinkled in Mr. Mycroft's eyes. "You've been talking with Brother Sherlock."

"Who seems to have been less than forthcoming with me. Did you happen to include any indirect message for him that he didn't tell me about?"

"Mlle. de Galais says that you saved her life. I think I should hear the details."

I was not going to answer Mr. Mycroft if he were not going to answer me, but Mlle. de Galais confided, "The driver of my carriage revealed himself just after we left Escalles. I do not know how the Moriarities learned what I was up to, but the driver was armed with a knife, a gun, and an air rifle, and he gave me two choices. I could agree to accept the package from M. Simonson and no harm would come to him, or the driver would dispose of me and take the package from M. Simonson's corpse." She turned my way, leaving it to me to pick up the reins. What could I do? "I tracked the carriage to Calais. I recognized the driver from my days in the Moriarity gang, but there was no opportunity to intercept them before they boarded the ferry. I made my move during the crossing and took these off of him." I removed the driver's sheath knife and Colt revolver from my pockets and laid them on Mr. Mycroft's desk. "Labuda probably left the air rifle in the carriage."

"That was his name?"

"Yes."

"What did you do to him?"

"I gave him two choices."

"I see. Did he tell you anything?"

"His instructions were to kill Mlle. de Galais before the ferry reached England and to deliver the key to London. Labuda also mentioned another agent named Bonvalot was supposed to have done all this but the poor chap has been ill and took a sudden turn. It seems he's suffering from tetanus."

Mr. Mycroft's eyebrows went up. "An interesting turn of events. So where is Labuda?"

"I'm afraid we ran into a gale halfway across the Channel."

"I see."

"It couldn't be helped." I did not want to go into details in front of Mlle. de Galais. She knew what I had done but had not seen me do it. Meanwhile Mr. Mycroft picked up the weapons, removed the knife from its sheath to examine its blade, and then opened the Colt's cylinder to count the bullets. "He had more of a chance than he was going to give the young lady."

Mr. Mycroft asked Mlle. de Galais if he could speak with me in private. When we were alone he said, "It is good to see you, Walter."

"And you, sir."

"I should tell you that Dr. Watson will be returning to London tomorrow."

"You think it's safe?"

"The man isn't giving us a choice. Sound familiar? We shall keep an eye on him. We owe him that. In any case Moran has other dogs to whip right now. The Moriarity gang teeters on the precipice."

"I'll believe that when I see Moran marching in Newgate's exercise yard. What about the Ash Stone?"

"It was eradicated along with Sergeant Connor Newcomb. You will hear the whole story once all statements and reports have been filed." He showed me the cable I had sent from Dover. "So which are you? Sword or arrow?"

"I am whichever you need, whenever you need it."

"Always the faithful servant." Mr. Mycroft stared at my cable. "'He made my mouth like a sharp sword; He hid me in the shadow of His hand. He made me like a polished arrow; He hid me in His quiver.'[133] There are days I feel the same way. Laboring here in vain as I spend my strength on futility and vanity." His drooped in his chair. "It's been an eventful day, but at what price?"

"You tell me. Was it necessary to use Jacinth de Galais as a decoy?"

"If it were only that."

"What do you mean?"

"I mean that in a world of sinners I am the worst." He stared out a window at Whitehall. "Meanwhile the daughter of Vernon de Galais willingly risked her life so England can remain upon her proper course and you would go unharmed."

"I'm still not sure what to make of that. She's no piker."

"No. Well, perhaps we shouldn't read so much into it. Sherlock warns against trusting even the best of women."

---

[133] Isaiah 49:2

It was an atrocious statement, but I had no appetite to argue when I could only imagine what dilemmas of high government Mr. Mycroft had been laboring with for three years. "This hasn't been easy for you, sir."

Mr. Mycroft contemptuously waved a hand. "Let's not get sentimental. I think Mlle. de Galais should remain in London a day or two until the smoke settles somewhat, and when the time comes I think it would be best if you returned to France with her. Get a lay of the land. Find out what you can about any Moriarity agents that may still be at liberty like this Bonvalot."

"All right. I have to admit I worry about her father. When he finds out what happened today, the poor lass might find herself out on her ear."

Mr. Mycroft trained his gaze at me. "She might. Just don't you forget your Kipling. 'He travels the fastest who travels alone.'"

"And don't you forget, 'A friend at a pinch is a friend, indeed.'"[134]

Mr. Mycroft apparently tapped into a reserve of vitality as he readied himself to return to work. "Keep me posted. Give my regards to Sherlock."

Our reunion was at an end, except to say, "Yes, sir."

The Notebook of Dr. John H. Watson

19 *February* – Strange to be in this house again.

Strange that it and the world look the same as they did a few days ago after everything that has happened.

---

[134] Both lines are from Rudyard Kipling's poem "The Winners" (1888).

Strange how persistence can be so different.

Simonson and Mlle. de Galais paid an unexpected visit this afternoon on their way back to Marseilles. Except for her attire the young woman looked the same as when we met, but as we shared what we could of our adventures I told her, "Lady Stanhope would be proud."

She blushed, but said nothing.

When I asked Simonson if he were returning to England soon he shrugged. "Will you be returning to your practice?"

"Yes. There is nothing else to do."

"Men like us always have options. For instance, you could start a detective practice."

Mlle. de Galais clutched her hands with a clap. "That makes perfect sense! Doctors purchase another doctor's practice. You could take over Mr. Holmes's practice."

"You're kind, but I couldn't."

Simonson asked, "Why not?"

"My training is in medicine, not crime."

"What were those years assisting Sherlock Holmes and documenting his cases if not training?"

I thanked them before changing the subject, but ever since they departed I can think of nothing else except Simonson's words:

"Men like us always have options."

In truth I had not realized how delimited and terminable my perspective has become since Holmes died and while I was caring for

Mary. I know I am incapable of Holmes's pragmatism and I am not a student of Pierce,[135] but I suddenly find that my doubtful outlook is inspiring me to consider alternatives in my life. The world changes, sometimes dramatically, even when change is not apparent.

For instance, it has just dawned on me that I am by myself in the house. Pleasantly and completely by myself.

VIII. SHERLOCK HOLMES'S FULL STATEMENT OF THE CASE

If Professor Moriarity bounding off a rock and splashing into the abyss of the Reichenbach Falls did not make it apparent, then Colonel Moran's bombardment of stones afterwards made it abundantly clear that the most powerful syndicate of criminals in Europe was not going to be eradicated by the death of its terrible chief. I realize now that I should have never left the game entirely in the hands of the London police. My brother, Mycroft, expressed reservations against my decision even as he was assisting Watson and me in our departure for the Continent, but I refused to listen. Perhaps exhaustion overruled my judgment. The Professor's assaults did press me beyond my limits. Whatever the reason there is no denying I failed to heed Robert Burns's counsel concerning even the best-laid schemes,[136] an oversight that not only led to Moriarty evading capture but Moran, who made his first try

---

[135] Charles Sanders Pierce (1839–1914). Mathematician, scientist, logician, and philosopher. Sometimes referred to as the father of pragmatism.

[136] 1759 – 1796. Often cited as the national poet of Scotland. One of Burns's his most famous poems is "To a Mouse, on Turning Her Up in Her Nest with the Plough, November 1785," which includes the line: "The best-laid schemes o' mice an' men Gang aft agly [Go often askew]."

on my life by utilizing the natural resources at hand along the Gemmi Pass.[137]/[138] As disappointing as this was, it was not as disheartening as when I later confirmed that at least two of the Professor's lieutenants and several subordinates also succeeded in giving the police the slip. I had been sincere when I told Moriarty that I would cheerfully accept my own destruction if it could assure his own,[139] but with so many members of his gang still at large it seemed as if I had risked total ruin for nothing. Thankfully Mycroft was able to steer me back on course after I made my way back to London.

"The Moriarities may not be defeated, but the official police did dwindle their ranks and you have beheaded their mastermind. It would be foolhardy to belittle the prowess of the Professor's underlings, but the fact is they represent the residuum of a once mighty organization and it is no hydra. The cleverest rogue of his generation is not about to be replaced by another of his intellect. Nevertheless a wounded animal is the most dangerous and the Moriarities would like nothing more than to track you down."

"So we are of like mind this time that I should forsake England?"

---

[137] Colonel Sebastian Moran is generally associated with using an air-gun and not rocks when committing murders. Holmes is concerned about air-guns as early as "The Final Problem" and in "The Adventure of the Empty House" Moran disposes of the Honorable Ronald Adair with an air-gun before trying to kill Holmes with the same weapon. Moran was nothing if not a practical assassin, not to mention an expert outdoorsman, so a large rock becomes the more practical weapon if Moran's aim was to make Holmes's death appear accidental. Holmes mentions in "Empty House" how Moriarty used Moran "in only one or two very high-class jobs, which no ordinary criminal could have overtaken," and references the 1887 death of a Mrs. Stewart of Lauder, Scotland. Holmes is certain Moran is responsible for Stewart's demise but could not even prove the woman had been murdered much less by whom.
[138] A mountain pass in west-central Switzerland.
[139] See "The Final Problem."

"Not only England but Europe. This gang's tentacles still possess a lengthy reach. On the other hand we cannot merely bide our time until the Moriarities lay themselves open. The British government has no intention of ignoring the repercussions of the *horror vacui* that shall inevitably result from Moriarty's death. There will be those within as well as outside the organization who shall seek to fill this void even as his gang retaliates, but we may be able to turn their aggression against them, much like the Mongols did to the Rus at the Kalka River."[140]

Something of the old zest for the hunt kindled inside my breast. "You've already worked out a battle plan."

"Professor Moriarity was not one to let the grass grow under his feet. I say we follow his example. That is, if you feel up to it." Mycroft grinned. "Your career has not reached its summit, Sherlock. Not yet. Colonel Moran hurled stones at you and I suggest you return the favor."

Mycroft's ability to store and process facts in regards to any matter at hand is the attribute that makes him most essential to the British government, and Moran's missiles in Switzerland had inspired a scheme to distract, disperse, and hopefully dispense with the Moriarities. Mycroft had read about the Ash Stone while researching the Safavid Dynasty's relation to Pontic Greeks[141] who had spent the better part of the nineteenth century constructing schools throughout the Trebizond

---

[140] Battle of the Kalka River, May 23, 1223. After the Rus's armies defeated the Mongols's rearguard, the Mongols feigned a retreat to spread out the Rus's armies before stopping on the banks of the Kalka River, where they defeated their overaggressive pursuers.
[141] An ethnically Greek group who traditionally lived in the region of Pontus.

Vilayet.[142] This put him in mind of the Ottoman occupation of Tabriz, which directed his thoughts to the Mongol invasions of Anatolia, which reminded him of the Battle of the Kalka River.

"Legends are as malleable as gold and there is no more relentless a mallet than Time. The Grail Stone is an exemplar of that. Almost everything about the Ash Stone is legendary, so its existence can neither be established nor denied, making it all the easier for us to persuade the Moriarties that they should dedicate some portion of their remaining resources on a quest to retrieve it."

The first step in Mycroft's gambit was to dispatch his own agent, Walter Simonson, to search for the Ash Stone. Simonson was not made privy to the subterfuge but instructed that it was imperative to prevent such a mineral from ever being employed against Great Britain. Furthermore Simonson was to assume the guise of an explorer named Sigerson. When Simonson expressed a preference to conduct the search surreptitiously, Mycroft's rebuttal was that Simonson could operate more efficiently hiding in the open, but in truth my brother was counting on news of Sigerson's exploits to persuade the Moriarties of our government's interest in the Ash Stone.

The second step commenced with me sequestering myself in the wilderness of Tibet to recuperate while establishing the persona of a Bonpos[143] named Haj. Eventually Haj traveled to Nepal where, much

---

[142] A vilayet was a province of the Ottoman Empire. The Trebizond Vilayet ran along the Black Sea and the interior highlands of the Pontic Alps of Northern Anatolia, Turkey.
[143] A follower of the Tibetan religion of Bon. Bonpos believe Bon originated in a land called Tanzig, which many scholars identify as Persia.

like Hugh Boone[144] on Threadneedle Street, he made himself a daily seat at the Great Northern Gate of Katmandu. There Haj traded in rumors and tales, one of which was the Ash Stone, but it didn't take long for Haj to also become a resource for those wanting or needing to know who passed through the Gate. When Simonson sought out Haj in his search for Damon Nostrand I knew the game was afoot and my sabbatical was at an end.

The third step was recruiting Herbert de Lernac. The Foreign Office has kept an open file on Lernac since 1890 when a financier and political agent named Louise Caratal vanished while on route to London. Caratal had commissioned a special after arriving in Liverpool from Central America and discovering he had missed the London express. Time was of the essence as Caratal was scheduled to present evidence he had amassed in South America at a Parisian trial involving some of the chief men of France, not a few of whom were members of the Société des Mines de Lorraine conglomerate. This group attempted to protect themselves by creating a syndicate that hired Lernac to prevent Caratal from reaching Paris.[145] Once hired, the French Lernac found it necessary to trespass into England and consult with the Moriarty gang. When the Caratal special disappeared between St. Helens and Manchester my brother insisted that I be brought in, and I was able to ascertain the train had been diverted onto a temporary sideline to crash into the abandoned

---

[144] The beggar persona of Neville St. Clair in "The Man with the Twisted Lip."
[145] See "The Lost Special."

Heartsease coal mine in Lancashire. From there it was a rudimentary matter to deduce those responsible and who had executed the plan.

What happened next transpired mostly within the murky realm of high international politics. The British government informed the French government about the lost special. More than one crime had been committed on English soil. Our government could not ignore these offenses, but exposing the syndicate's plot would financially and politically cripple France, which would have catastrophic consequences for all Europe. To prevent this an unwritten deal was cut. The British government would excuse Lernac's crimes in trade for reparation from the French government of a type and time of England's choosing. As soon as this deal was agreed to any further investigations into the lost special were discouraged without flurry but without delay, but a curious public still had to be thrown off the scent. To that end it was requested that I publish a theory of the crime suggesting an English Camorra of colliers might be responsible. Such a theory coming from a respected authority generated considerable interest, but it also elicited accusations that I had preposterously libeled an honest and deserving set of men, and as weeks passed with no resolution to the mystery my reputation and business suffered. I had done what should be expected of any British citizen, but I was nevertheless grateful when providence provided an opportunity for me to redeem myself by solving the disappearance of the popular race horse Silver Blaze.[146]

---

[146] See "Silver Blaze."

There were risks in recruiting Lernac, but Mycroft's scheme depended on the arch-criminal's participation. It was inconceivable the Moriarities would not enlist his aid the way he had theirs if they believed the Ash Stone were in France.

At the outset there was no assumption that the Ash Stone might be real. Sigerson's search was a stratagem and nothing more. So when Simonson and I departed Khartoum for France, I thought nothing of it when our new companion, Nadir Khan, entertained us with tales about a remarkable gentleman whose life he had spared. Even when Nadir mentioned this rogue had fled the Sudan with some of the Shah's possessions, which included a curious box with three locks, I dismissed it as coincidence, the same way I had when one of Watson's university friends turned up after Moriarty's death only to turn out to be the son of one of the gang's assassins. Simonson, on the other hand, knew about Pari Khan Khanum's three-lock box and insisted that it and the Shah's stolen property must be one and the same. There was nothing to gain but possibly much to lose by attempting to dissuade him, so we detoured to Constantinople to try to track down Nadir's rogue friend only to reach an impasse with the wreck of the *Kettleness*. There things stood until I assisted the Foreign Office regarding the Russo-French alliance. While in Paris I called on Nadir, who informed me that he had been in contact with his friend, the shipwreck's lone survivor, who came to Paris afterwards to begin a new life as a contractor.

"He seems content so I am happy for him, although I fear he shall never abandon his old ways completely. He recently became one of two silent partners in a pair of Montmartre cafes, and the other partner is a *majrim*[147] named Herbert de Lernac."

Another coincidence, one I shared only with Mycroft, but word of my visit with Nadir still made its way to Lernac. A few weeks later it was decided that Watson should leave London and come to Montpellier, which I felt was wise, but I disagreed with sending the doctor to Providence even with a guardian. The government had its way, as it always does, and Watson more than adequately represented our concern, but Lernac would never have set the events that began at the *Cabaret l'Enfer* into motion if Benajah Place had not been murdered.

Needless to say Mycroft was as mortified as I to discover that the Ash Stone was genuine. This was more than a coincidence, it was a catastrophe. Drastic action was called for, but Mycroft lost sight of our mission's practical points and insisted the stone be transported to England so he could oversee its destruction. Our government made contact with the French government, who made contact with the Société, whose investments in the rolling stock of the Chemins de Fer du Nord amounted to a partnership in the company. The Saxton special was arranged with the conglomerate's guarantee that only Watson, Lernac, and Lernac's handpicked comrades would be allowed to board the train, and sentries were concealed in strategic positions along the track to Calais with instructions to intervene if prearranged signals from the special were not executed. As a further safeguard the original lock and keys on Pari Khan Khanum's box were replaced by Nadir's friend,

---

[147] "Criminal"

who kept a master set of all three keys. One copy of a new key was conveyed by an *estafette*[148] to Whitehall, a copy of the second key was delivered to Simonson, and Lernac held on to a copy of the third key. What Mycroft was not told was that his superiors made ancillary arrangements with Lernac and the Société. With Lernac they commissioned to have Nadir's friend implant an explosive in the box. With the Société they arranged that an agent of the Moriarities be allowed to board the train in Paris and escape with the box to England.

What the Société didn't tell Mycroft's superiors was that it made supplementary arrangements with the Moriarty gang and Lernac. With the gang it not only agreed to permit one of their agents to board the train and get away with the box to England, but to substitute Lernac's guard with a second Moriarity agent as a precaution. With Lernac it agreed to give a Moriarty agent safe passage to board the train and get away with the box, but only if this agent was Connor Newcomb.

What Lernac didn't tell anyone was he had Nadir's friend incorporate a trigger combination for the explosive into the box's new locks. Furthermore Lernac's arrangement with the Société stipulated that under no circumstances was the Ash Stone to leave France. In fact the stone was to be destroyed as soon as possible after Newcomb acquired it. In exchange for all this Lernac agreed to perform a favor for the Société if the special had to be derailed.

What Mycroft and I didn't tell anyone was that Lernac presenting me the shard from the Ash Stone struck us as suspicious, coming as it

---

[148] A military courier.

did so soon after Lernac learned of Place's murder. Lernac is notorious for being patient but not cautious, and his assault on Brunel and his remark about justice or retribution concerned me. So Mycroft and I contacted the Société to make our own arrangements, which ended up involving a rescue of Lernac's guard and my substituting for him.

Mycroft saw to it that the man assigned to fetch the second key from Lernac and deliver it to Simonson was not a Queen's Messenger but Justin Beahm of Ipswich, who proved his mettle, quick-thinking, and fidelity to our house during the treacherous pursuit of the forger Victor Lynch.[149] What Beahm not did tell Simonson was that his first stop upon arriving in Montpellier was the home of Vernon de Galais, where he delivered a humbug message from Colonel Sebastian Moran. Mycroft worded this message so that Mlle. Jacinth de Galais could recognize it as a pretense, most notably by slipping in the passphrase she had given to Watson in Providence: "Fidelity is my glory." Mlle. de Galais acquiesced to the sham request to come to London, but met Beahm after departing on her mission to go over her true instructions. From that moment her life was in peril and in the hands of an unsuspecting Simonson. According to Mycroft they both behaved magnificently.

Beahm returned to Benet's home after Simonson's departure and we left soon after for Paris, where the Société provided me with a guard's uniform and a photograph of the real Jacob Michael. I supplemented the uniform with a short-barrel bull dog[150] in a shoulder holster. I was able

---

[149] Holmes mentions this untold case in "The Adventure of the Sussex Vampire."
[150] A Webley Metropolitan Police RIC revolver.

to avoid Watson for most of the journey, although it was frustrating to be so near my old friend and colleague. I was actually overjoyed when Newcomb marched him into the guard van with Lernac, although my enthusiasm was tempered by the circumstances. Then there was the matter of my being thrown from the guard van after I failed to prevent the derailment.

It is an unpleasant and humbling experience to have your fate utterly out of your control. This experience was mercifully brief, but the brain acts rapidly and in that incandescent moment I appreciated that I had a small yet realistic chance of survival, but how I landed would determine my destiny. I did find comfort that such hopes would have been unavailable to Professor Moriarty during his long plummet to the bottom of the Reichenbach Falls.

As providence would have it I avoided the fates of Icarus and Phaethon by landing in the giving boughs of one of the poplars dotting the Avre's eastern bank. Even more amazingly my injuries were confined to a momentary bout of dizziness and some scrapes and scratches. My uniform also suffered only minor damage but my cap and the wig and moustache to my disguise were missing. Meanwhile the poplar provided an excellent vantage point to survey the wreckage. I could see that the engine was completely submerged and the tender mostly so, while the luggage car had uncoupled and remained upright after it descended onto the collapsed bridge. The passenger car and guard van lay on their sides upon the tracks, the passenger car having collided with the luggage car and the guard van with the passenger car. Comte and Roulet must have jumped from the engine prior to reaching the bridge, for they were dry and mostly unscathed as they crawled into the guard van through a window while calling out to Lernac and Watson. The pair was as yet unaware of Newcomb's presence aboard the special and failed to notice him getting out of the luggage car through a roof hatch. Newcomb had the three-lock box tucked under one arm but was not carrying his pistol, and I could not see if it was concealed on his person. While Newcomb busied himself clambering off the luggage car and over the remnants of the bridge, I lowered myself from the poplar and by the time I stood upon solid ground once more my quarry was moving northward towards a hedge of pines, limping with his left leg. His intentions were clear, as was my duty, but it pains me still that I abandoned Watson at such a moment, even though he would have insisted I pursue Newcomb. I took some solace that I was confident Lernac would make good on his debt to Watson and see that my friend received whatever care he required, which he did.

Intercepting Newcomb was the simplest of my dilemmas. There was nothing for the man to do but to try to make his way to Amiens and from there Calais before Lernac alerted his comrades in those cities, but time was not on Newcomb's side. He likely had three hours to reach Calais. If he could do it in two so much the better, but either would have been a challenge with two healthy legs. Newcomb would have to hike the road to Moreuil, which was more accessible than keeping to the trees but also exposed him to view; however, he might be able to beg a ride on a cart if one chanced to pass his way. Once in Moreuil, Newcomb could hire conveyance to carry him to Amiens, but getting to the road necessitated cutting through the pines. The uneven terrain through the trees slowed him down and by the time he had trekked to a glade near the middle of the hedge I was waiting for him, seated upon a fallen trunk and smoking a cigarette. You're surprised to see me, sir."

The Professor had selected well when he recruited this man. Newcomb displayed no hint of being taken aback, but swiftly and smoothly drew his pistol. If anything I was the startled one when Newcomb said, "So it's your eyes I've been feeling on the back of my neck."

I peered through the pines but spied no one. "It couldn't have been me."

"Listen to the great detective! He thinks even an old campaigner can't pick up his scent."

"I arrived first and did so by anticipating your course. If anyone is following you, I suspect – "

A report cut me off as a patch of earth erupted in the approximate equidistant of the glade.

Newcomb and I ossified.

I was certain that Newcomb, like myself, presumed the shot had been fired by an agent from the Société des Mines de Lorraine, which presented the chess problem of which of us—or if either of us—was in greater peril. Newcomb made the first move, keeping his pistol aimed at me while clutching the three-lock box in a way that shielded his chest.

"My compliments on another effective disguise. Even Dr. Watson was taken in, but there you had an advantage. He still thinks you're dead."

"He also never met Jacob Michael."

"I would have thought Lernac or one of his comrades would have."

"Michael has no association with the Paris underworld, so it seemed unlikely that Lernac would know him. As for the train crew, I kept enough distance between them and myself that my disguise would suffice if they were familiar with him."

"What about our doppelgänger? Is he being held by the Sûreté or the Yard's Special Branch?"

"All I can say is he is receiving better treatment than he intended to give M. Martini."

"You can't fault us if your side insists on obeying Queensberry rules or the Geneva Convention."

"We only insist up to a point."

"That's true. The Professor found that out."

"Moriarty brought his fate upon himself."

"Who was it that commissioned you to make him your business? The Professor begged you to drop it but you refused to stand clear."[151]

"'The fault, dear Brutus, is not in our stars, But in ourselves, that we are underlings.'[152] May I offer you my compliments on boarding the special? You had the blessing of the Société, of course. I know from

---

[151] See "The Final Problem."
[152] *Julius Caesar*, Act I, Scene III.

personal experience that no one could have gotten onboard without it. Was petitioning them to double-cross Lernac your idea?"

"With Colonel Moran's say so. The Société wouldn't agree without it even though many of its principals believe Lernac is a greater risk because of that Caratal business."[153]

"Did Moran also agree to their betraying you?"

"I thought you might take a stab at that."

"I won't deny it is nothing more than a supposition." I tossed away my cigarette and cautiously crossed my arms over my chest, bringing my hand within reach of the bull dog. "In any case they needn't have bothered. There never was an Ash Stone. It's all been a goose chase."

"Of course it has. Well, what can I say? *Errare humanum est.*"[154]

"*Persevere diabolcum.*[155] The British government wanted your organization to scatter your agents and squander your assets."

"And in the process you've done us a favor! It is more clear than ever that our leadership needs new blood. It is results that count, and I have this." Newcomb patted the box.

"The only thing that box contains is a hunk of gravel dipped in coal-tar. Look for yourself."

"I did."

"Look again."

---

[153] See "The Lost Special."
[154] "To err is human … "
[155] "… but to persist in error is diabolical."

"I can wait. It might be safer having someone who knows about such things give the box a good once-over first. Game effort, though, Mr. Holmes."

"Have it your way, Sergeant Newcomb. 'What's to come is still unsure.'"[156]

"So you say." Seeing nothing further to be gleaned from our conversation Newcomb shouted to the trees, "What's it to be then?"

There was no response.

"All right. You can have it your way, too, but I'm off and I'll be taking the stone with me. But first …" Newcomb started to aim at me, but before I could snatch my revolver he was swallowed by a column of thunder, fire, and debris.

A concentration of air simultaneously backhanded me over the trunk and squeezed the wind from my breast. It was not as debilitating an experience as the House of Commons,[157] but mustering the wherewithal to stand was neither easy nor quick. I looked where Newcomb had been, but there was only a broad depression. Nothing remained of him or the three-lock box. I bowed my head and shut my eyes to clear my thoughts for I know not how long, and when I opened them again a tall, very powerful man was standing near the fallen trunk considering the cavity without admiration or disgust. He was hardly of middle age, dark with a thin mouth, black eyes, and no ear lobes. His

---

[156] *Twelfth Night*: Act II, Scene III.
[157] It is possible that Holmes is referring to the dynamite bombing of the House of Commons chamber on January 24, 1885. This was one of the last attacks in the Fenian Bombing Campaign, but what Holmes's involvement may have been with this incident remains a mystery.

jacket sleeves covered his forearms, which cradled a Winchester rifle with "1 of 1000" engraved on the octagonal barrel.[158] I asked if he were: "Horace Moore?"

"That name serves as well as any." His voice was intelligent and confident with a tint of Polish stress.

"That is an admirable weapon."

"I had doubts a .44-40 cartridge could penetrate that strongbox." Moore sighed through his nostrils. "I am sure you are aware that some in your government would have been overjoyed if this had happened in London. I suppose they would have blamed the Fenians. *Quorum igitur scelerati?*[159] Still, this makes things easier for you and me. Doesn't it?"

"Well, what I told Newcomb is certainly truer. He is dead and the Ash Stone destroyed. Meanwhile you surely didn't come here alone. If not, then the passivity of your comrades suggests that they have changed their allegiance to you, Moran's logical successor, or have been enlisted by the Société des Mines de Lorraine. As for your passivity these past three years, that suggests you have been waiting for the total collapse of the Professor's once mighty organization."

"'Once in, never out' has no teeth when there is no gang to enforce it."

"Your allegiance was with the man and not his organization?"

---

[158] The One in One Thousand grade Winchester was limited to its model 1873 lever-action repeating rifle. The barrel of these almost perfect rifles produced targets of extra merit (smaller than average groupings) during test-firing.
[159] "Who, then, are the villains?"

"There is no gang without the man. No one seems to understand that. While the Professor's ambitions were sometimes hampered by his delight with peril, no one was his equal much less his better."

"I, too, hold a very high opinion of the Professor's abilities, as I'm sure does the Société, who must be anxious for the elimination of its chief European competitor. They did betray Lernac, but I hardly suspect he will care."

"Lernac will be remunerated. As for me, I admired the Professor but I am not a slave to devotion. Only two of the Professor's officers ever wished to avenge his death.[160] You won fair and square." Moore propped his Winchester against the trunk and strolled to the depression. It was a gesture, but one I appreciated. When Moore reached the depression his face—a *tabula rasa* until now—radiated with anticipation. "This spot is a crossroads. It is not so fearful a place as the fall of Reichenbach nor as treacherous a path as the one where you overpowered the Professor, but what we do next and where we go from here is up to us. You said I've been passive since the Professor's death. I would say that I have been practical in your own fashion. I shan't bore you with my feats these past months, except that they have been no less perilous than yours." Moore surveyed our surroundings like an indentured man on the cusp of release. "The final labor falls to you. If

---

[160] In "The Adventure of the Empty House" Holmes tells Watson that one of the reasons he decided to go into hiding is because he knew "Moriarty was not the only man who had sworn my death. There were at least three others whose desire for vengeance upon me would only be increased by the death of their leader. They were all most dangerous men. One or the other would certainly get me." It appears Holmes believed these three men were Moran, Newcomb, and Moore.

you can accomplish it we will be free men. So will your helper Simonson. As for your friend Watson, Moran harbors no grudge against him. If anything he admires the doctor and sympathizes with how your government seems to see him merely as a pawn. So do I. In any case the Colonel remains a frightful adversary. I am not ashamed to admit one reason I have been keeping a low profile is that Moran has never forgiven me for superseding him with the Professor. It has been healthier to keep my distance."

"I see. Then perhaps you are right and there is nothing left but to return to London and beard the wily tiger." Instead of the customary dread, I found myself tingling with suppressed zeal. "Where do you go from here?"

"Back to Gdynia.[161] Once you have exorcised the Moriarities."

A realization dampened my enthusiasm. "Only to have another organization arise to take its place."

"You can take solace that the Bible says the world lies in the power of the Devil,[162] so the specter of evil can never be vanquished. Go snare Moran and do your bit for Queen and Country. Leave the Société to France. Who knows? Perhaps Lernac will not be as forgiving to them as I suppose. Or maybe another competitor will spring forth to challenge them. Such is the way of hydras."

We parted ways soon after that. There was nothing more to say.

---

[161] City in northern Poland.
[162] 1 John 5:19: "We know we are from God, and the whole world lies in the power of the evil one."

A few days later, news that the train crash had taken a peculiar (if somewhat familiar) turn reached the public:

THE DAILY NEWS
TUESDAY, FEBRUARY 20, 1894

FRENCH LOCOMOTIVE VANISHES
AFTER DERAILMENT.

——·——

(Through Reuter's Agency)

BRACHES

The derailment of a Nord company train commissioned as a special by the British Museum has turned mysterious with the disappearance of the train's locomotive. Investigators that arrived within hours of the derailment on 16 February discovered the locomotive and coal car had fallen into the Avre River after a bridge near the train station in the hamlet of Braches collapsed. Surging river waters resulting from heavy rains and melting snow to the north are believed to have caused the collapse. The passenger car, luggage car, and guard car did remain on land, but the passenger car and guard car were overturned. Due to the late hour when the track was finally cleared of these cars, it was decided to wait until the next morning to begin building a temporary spur and salvaging the submerged cars, but when the crew returned the following morning they found only the coal car. Engineers suspect that the locomotive was carried away during the night by the surging waters and may now be some miles downstream or buried in quicksand.

Traveling on board the special when it derailed were Professor Sir Christopher Saxton and Captain Peter Wells, who were returning from an expedition sponsored by the British Museum from the Yark and River Valley in China with several precious frozen specimens. Also on board were engineer Herni Comte, stoker Etienne Roulet, and guard Jacob Michael, all long-time employees with the Nord

Company. At first it was feared that Michael was a casualty
when he could not be found after the crash, but the guard
made his way to Braches the following day having
suffered no injuries from his experience.

As the rails were cleared and the Braches bridge was being repaired, an
expedited insurance claim was filed and in a relatively short amount of
time another French class 120 steam engine, No. 921, was added to the
company's register. To date No. 721 has not been recovered and no
investigation into the engine is under way.

EPILOGUE: PALL MALL EAST
23 March 1894

THE BEGATELLE, an admirably conducted card-playing club, opened as it did each day at two in the afternoon. The stakes here are small and so is its membership, which permits no strangers. Not every member knows the other but on the whole they are familiar with one another's exploits, which is the case at the table where Colonel Sebastian Moran sits playing whist.

To his right is the noted Trinitarian, amateur conjurer, and rover Simon Melas, a very tall, broad-shoulder young Norman with blond hair, wind-weathered face, and a scar over his left eye.

To Moran's left is Melas's frequent associate Cyprian Nightlinger, a spry, scholarly gentleman whose universal ambition has prompted him to aim at distinction in many subjects rather than preeminence in one.

Moran's partner is William Havelock-Smith, the epistemologist and remittance man who recently returned from America after less recently becoming the last living member of his family line.

There is not much in the way of conversation during the first hand, but as Melas deals the second and Moran updates his whist counter, the Colonel suggest to his partner, "Wouldn't the Travellers Club have been more to your liking."[163]

---

[163] Founded in the early nineteenth century by the Anglo-Irish statesman and British Foreign Secretary Robert Stewart (1769-1822) the Travellers Club is London's oldest surviving club. It was created to be a resort for gentlemen who had resided or travelled abroad as well as an

"I heard where one of their waiters recently turned up his nose at a soldier who simply asked for a pack of cards and a racing paper. Imagine what they'd do if they saw me?"

Melas turns up spade for the trump. "The place is a bit cold and bare. Except for the library."

"Yes, the library is a wonder, but I'll be staying at my father's rooms in London. In any case, I wanted to play whist. All the Americans wanted to play is faro."

Moran plays a singleton, the jack of hearts. "I don't recall reading about your return in *The Sportsman* or *Daily News.*"

Nightlinger follows with the three of hearts, Havelock-Smith the five of hearts, and Melas the eight of hearts. As Moran takes the trick his partner says, "The screeds must be slipping. It's getting so even explorers in the back of beyond have no privacy."

Moran deals and turns up clubs for trump. "I couldn't agree more. Nansen on the *Fram* sailing for the North Pole.[164] Peary scouring Greenland for the Great Iron meteorite.[165] Sigerson in Asia and the Sudan hunting for the Ash Stone."

Nightlinger leads with the seven of clubs.

---

accommodation for foreigners who were given an invitation during their stay. One qualification for membership is that candidates must have travelled outside the British Isle to no less a distance of five hundred miles in a straight line from London.

[164] Fridtjof Wedel-Jarlsberg Nansen (1861-1930). Diplomat, scientist, and explorer. Led the first crossing of the interior of Greenland in 1881. Awarded the Noble Peace Prize in 1922 for his humanitarian work assisting displaced refugees from World War I and other conflicts. The *Fram* Expedition (1893-1896) was named after the ship Nansen used in his attempt to reach the geographical North Pole.

[165] Robert Peary (1856-1920). US Naval officer and Artic explorer. In 1894 Peary became the first Western explorer to reach what later became known as the Cape York meteorite.

Havelock-Smith plays the nine of clubs. "Even when I was in Arizona with only the *Tombstone Epitaph* at my disposal, I still knew most days what any of those fellows had for dinner the night before."

Melas plays the four of spades and picks up the trick as Nightlinger asks, "Were you really in Tombstone? Did you see the O.K. Corral?"

"I walked past its front entrance a few times. The corral was only one block from the Grand Hotel on Allen Street where I stayed. But I am afraid the gunfight took place in the rear along Fremont Street and I never walked that way." Nightlinger deals the next hand and turns up diamonds for trump as Havelock-Smith continued. "Funny thing about the gunfight. Virgil Earp, Ike Clanton, and Tom McLaury spent the night before playing poker with the county sheriff and one other man. Eight hours later Earp participated in the death of Clanton and McLaury."

"Such things are not unheard of," Moran comments as he orders his cards. "There is a time for every purpose."

"I see your point, Colonel. A time to cast away stones and a time to gather stones together as it were."[166]

The partners peer at one another for several seconds.

Finally, Havelock-Smith says, "Yes, I see your point and I couldn't agree more."

* * * *

---

[166] Moran is paraphrasing Ecclesiastes 3:1-3.

Four hours later Havelock-Smith departs the Begatelle, five pounds richer and ready to move on to his next club. Not the Travellers but the Diogenes, where he checks into his father Jonas's rooms.

After supper Havelock-Smith relaxes by perusing the agony columns of various newspapers in the reading room until seven o'clock, when he leaves to keep an appointment in The Stranger's Room. Waiting for him is Mycroft Holmes, who frowns at the newcomer. "I shall never get your penchant for theatrics, Sherlock."

"I seem to recall you once had ambitions of being a countertenor."

"When I was a student. Grown men should indulge in common sense. It was bad enough the time you came here dressed like a cabbie. Now you've wormed your way into one of our deceased's member's rooms!"

"I have no intention of imposing upon you much longer."

"Just how long do you think it will be before Moran realizes Havelock-Smith is still on route from America and you're in London?"

"He already knows, Mycroft. You know that. Just like you know that the Colonel and I passed the afternoon playing whist at the Begatelle."

"Which was a foolish risk! What did you benefit by it? He might have moved against you right then. What if he had followed you here?"

"Moran is too club-footed[167] to dare anything untoward in the Begatelle or the Diogenes. The only time I may have been in danger was

---

[167] There is no evidence that Moran suffered from talipes equinovarus, so it appears Holmes is making a point by referencing the satirical poem "Clubs" by Theodore Hook (1788 – 1841) in which members of the Travellers Club are described as men who "smoke cigars so cosily" and have "explor'd all parts" of the world, but "now they are club-footed! and they sit and look at charts of it."

when I was in transit. As for what I benefited, the Colonel and I made a tidy though not considerable profit. He is a fairly competent card cheat."

"Sometimes you can be too bold by half."

"All right, Mycroft, it benefits me to have Moran worry that the hounds may be closing upon his heels. Let him be the one to lose sleep while I make preparations for the last hand."

"And what preparations might those be?"

"First, I return to France to settle Benet's affairs, including a commission made with Oscar Meunier."

"The wax sculptor?"

"He comes highly recommended by the university and the Sûreté."

"We have used his services as well. What are you up to, Sherlock?"

"You shall see when I return to England, but that will not be for a few days. When I do, however, our war with the Moriarities will be ended. One way or the other it shall be ended."

ADDENDUM

> "Work is the best antidote to sorrow, my dear Watson," said he,
> "and I have a piece of work for us both to-night which, if we
> can bring it to a successful conclusion, will in itself justify a
> man's life on this planet." In vain I begged him to tell me more.
> "You will hear and see enough before morning," he answered.
> "We have three years of the past to discuss. Let that suffice until
> half-pastnine, when we start upon the notable adventure of the
> emptyhouse."
>
> - "The Adventure of the Empty House"

IN 1898 Herbert de Lernac was arrested by the Marseilles police and convicted of murdering a local merchant named Bonvalot. There was no apparent motive and if a chance accident had not prevented Lernac from immediately escaping the scene he might have returned to Paris with no one the wiser of his involvement. Nevertheless Lernac confessed that he killed Bonvalot, claiming, "To do otherwise would be an even greater crime." In hopes of gaining a reprieve Lernac gave a widely published statement in which he explained his role in the 1890 disappearance of the Caratal special and then threatened to expose the members of the powerful syndicate that had hired him. "Messieurs, you may believe that Herbert de Lernac is quite as formidable when he is against you as when he is with you, and that he is not a man to go to the guillotine until he has seen that every one of you is en route for New Caledonia." There are no records that Lernac was ever executed or if his sentence was commuted or that he was released, so the ultimate fate of Herbert de Lernac remains a mystery to this day.

THE TRAGEDY OF THE PETTY CURSES

FEW OF Sherlock Holmes's cases have started so bizarrely, or ended so tragically, as the affair of the Angus-Burtons of Notting Hill, which began for me with a letter from my friend that arrived at my Paddington practice with the four-o'clock post on a blistering afternoon in August of 1889. It read,

Watson,

If you happen to be free this evening, could you come round to Baker Street at seven? A young woman has presented me with a problem ripe with those unusual and outré features so dear to us both. Also, since the fair sex is your department, your opinions of this new client might prove beneficial to my investigation.

Holmes

My wife Mary was in Whitby for a few days as a favor to my predecessor, old Mr. Farquhar. It turned out to be an excellent opportunity for her to escape the extreme summer heat, but I had no choice but to remain behind to attend to my new medical practice. I was feeling quite forsaken and therefore was delighted by Holmes's request.

A storm was beginning to brew when I arrived at Baker Street. The wind had picked up, the air was thick and humid, and the sky was beginning to churn with purple clouds piled high over grey clouds. Holmes was standing at the curb waiting for me, careful to keep a tight hold of his hat, and gratefully climbed in my cab while giving the driver our destination, 17 Kensington Place Road. After settling in, he commented, "I see that your wife is away, Waston, and has left you to fend for yourself."

"And how exactly do you deduce that?"

"A few little things told me, but primarily your tie. It is not perfectly straight as when Mrs. Watson brings it into regulation for you. Though circumstances have prevented us from seeing more than little of each other since your recent marriage, I am nevertheless confident that your tie has not looked quite this off-balanced since you resided at Baker Street."

"I see. Well, I won't bother asking about the other little things. You're right, as usual." I imagine it was the heat that put me in as petulant a mood to add, "Of course your deductions always seem simple after you explain them."

A nettled expression came over Holmes. "Yes, the obvious always seems simple when it is explained."

Realizing my rudeness I apologized and asked about the facts of this new case.

Holmes unexpectedly looked less than sure of himself. "I shall, but first, Watson, may I ask you a theoretical question?"

"Of course."

"What would you do if your wife insisted that you had placed a curse upon her?"

For several moments I was speechless, the question being so nonsensical. All I could muster was to mumble, "Pardon me?"

"What would you do if the person you vowed to love, honor, and cherish so long as you live was convinced that you had cursed her?"

"I would seek professional help. An alienist. It's preposterous, though."

"In the abstract I would agree, but this is not a theoretical problem for the young lady that I wrote to you about, Mrs. Halima Angus-Burton. She is seeking professional help, but, rather than an alienist, she has sought my aid."

"Holmes, if you're serious, then a situation like this definitely requires skills outside your talents."

"That may turn out to be so, but consider that her husband, Malcolm Angus-Burton, is the sole heir of a respected family, holds a high position with the Foreign Office, and is one of the Queen's most trusted advisers in matters regarding China. Under the circumstances, wouldn't you eliminate all alternative explanations before you irrevocably stained the character of the person you most loved?"

"Under those circumstances, but how could anyone even entertain such a thing? It's irrational!"

"I'm afraid the explanation I've been given will not sound any more rational." Holmes looked at the gathering clouds as if to collect his thoughts. "To begin with, Mr. and Mrs. Angus-Burton share the distinction of being raised in foreign lands. He was born in China to British parents, but Mrs. Angus-Burton is a pureblooded Egyptian who was adopted by a British father who married her widowed mother."

"'Halima.' I thought the name sounded foreign, but I couldn't recollect its origin"

"It means 'gentle,' and if I am any judge of character Mrs. Angus-Burton is precisely that. She is also loyal, levelheaded, and I would be remiss not to mention that she is a bonnie thing."

"Appreciating a woman's beauty? That isn't like you."

"On the contrary, Watson. My living is made by observing, and all I've done is state an obvious assessment. Tell me if you disagree when you meet the lady."

"Fair enough. I suspect this observation plays a part in whatever theories you may have buzzing in your head about this case."

As I should have expected, Holmes was appalled at my suggestion. "You know my methods. I never hypothesize before I have all the facts."

"Yes. I stand corrected."

"Angus-Burton's father was a representative of the British East India Trading Company in Canton, where his family lived until Angus-Burton entered university in 1878. Angus-Burton's father retired to London at that same time, but both he and Angus-Burton's mother have passed away within the last three years." Holmes paused to consider his thoughts again. "Make careful note of this, Watson. The reason shall be made clear when we meet Mrs. Angus-Burton. Ten years before Angus-Burton was born, his parents took charge of a Chinese boy named Tseng. Apparently Tseng's family was massacred by Muslim Chinese in Chinese Turkestan, and the boy wandered east where he managed to survive in the port cities of Kowloon, Hong Kong, and Macao until his plight came to the Angus-Burtonss' attention. They raised Tseng, who has been the head of the family's household staff since he turned twenty-one."

"So noted. Now what about Mrs. Angus-Burton?"

"Her adopted father worked in banking and was part of the Goschen-Joubert Mission that established the Caisse de la Dette Publique in Egypt in 1875. This is when he met his wife, whose family reputedly once practiced black magic beginning with their service to the Eleventh Dynasty of Egyptian Kings against the Theban priesthood."

I shook my head. "That sounds like something concocted by Haggard for one of his wild adventures."

"Nevertheless the rumor is an element in this case, as is this. Our client met Angus-Burton while he was touring Cairo during the summer holiday prior to his final year at Cambridge, and when their plans to be wed were announced only Mrs. Angus-Burton's father approved."

"On what grounds did the other three parents object?"

"Angus-Burton's parents wanted to see their only child marry a lady of pure British stock, while Mrs. Angus-Burton's mother was adamant that her daughter remain in Egypt rather than move away to England. Eventually Angus-Burton's parents accepted their daughter-in-law, but the relationship between Mrs. Angus-Burton and her mother remained strained. Then, last June, Mrs. Angus-Burton's parents were killed in a railway accident near El Mahalla el Kubra. Any possibility of reconciliation between mother and daughter died with them, in this world at least. Mr. Angus-Burton insists this accident motivated his wife to curse him."

Abruptly something about Holmes's tale followed some train of logic. "I presume he believes her capable of such a feat because of her alleged hereditary strain of black magic?"

"Once more I caution against the practice of presuming, Watson, but you are correct in this instance. I warned you that this would not sound rational"

"Does it really matter, so long as Angus-Burton sincerely believes it is true?"

Holmes started to concur when the cab came to a halt. We had stopped on the Notting Hill end of Kensington Place Road. Holmes instructed to driver to wait then asked me for the time. Looking at my watch, I informed him, "Seven twenty-eight. What is this place?"

"The home of Mr. and Mrs. Angus-Burton."

During our journey the wind had grown stronger as the storm clouds grew thicker and the evening darker, but I could still make out that the Angus-Burton home was grand in scale and architecture, common attributes of the houses in this district. As we approached the front door, Holmes said, "Mrs. Angus-Burton informed me that her husband routinely leaves for his Pall Mall club at seven-fifteen each Monday evening. She assured me that he intended to keep to his routine tonight, giving us the opportunity to inspect the home without alarming him. I am particularly anxious to examine his study."

"Why the study?"

"Because Angus-Burton believes his wife has incorporated the study into her curse. Attend to the knocker, would you, Watson?"

The door opened, we were invited inside, and Holmes introduced me to Mrs. Angus-Burton. She greeted me warmly, but I was struck speechless. Neither before nor since have I beheld so handsome a creature. Her sunset complexion, regal cheekbones, and large russet eyes were at the very least enthralling. If Medusa's loveliness was in any way comparable to Mrs. Angus-Burton's beauty, I can understand why the insecure Athena cursed that vain mortal woman. At Holmes's gentle prodding I regained my composure. "I beg your pardon. My mind went elsewhere for a moment. I'm afraid I think too much at times."

"Yes, I'm forever admonishing Watson about thinking too much." Holmes then asked the mistress if she had given her staff the evening off.

"I did just as you instructed."

"Excellent. May I look about the house while you and Dr. Watson become acquainted?"

Mrs. Angus-Burton had barely given her leave before Holmes dashed away, asking over his shoulder, "Has there been any word from your butler, Tseng?"

"No. The police have still found no trace of him."

Recollecting Holmes's comments about the man, I asked, "Your butler is missing?"

"Yes, Doctor."

"For how long?"

"At least a month. Possibly two. As I told Mr. Holmes this afternoon, my husband and I departed for China in March and did not return until two weeks ago. It was our third trip there in as many years, but the Foreign Office insisted my husband investigate the possibility of Britain leasing the New Territories in the near future. While we were away, Tseng vanished."

"When was he last seen?"

"In July, so far as we know. When my husband and I are away for any extended time our staff, with the exception of Tseng, is sent to work at an estate near Withyham that belongs to a friend of my late father-in-law. Tseng remains here by himself, except for a few days at the beginning of each month when the staff returns to help him clean the house. The rest of the time he spends tending to upkeep and repairs. He is a superb handyman." I asked if it would be simpler to shut up the house during their absences, but Mrs. Angus-Burton explained her husband preferred that Tseng remain to guard the home. "Our staff saw Tseng in July, but when they returned at the beginning of this month he was gone. Nothing had been stolen. There was no sign of violence. It was almost as if Tseng left without giving notice, except that his clothes and everything he owned is still here."

"Did he have any provocation to leave? Perhaps a disagreement prior to your leaving in March?"

"No. Tseng never disagrees with anyone and my husband adores him like an uncle."

A rude pounding interrupted our conversation, accompanied by Holmes calling out for Mrs. Angus-Burton to unlock the door to the study.

Excusing herself while I joined Holmes, the lady fetched a key ring from one of the servant's quarters. "Malcolm keeps this room locked these days. He apparently forgets that Tseng has a spare key." As she set to work finding the correct key, Holmes inquired, "You told me before that everything your butler owns is still in his room. I just looked at it. It's quite barren. Nothing really in the way of personal belongings except his clothes and some Chinese books."

"Yes, Tseng lived very simply." Unlocking the study, her expression, restrained to this point, became anxious. "I pray you will find some sort of clue to explain why my husband doubts me."

"Dr. Watson and I shall make every endeavor to do so. Now if you will excuse us." Holmes ushered me into the study and shut the door behind us. I began to reprimand Holmes for his impoliteness before being enthralled for the second time since entering the grand house. "My word. This is like a private museum."

"As you can see, Mr. Angus-Burton owns an outstanding collection of ancient Chinese furniture, curios, and art."

"Now it makes sense why he wanted his butler to guard the house whenever he and his wife were away. You knew this was in here?"

"I did. According to Mrs. Angus-Burton, her father-in-law collected these treasures during his tenure in China, and they are her husband's prize possessions."

Without forethought, I found myself bemoaning the injustice of one man being blessed with such beautiful objects and an equally beautiful wife.

This delighted Holmes. "Ah! So you agree with my observation of the lady?"

There was no point denying it. "You know I do. As does she, I'm embarrassed to say."

Thus appeased, Holmes took some pity on me. "Think nothing of it, Watson. You were the model of politesse. Now, as I mentioned, Angus-Burton believes his wife has incorporated his study into her curse. Before he left in March Angus-Burton would work in this sanctorum for hours, but since returning he finds that spending more than a few moments in here arouses an uneasiness whose persistence drives him out of the room."

"If the curse were true I suppose that would make a bizarre sense. The wife lost her mother, so in vengeance she bars her husband from the objects he cherishes most. But surely there must be a logical explanation. Perhaps Angus-Burton's anxiety about Tseng manifests itself in a subconscious way through the uneasiness he feels when in this room."

"You may be on to something, Watson," Holmes permitted. "My search of the rest of the house found nothing untoward, so..." Without another word, Holmes set about poking, prodding, and crawling throughout the study. I had seen him perform this bloodhound style of investigation a number of times, and, as on those occasions, Holmes rummaged mostly in quiet, permitting himself only an occasional grunt or hum. As time passed Holmes grew frustrated and may have been about to forsake this tactic when his attention fixated on a small cabinet. Holmes craned his neck to stare at the study's only window, which had its curtains drawn, and then looked back at the cabinet. He rubbed the side of the cabinet, rubbed his fingers together, leaned his hawk-billed nose close to the cabinet, sniffed, then smiled. Then Holmes dropped flat on the floor to examine the carpet underneath the cabinet before standing to reexamine many of the surrounding pieces. He seemed to be seeing the collection from a totally fresh perspective, though I had no idea what that might be. Finally Holmes paced the room to make what I assumed were a series of mental measurements in relation to the study's treasures, the room's dimensions, and the window. When he was finished he looked at nothing in particular and said more to himself than me, "Remarkable."

"Remarkable?"

"Yes. Elegantly remarkable, and yet there is the suggestion of bitterness. Resentment, I think."

"You're not making sense."

"Patience, Watson." Opening the door, Holmes called Mrs. Angus-Burton into the study to ask if anything in the room had been disturbed since their return two weeks earlier. After looking about, she said, "No. Everything is in its normal place."

"Can you recall when your husband last changed the location of anything in this room?"

"Never. As far as I know this study is arranged as it was on the day Malcolm's father moved into it."

"I see. That window? Are those curtains ever drawn back to permit sunlight into the study?"

"Quite frequently."

Holmes appeared more than satisfied and thanked the lady, adding, "If you would give the doctor and I another minute alone, we will be on our way."

Concern broke through Mrs. Angus-Burton's resolve once more. "I don't understand. You've found nothing?"

"Quite the contrary, but it is merely a thread. A thin, frail thread we will follow as best we can to see where it leads."

"So there is an explanation?"

"I did not say that."

"But there is hope?"

"There is always hope, madam. Never lose faith in hope."

Once alone again, I asked, "What thread did you find, Holmes?"

My friend ushered me to the cabinet he had been examining. "Come look at this. Specifically this faded elm wood along the side. Does it look natural to you?"

It did at first, but then something struck my eye as being amiss.

"You see it, don't you, Watson? Go ahead and touch it."

I did. It wasn't faded wood but paint. "Someone's painted the wood to appear faded."

"Faded from the sunlight shining through that window, as any wood in that location would be after years of exposure. I discovered similar camouflaging on that vase and this marble statue."

"These three pieces are frauds?"

"Expert copies of the genuine pieces that were here before the Angus-Burtons left for the New Territories." Holmes's eyes kindled with the thrill of this discovery. "The other cabinets in this room are either lacquered or are covered with decorative paint, so we were fortunate that the elm wood on the sides of this one cabinet were left to patina."

"Then there's been a robbery! Why didn't you tell Mrs. Angus-Burton?"

"Because this is not an answer. It is a clue. There is still much to discover. These forgeries and the disappearance of the butler make up the thread we must follow. If we can trace it back to its skein, then I believe we can confirm what happened to Tseng and the explanation for Angus-Burton's uneasiness whenever in this study."

"Surely you have some idea."

Apprehension dampened the spark in Holmes's eyes. "What I have is an errand that I must attend to while you return to Paddington."

"Why should I return home? Don't you need my help?"

"As always when the hour of action arrives," Holmes assured. "Unless I'm mistaken, we will have to make a dark descent into a perilous place this night and so we best prepare ourselves. We'll meet at Baker Street at ten o'clock, and be sure to bring along your revolver."

* * * *

Doing as Holmes instructed, I returned to our old rooms in Baker Street as the familiar clock above the mantle struck ten. Through a miasma of blue smoke I spotted Holmes sitting on the floor wearing his dressing-gown, legs crossed, a pouch of tobacco and a telegram in his lap as he puffed on his briar pipe. Taking my familiar seat by the fireplace, I felt most at home. Perhaps too much so, as I said, "Something is weighing on your mind."

"And how exactly do you deduce that?"

"A few little things. For instance, you always smoke your black clay pipe unless your mood is blue, then you smoke your old briar pipe. You have also kept the windows closed despite the heat, most likely for the sense of confinement, which you insist aids your concentration."

"Excellent, Watson. Of course, it all seems so simple after you explain it."

My friend's tone prodded me to acquiesce. "Does that telegraph have anything to do with where we are going tonight?"

"It does. It is from the Wapping headquarters of the Thames River Police to inform us that safe passage has been arranged for you and I tonight to enter a certain shop in the Dockland."

"Why go there? And why should we need any sort of safe passage?"

Holmes inhaled deeply upon his pipe. "I fear I am asking you to risk a great deal by accompanying me tonight. That is what weighs on my mind. We must go to this shop because it is only there that the confirmations I spoke of earlier can be established." He pointed to the telegraph. "The necessity of the safe passage is because this shop is under the protection of the city's most notorious Oriental society, the Triad, who guard it as vigilantly as the Crown Jewels are guarded in the Tower of London. Without this safe passage it would take the assistance of a regiment for us to reach this shop, and if for any reason the Triad would decide to rescind it during our visit the chances of us escaping are perilously slim."

I don't know if I had ever heard Holmes sound so worried, but there was never any question that he could depend upon me and I told him so.

"Good old Watson. Our safe passage begins at midnight, so until then I'm afraid all we can do is smoke a quiet pipe and wait." He said not another word until the time arrived to depart.

From Baker Street we traveled to the East End and descended into that other London. Whitechapel. Aldgate. Spitalfields. Mile End. Ratcliffe Highway. Even at that hour those mazes of alleys and wharves were brimming with the bawdy music from pubs, the luring aromas of food from around the world drifting from restaurants, the crude voices from various sailor boarding houses, and everywhere the children, those street Arabs who were "pale and always ailing."[168] The temperature had precipitately cooled when Holmes stopped to fix his bearings and then look at the sky again. "By the look of that lightning, Watson, it appears this storm is finally going to break. Thank goodness we've about reached our destination."

"Which is where? You haven't even told me the name of the place."

---

[168] As of this writing I have been unable to locate the source for this quote.

Instead of answering, Holmes pressed on. "Down this direction."

"This way is even bleaker," I said, convinced after a few steps we must be lost. "Where's everyone gone? All I see are courtyards, backyard slaughter houses – "

"And our destination. That rather exotic shop."

Through a brick archway that I failed to notice before I dimly perceived the bland green painted façade of a waterfront shop. From this angle the shop appeared to be tucked away by itself with the exception of a large warehouse it abutted. Above the door was a sign. "'The Way to Heaven.' Scarcely an apt name, I would wager."

"Let's pray it is not a prophetic one for us." At that second the skies opened. "Here's the rain! Inside, Watson, before we're drenched!"

Upon entering the shop I realized that Holmes had been right to call it exotic. Walking through its rooms was, I imagine, like walking through the Great Yarmark, the famous summer fair at Nizhny Novgorod.[169] Among the collectibles I saw were Javanese pottery, cow-tail coats, jeweled idols, and bizarre arms and armors. In the back rooms was a zoo stocked with animals from the four corners of the globe, including a black swan, a Sumatra civet cat, a black panther, even a pair of petulant crocodiles. We spotted no other human beings until we reached the rear of the shop, where an ancient-looking Chinese man waited for us beside a large ornate drapery.

"Mister Holmes. Doctor Watson. Welcome to the Way to Heaven. I am Hip Yee. This is my shop."

---

[169] City in western Russia on the Volga River.

"Good evening," said Holmes. "I believe we're expected."

"Yes, sirs. Tseng is waiting. Through this passage, please. The way is dark, but not too dark. I will take you." The proprietor drew back the drapery to reveal a red-brick groined tunnel. We followed Hip Yee in, and, as we descended, I asked Holmes, "Tseng is here? How did you find him?"

"We have the Thames River Police to thank for that. I deduced that Tseng is involved with the Triad, so it seemed likely that they would be hiding him somewhere in the Dockland, where the Triad is strongest in London. I presented what details I had to the River Police, who used that information and their expertise of the Dockland to locate Tseng and contact him. We are here because the Triad agreed to give us safe passage after Tseng consented to speak with us."

"And here you are, gentlemen." Hip Yee stopped before a great oxidized iron door, which he opened with far less effort than I would have supposed. "Inside, please, gentlemen. Please wait here for Tseng." We passed through, the door closed behind us, and we found ourselves in a large chamber. What I saw was beyond belief.

"Holmes. This room. It's – it's – "

"Remarkable?"

"It's Angus-Burton's collection! Every piece of it! But this … this is incredible. No, it's impossible! Tseng could never have stolen it all and replaced it by himself."

"You are correct. He couldn't. And he didn't."

Before Holmes could explicate, the great door opened and we were joined by a Chinese man of proud bearing wearing a long loose white garment. Like many middle-aged men of Asiatic heritage, it was difficult to decipher his exact age. The newcomer could just as easily been in his early forties as his early sixties. His hair was black, his green eyes were bright and perceptive, and I appraised that he had likely been quite handsome in his youth. Speaking with a voice tinged by an accent, the man said, "I am Tseng. Welcome to my home."

Forgetting our circumstances, I retorted, "'Your' home? Everything in this room, sir, has been taken from the study of Malcolm Angus-Burton!"

"What you say is true, Doctor."

"Then you admit you're a thief!"

"I admit I have committed a crime, but I have no qualms about how other men shall judge me. I am content in my heart." Having dismissed me, Tseng turned towards my companion. "I am curious, Mr. Holmes. How did you know to have the River Police search for me here? Pains were taken to leave no trail."

With the respectful voice of a patient schoolteacher, Holmes told Tseng, "A man leaves trails throughout his life that can be followed by someone who knows how. In your case, when you were an orphan you lived for a time in Macao."

"I fail to see anything revealing in that."

"No, but I am a student of crime. Not only in England but across the world. So I know that for the past several years a Triad branch has operated in Macao and that they often attempt to recruit orphans into their society."

Tseng pondered this, perhaps recollecting moments from his past, then nodded. "Lost souls can make dedicated if mindless soldiers, however I never joined the Triad as a child. Instead I fled to Canton."

"I must confess I was uncertain if you joined them then, although it seemed logical that you did not. If you had there would have been no need for you to be taken in by the Angus-Burtons."

"Living with them was indeed a better option than joining the Triad. The Angus-Burtons cared for me well and saw to my education. No one could have been more grateful to his benefactors than I."

"Mrs. Angus-Burton sings your praises as a handyman. I see from the calluses on your palms and fingers that you are more than that. You are a sculptor as well as a carpenter."

"And he would have to be to make all the forgeries in Angus-Burton's study," I said.

"But he didn't make them all," Holmes told me, then returned to Tseng. "That is how I knew you had joined the Triad. The number of forgeries involved with this grand substitution was too great for one person to create even if he had a lifetime to complete them, much less three years."

This piqued Tseng. "Why do you say three years?"

"That is how long both of Malcolm Angus-Burton's parents have been dead. That is when your former master inherited the family's estate and all its possessions, including these treasures taken from your homeland."

"So you think that was my motive for wanting to possess this collection? Because these treasures were taken from China?" Tseng appeared to be almost disappointed with Holmes.

"No. You lived in the Angus-Burton household ten years longer than their only son, but you received nothing in their will. Your motive was that you were not remembered."

This stunned Tseng, who remained silent for several moments. When he found his voice, he stammered, "How could you know that?"

"Mrs. Angus-Burton told me you left all your belongings behind when you disappeared, which is a most telling act in and of itself. To stay on point, however, when I searched the Angus-Burton home earlier this evening I found nothing in your room that could be construed as an heirloom."

"It is a plain and mostly empty room. Tell me, why was leaving my belongings behind so telling?"

"To borrow a gambling phrase, you overplayed your hand. If you had taken your belongings and left a letter of resignation, then your disappearance would have been dismissed as unexpected but not unusual. Logically that would have been the preferable effect if your substitution of the collection were successful. This would mean, though, that your former master would not suffer as you suffered when his parents forgot about you. Mrs. Angus-Burton told us her husband loves you like an uncle, so if you vanished inexplicably then Angus-Burton would always wonder and worry what happened to you."

What Holmes was describing struck me as reprehensible. "If that's true, it's more malicious then the robbery!"

Instead of refuting, Tseng queried Holmes, "What evidence do you have to suggest that I could be so vindictive?"

"Evidence? How about the pieces in Angus-Burton's study that are not forgeries?"

This made even less sense to me. "Tseng didn't steal the entire collection?"

"Oh, I did, Dr. Watson. You have my word that every piece of the collection accumulated by Angus-Burton *père* is here."

Holmes explained, "Whenever possible I put myself in the shoes of the criminal, as it were, to try to think as he thinks. When I recognized that the small cabinet was a forgery I searched the collection for more. To my surprise most but not all of the treasures had been substituted. This puzzled me. Why only steal the vast majority of the treasure instead of all of it? Then I noticed that the authentic pieces were among the most intricate and detailed of the collection. That was when it became obvious that all of the collection had indeed been stolen. These authentic pieces would have been virtually impossible to accurately duplicate, so they were replaced with genuine identicals."

"I'm trying," I said, "but I can't see any reason for doing that. The trouble and expense of replacing a few items with genuine twins could not have been worth the effort."

"My friend is correct, Tseng. Such an action suggested bitterness and resentment. You could not permit Angus-Burton to keep one single item from his father's collection if it was in any way possible to leave him with none of it."

Tseng paced a bit, his faced turned from us all the while. "I repeat, I have no qualms about how other men shall judge my actions. Still, you have not told me how you knew I had joined the Triad."

"To accomplish this robbery, you needed the aid of artisans familiar with Chinese furniture and art. These would have to be men that you could trust not to talk about your plan. You also needed access to a good deal of capital, not just for these artisans but to pay for materials. What other resource was available to you that had access to all of this than the Triad? Especially when in return you could offer them access to everything you had learned from your years of service to one of the Queen's own advisors."

"Ah. I see." Tseng halted and let everything he had just heard go round his head again before speaking further. "It is a rather obvious trail once it is explained, but one that requires extraordinary perception and skill to follow." He smiled at Holmes. "I congratulate you on your abilities."

"You are aware of the unexpected affect your robbery has had on your former master?"

"Which is?" Tseng asked half-heartedly.

"He senses that things are not as they appear to be in his study, but he cannot see what is out of place. This coupled with your mysterious disappearance and, I suspect, the fatigue of three journeys to China in three years have deluded him to believe his wife has cursed him."

Tseng started to raise his arms in alarm before catching himself. "He thinks the mistress could…that is absurd!" I assured Tseng it was true and his anger blazed. In a quiet voice, he cursed, "That fool." Then his calm demeanor returned. "Well, it does not matter. Your deductions are correct, Mr. Holmes. Go and tell him everything. When you do he will see that there is no curse. The mistress is most innocent."

I suggested, "Perhaps it would be better if you returned what belonged to him?"

"No, Doctor. I couldn't do that even if I wanted. The Triad owns this collection and they own me. That is the price I paid for their help. Their wish is that I return these treasures to China and I must obey. As must Malcolm Angus-Burton. He has more in his life than this collection. He has influence. He has wealth. And he is married to the most beautiful and gracious woman in England. I ask you, how much fortune does one man deserve in a lifetime?"

Holmes interjected, "Such decisions are for providence, not men, to decide."

"I have decided. I only agreed to your request because my masters in the Triad believe it was the simplest way to bring this matter to a conclusion. Now it is time for you to go."

"Wait!" I said. "What did you mean that Angus-Burton must obey the Triad?"

A solemn but determined glint hardened Tseng's eyes. "The Triad defends what is theirs, Doctor. If Malcolm Angus-Burton does not wish to lose the abundance of all he still possesses, then he must be satisfied with matters as they stand and move on with his life, as I now must move on with mine."

* * * *

The following day, with Mrs. Angus-Burton's permission, Holmes presented Tseng's warning to her husband. That should have been the end of the matter, but Angus-Burton was outraged to learn of the betrayal.

The next night Scotland Yard stormed the Way to Heaven and after a fierce struggle recovered the stolen collection. They also found Tseng, murdered in the gruesome ritualistic way of the Triad to prevent the organization from losing possession of him to the police. As for the Angus-Burtons, a few nights later their Notting Hill home was broken into and upon the morning they were discovered by their servants in the same condition as their former servant.

The tragedy shook the grand old city, inspiring magistrates to begin the clean up of the slums that grew in earnest during the Nineties. I like to think that because of this the Angus-Burtons did not die in vain, something that I mentioned to Holmes while we looked back upon this sad case a short time later.

"It's a fine thought, Watson, but for myself I am convinced that there was indeed a curse at work in this case. Two of them, actually. The petty curses of hubris and desire. Angus-Burton's hubris not to accept what was lost and be thankful for what he still possessed, and Tseng's desire to take what he could when he couldn't have what he coveted, all to hurt a man who had never done anything but love him. It cost them both dearly, but not as dearly as it cost a dear young woman whose only sin was to be caught between the folly of two men's pointless inhumanity to one another."

THE ADVENTURE OF THE AMBITIOUS TASK

"In a modest way I have combatted evil, but to take on the
Father of Evil himself would, perhaps, be too ambitious a
task."
-Sherlock Holmes, "The Hound of the Baskervilles"

I. *The Danseuse*

READERS OF *The Sign of Four* will recall that I met Miss Mary Morstan
when she consulted Sherlock Holmes upon the recommendation of one
of his former clients, her employer Mrs. Cecil Forrester. Miss Morstan
accepted my proposal of marriage after this adventure, but it was not
until several years after my wife's death that I heard from Mrs. Forrester
again when she advised another young woman to seek my friend's
assistance.

It began on an unseasonably balmy afternoon in late October 1920
when a telegram from Mrs. Forrester arrived at my Queen Anne Street
residence asking that I call at the earliest opportunity. I was semi-retired
from civil practice and had no more patients that day, so—with some
reservation—I took a cab to the Metropolitan Borough of Camberwell,
where I was confronted by the tranquil home to which I had escorted
my blonde, small, and dainty Mary on that first drizzly September
evening. Even the stark autumn sunlight blistering through wafts of
smoky-colored clouds could not dispel the image of Mary standing with
Mrs. Forrester on the step that night before I returned to Pondicherry
Lodge, the women's graceful, clinging figures silhouetted within the half-
open door.

My knock was answered by a lovely woman of no more than two and twenty possessed of a melancholy air. Obsidian hair in an Eaton bob framed a clear-cut oval face and emerald eyes that were as penetrating as they were translucent, and a dark pleated skirt with matching loose jumper and cardigan draped an exceptionally lithe yet sinewy physique. "Dr. Watson?" she asked with a suggestion of a French accent.

"Yes, I'm Dr. John Watson."

"Mrs. Forrester has been expecting you." The woman grasped my wrist, tugged me inside, and led me down the familiar hallway with its stained glass, barometer, and bright stair-rods to the drawing-room, where Mrs. Forrester was sitting in the basket chair near the window, a volume of Dickens's winter tales in her lap and an empty Gothic chair with Dragon and Peacock fabric facing her. Now in her seventies and dressed in an Edwardian ivory tea dress, she appeared fit and alert while her voice retained most of its timbre as she greeted me. "My dear John, it does my heart good to see you." She held a hand out towards my escort, who clutched it and stood beside her. "This is my granddaughter, Ivy Forrester."

I considered the young woman again. "Forgive me, but your name seems familiar."

"Most likely because I was engaged to Nathaniel Hayes."

Mrs. Forrester added, "The son of the American circus impresario Bartholomew Elroy Hayes."

"Yes, that's it." A torrent of recent newspaper obituaries tumbled through my memory as I added, "My sincere condolences."

Ivy Forrester thanked me and in the next beat asked, "Do you think it possible to persuade Mr. Holmes to look into what happened to Nathaniel?"

Without thinking I replied, "Mr. Holmes is retired."

"We know," Mrs. Forrester intervened, "but if you could present Mr. Holmes with the relevant circumstances—which are so strange, so utterly inexplicable—might he at least be willing to offer advice as a consulting detective?"

Age had not robbed Mrs. Forrester of her wit much less her charm. "I am afraid I have never been able to predict what Mr. Holmes will do. However ..." I made myself comfortable in the Gothic chair. "You say the circumstances are inexplicable?"

"Most outré." Mrs. Forrester gazed at her granddaughter. "Are you up to this, my dear?"

A resolute fire kindled in the young woman's eyes. "I am." She stared at me. "I'm a *danseuse*, Doctor."

All I could think to say was, "I had assumed something of the sort by your carriage."

"You are not the first man to notice. I was a *petit rat* and then a *ballerine* in the *corps de ballet* for several years at the Opéra National de Paris." She paused, weighing her next words carefully. "My father passed away when I was five. He began boarding school before Mrs. Watson was hired here as governess, but *Grand-mère* tells me your wife was a wonderful woman whom my aunts adored."

"Thank you."

"I am not at liberty to discuss the circumstances, but I recently reached a crossroads concerning my career at the Opéra, and because of that I was dismissed after the run of *Le Domaine d'Arnheim* last spring. I also found myself a pariah from my family until *Grand-mère* offered me sanctuary." Miss Forrester kissed her benefactor's hand. "I was auditioning at the Royal Coburg when I met Nathaniel last June and soon after he offered me a position with his family's circus."

I paused, weighing my next words carefully. "I was unaware that B.E. Hayes's Circus and Great London Show features ballet dancing."

A wistful smile rippled across Ivy Forrester's lips. "I appreciate your diplomacy. The particulars shouldn't matter, but by the time Nathaniel presented me with his offer I was already as much in love with him as he was with me." With a tremble in her voice, "From what *Grand-mère* tells me, you can appreciate that."

I cautiously nodded.

"Our engagement was announced in early July, but hardly two weeks passed before Nathaniel started evidencing a remorseless withering that eventually killed him."

"May I ask the cause?" No disease or symptoms were reported in any newspaper account I had read.

"No disease was identified. Nathaniel wasted away without explanation until his will gave out."

Mrs. Forrester interjected, "We know the Hayes's doctor ruled out consumption. For a time anemia was considered the likeliest cause because Nathaniel suffered from active kaleidoscopic dreaming as well sleepwalking."

"Well, the former can be an indicator. Was Mr. Hayes's red blood count tested?"

Ivy Forrester answered, "Yes."

"It was low?"

"No."

This surprised me. "Did he suffer from air hunger or complain often of being cold?"

"Neither."

"Then I fail to see a reason for this diagnosis."

"The doctor gave none for it or why he later suspected cerebral hypoxia."

I was confounded. "Was Mr. Hayes epileptic or asthmatic?"

"Nathaniel was an active sporting man beginning with his childhood in the United States."

This triggered a thought. "Was he a mountaineer? Or fond of skiing?"

"Neither. Why?"

"Cerebral hypoxia can be triggered by intense exercise in high altitude before one becomes acclimated to the thinner air. Did his doctor find any evidence that Mr. Hayes's brain was being hindered in receiving or processing oxygen?"

"None except his symptoms."

The more I heard the more I suspected this physician had been clutching at straws. "You say Mr. Hayes walked in his sleep?"

"Every night. Even after he became too weak to stand while awake."

A bit of light! This struck me as a psychosomatic symptom induced by hysteria, possibly brought on by the sudden betrothal. "Did he ever sleepwalk prior to becoming ill?"

"Never, according to his family."

Mrs. Forrester added, "Nathaniel proved to be something of an artful dodger as a somnambulist. He nearly always escaped his house regardless of precautions. Fortunately he never wandered further than their landscape garden. His family does not live in the safest neighborhood." It was common knowledge that the Hayeses owned four opulent mansions in America and Europe, but spent most of their time in their London residence, a renovated three-story brick pub named Tannhäuser Gate at the corner of Landor Lane and Cottage Way in Wapping near where Nathaniel's mother Jorun had grown up. "Which brings us to Dr. Hell."

"Who?" I asked.

A frost chilled the room as Ivy Forrester's bearing turned rigid. "Dr. Ianthe Hell of New Orleans."

"An American?"

"That's where she lives. The Devil only knows where she came from."

I had never heard of a woman neurologist or psychoanalyst. "Is she a specialist?"

"The *devin-guérisseur*[170] claims to be many things, in particular an occultist."

Mrs. Forrester explained, "Dr. Hell is not yet thirty but has been a *célèbre* since the end of the Great War, for much the same tragic reason spiritualists and cunning folk became popular after the American Civil War."

"The Hayeses behaved as if only she could help Nathaniel, though they never explained why. Now she is furious and has brought suit against Scotland Yard because they are proscribing her from leaving London, as they have with everyone else involved." Ivy Forrester scowled irritably. "It is ironic, really, since Dr. Hell prohibited anyone from seeing Nathaniel except for her and his parents after she arrived. I never saw him alive again after that." Without forewarning, her resolve cracked. Tears swelled her eyes and she began to noticeably tremble. Mrs. Forrester recommended she try to rest and the young woman acquiesced. Once we were alone Mrs. Forrester confided, "I don't know how much more poor Ivy can bear. She is strong, but Nathaniel's body is missing."

"Good Lord! When did it happen? I haven't read anything about this."

"This news has not been released to the public. Nathaniel was interred in Brompton Cemetery in a mausoleum commissioned by his father to safeguard his body. It stands not far from where our Mary lies."

---

[170] "Diviner-healer"

"I see." A frightful thought struck me. "Did Dr. Hell suspect catatonia?"

"All we know is Mr. Hayes had the mausoleum equipped with a lock that was guaranteed to be far superior to even a Bramah. The lock is installed on the inside of the door and Mr. Hayes made certain that the only key manufactured for it was melted. Once the mausoleum was sealed it should have been impossible to open again even from within, but when Mrs. Hayes visited her son this morning the door was ajar. When she entered the mausoleum Nathaniel's body was gone."

"What does Scotland Yard suspect?"

"They have disclosed nothing beyond their displeasure over Mr. Hayes enlisting Sheridan Nightlinger to examine the mausoleum prior to their being notified."

"Nightlinger the stage magician?"

"Also Nightlinger the escapologist and spiritual debunker. He attended Nathaniel's funeral as a friend of the Hayes family and Ivy is also familiar with him. *Le Domaine d'Arnheim* was a spectacle and Mr. Nightlinger designed its stage effects. Since then he has been performing at the Théâtre Art Déco de Cheminot, but he keeps a flat at The Scheherazade in Mayfair and is residing there while remaining in London. He strongly disapproved of asking you and Mr. Holmes for assistance, insisting it would be better if Scotland Yard were permitted to handle the matter without interference. But how can I do nothing with Ivy suffering so?"

* * * *

245

II. *The Magician*

I went to Mayfair after leaving the Forrester home and stopped at a district telegraph office on Davies Street to send a message to Holmes regarding the matter. From there I proceeded towards Brooks Street to The Scheherazade Residential Mansions and Hotel, and at the front desk requested to speak with Sheridan Nightlinger at the behest of Miss Ivy Forrester. I was escorted to the uppermost level and when I stepped out of the elevator, my eyes were drawn to an enormous man talking to an incongruous pair of street Arabs outside the door to the furthest flat.

This, I was told, was Sheridan Nightlinger.

Half a foot over six feet in height and well over eighteen stone, he appeared to be scarcely middle age. His rugged face was crowned by long unkempt blond hair and scored by a scar running over his left eyebrow and partially down the same cheek, but his viridescent eyes were warm and fiercely intelligent. He wore an unbuttoned black vest, a white shirt unfastened at the collar with no tie, dark grey slacks, and black boots, all of exquisite quality. The urchins scurried into a stairwell as I approached while the man reached out and in a dramatic tenor voice said, "Dr. John Watson! This is a privilege!" His calloused hand enveloped mine and shook it with unprecedented strength.

"Sheridan Nightlinger?"

"I am. Welcome! Feel free to come here any time. Please enter."

Footsteps suddenly galloped above us. "Have those children gotten onto the roof? We're twelve floors up!"

"I promise you there are no young ones on the roof."

I followed Nightlinger into a sitting room decorated as much for a man-at-arms as a man of letters. An eclectic collection of ancient and antique armor and weaponry was systematically scattered between arrays of shelves brimming with books on a multitude of religious, legal, scientific, and pseudoscientific topics. More books along with maps, charts, scrolls, and codices blanketed two medieval trestle tables near the fireplace. Over the mantle hung a large painting by Alphonse de Neuville showing Alaric before Rome,[171] and to my amazement Sherlock Holmes was standing beneath the painting, enthralled in a copy of *Bybel der natuure*. As Nightlinger closed the door to his rooms he said, "I believe you two know each other."

Holmes glanced up, his grey eyes twinkling with amusement. "Good to see you, Watson!" He turned to Nightlinger and patted the book before putting it down. "Swammerdam and de Réaumur were invaluable companions while I was preparing my own study on bee culture."

"I thought I detected their influence. Along with Vidocq, of course."

Holmes almost smiled. "You read it?"

"I read everything of yours. I'd be honored if you'd sign my first edition."

"I should be delighted! Are you interested in melittology?"

---

[171] 370-410. First king of the Visigoths from 395 to his death. Led the sack of Rome on August 24, 410.

"I am more what you might call a frustrated Johnny-do-it-all. For example, Swammerdam is an undeniably brilliant and insightful biologist and microscopist, but just as fascinating to me are his physico-theological observations such as the omnipotent finger of God being visible in the anatomy of a louse."

"'Wherein you will find miracle heaped on miracle and see the wisdom of God clearly manifested in a minute point.'"

"That's it! Perhaps you observed something of that while watching your bees?"

"No more than I did watching the criminals of London." Holmes acted somewhat chagrined as he turned back to me. "Forgive me, Watson. I lose track more easily these days. You've come on urgent business and I am anxious to hear about your visit with Mrs. Forrester and her granddaughter."

All I could think to say, however, was: "How on earth are you here?"

"I asked Mr. Holmes for his help. It seemed the best course of action since Mrs. Forrester was determined to bring you into the matter." Nightlinger tucked two fingers into his right vest pocket and removed a piece of paper wrapped around two coins and presented them to me. The paper was my message to Holmes along with the price for the telegram. "How did ...?" Then I recalled the street Arabs.

"It made no sense to let you toss away good money."

Sherlock Holmes lit a cigarette, inhaled deeply, and absently rubbed a finger over his right eyebrow. "You remember Inspector Jones of the

Metropolitan Police? He is of the opinion that Mr. Nightlinger and Miss Forrester played a hand in the unpleasant circumstances surrounding Nathaniel Hayes. As you know, Watson, my method is founded upon the observation of trifles, but the only trifle Jones admits he has found is the fact that Mr. Nightlinger worked at the Opéra National de Paris prior to Miss Forrester's dismissal. I must confess such threadbare reasoning has me pining for the solid roast beef ratiocinations of our old friend Lestrade, misguided though the Inspector may have often been." Holmes drew upon his cigarette and tossed it into the fireplace as I went into my report on all Mrs. Forrester and her granddaughter had informed me, concluding with, "Neither mentioned Inspector Jones's suspicions, I'm afraid."

Nightlinger said, "They don't know about them. I haven't even told Nate's parents. They've been through so much. I'm also afraid I don't know why Miss Forrester was dismissed, either, although I've heard rumors." Nightlinger paused, weighing his next words. "You're both familiar with Edgar Degas's[172] paintings of the Opéra's ballerinas and dancing students? Some of them like 'L'Etoile' and 'The Ballet Rehearsal on Stage' feature black figures lurking in the background."

"The *abonnés*."[173]

"Yes. There are those who believe a murdering ghost prowled the Opéra not long ago, but these blackguards always have blighted the place. Every enterprise has its shadows and these are indispensable to

---

[172] 1834 – 1917. Over half of Degas's' works depict dancers.
[173] "Subscribers"

the Opéra. The management expects absolute obedience from its students and dancers when it comes to the *abonnés*, especially in the *foyer de la dance*." I recollected another painter, Jean Beraud,[174] and his 'In the Wings of the Opera' as Nightlinger sighed in a world-weary way. "The scuttlebutt is that Miss Forrester was becoming uncooperative despite pressure from the management and her family. If that's true, then I say hurrah for her."

Holmes appeared to muse upon this as he asked, "What about Dr. Hell? Do you know why her aid was enlisted?"

Nightlinger shrugged. "The Hayeses never mentioned her to me before and we've been friends since the circus started making its winter camp in Minnesota. I do know she has the police somewhat cowed."

This disenchanted me. "I thought the professionals were made of sterner stuff than to be nervous about lawsuits."

Holmes said, "Don't forget how well the threat of slander and libel served Professor Moriarty."

Nightlinger added, "I wasn't referring to constables and detectives, but rather their superiors at New Scotland Yard. Even the bravest soldier must obey orders, but it's my neck on the block so I've been making discreet inquiries with some of my colleagues in America like Moro Frost and Prince Abdul Omar. There's no lack of public information on Dr. Hell, but the lady guards her reputation jealously. She beats down any probing into her private life the way a brute might whip some poor cur."

---

[174] 1849 – 1935.

This brought to mind the disingenuous Isadora Klein[175] as Holmes began to pace. "You mentioned the rumor about Miss Forrester. Are there rumors about Dr. Hell? A pattern of hearsay can sometimes be revealing if judiciously dissected."

"Practitioners like Dr. Hell attract rumors like flies, Mr. Holmes. They will even encourage the most popular gossip if it can promote their services, much like the tittle-tattle currently whirling around that Harley Street miracle man Dr. Herbert."

I had heard about Dr. Herbert, as had most of London. "Some of those claims are rather farfetched, though, such as his resuscitating the recently deceased."

"And communicating with the dead is less incredible? Dr. Hell is a medium and mesmerist in good standing with the National Spiritualist Association of Churches, which claims she follows their Declaration of Principles, although from what I've found out so far they appear to give her a longer leash than they do other members. For example, you are familiar with Poe's 'Facts in the Case of M. Valdemar'? There are whispers Dr. Hell has taken part in comparable experiments, although always at a client's request and supposedly without such ghastly results. Where Moro and Prince Omar have proven most beneficial, however, is with Hell's dalliances. She has never married but she's purportedly left a swath of 'pale kings and princes,' each one claiming her 'faery song' corrupted them body and soul. Even so, these wretches were unable or unwilling to resist her until they succumbed or took their own life."

---

[175] See "The Adventure of the Three Gables."

Holmes ceased his pacing to gaze out at London. "'*La belle dame sans merci* hath thee in thrall!' It appears the world still has much to learn from the poets."[176]

"Normally I'd have doubts about Nate's parents asking for Hell's assistance if they knew about these rumors, but I've learned never to underestimate what desperate parents will risk. In any case, though, I should be telling them about Jones's suspicions."

Holmes agreed. "Meanwhile I would like to take a look at Nathaniel Hayes's mausoleum."

"Of course. You can leave your valise here if you wish and I'd be glad to escort you."

III. *The Cemetery*

Holmes excused himself outside The Scheherazade to dispatch some letters and telegrams, promising to join up with us at Brompton Cemetery in a few minutes. By the time Nightlinger and I arrived at the graveyard, slashes of purple clouds drifting across the dimming orange sunlight were transforming the horizon into a jack-o'-lantern squatting on a hedge beneath the darkling sky. I pulled my overcoat closer around me as the night grew colder and damp, but Nightlinger was content in only a black frock coat. As we walked down the cemetery's main avenue he scanned the headstones and railed-off tombs. Pointing towards a particular cluster, he said, "A Dakota Sioux chief named Shoot Holy lies

---

[176] Nightlinger and Holmes are quoting John Keat's *femme fatale* ballad 'La Belle Dame sans Merci,' first written in 1819 and revised in 1820.

over there. Pneumonia took him soon after Bartholomew brought the circus to London the first time. A girl named Snow Bird lies with him. She was not quite two years old when she fell while riding horseback with her mother."

"You knew them?"

"In the United States. We were neighbors. So were several First Nation performers also buried there who came with *Buffalo Bill's Wild West Show* when it played at the Exhibition Grounds near here." Sadness glazed his eyes. "Europe welcomed them but it was none too kind to them."

We kept walking until we were a little more than halfway down the avenue, where I excused myself and ventured off the path towards the east while Nightlinger continued alone. Mary and I had been living in Kensington at the time of her passing and she was buried in Brompton Cemetery because of its proximity. Even so I never visited her grave this late in the autumn before and was surprised to spy garlic flowers interspersed among the lush grass. There was also an unusual lack of spider webs for the time of year.

A shadow or sound attracted my attention towards the Indian burials and I spotted a small woman standing amongst the graves. Her back was towards me, but her bearing denoted stern elegance while her lengthy white hair, woven into a braid, contrasted prominently against her *purpura* cloak. I turned back around and bowed my head, but glanced up again when I sensed I was being watched. A red fox trotting up the avenue warily glared at me, its eyes shining black in the gloaming. For an instant or longer I felt lost in thought and then I finished my prayers, by which time both woman and fox were gone.

A fantastically gibbous moon was nearly overhead when I found Holmes and a night constable conversing in front of Nathaniel Hayes's mausoleum in the shadow of the graveyard's domed chapel. The sepulcher was coffee brown granite with four Ionic columns supporting cornices overhanging a short portico with a pentagram engraved in the triangular pediment in place of a name. Nightlinger was nowhere in sight as I approached and overheard the young constable tell Holmes what an honor it was to meet the famous detective before he noticed me. "This is truly a delight, sir. I've been reading your adventures since I was a tot."

I thanked him as Holmes requested to look inside.

The constable fidgeted, caught betwixt adulation and duty, but finally acquiesced. "You won't tell the Inspector, will you, sirs?"

"It shall remain our secret."

Holmes and I entered the mausoleum, which was so dark that my companion had no choice but to pull an electric torch from one of his overcoat's pockets. It provided some radiance, but I could not help commenting that I wished we had another. Instantly I felt a tap on my shoulder and nearly shouted as Nightlinger's illumined face appeared. He motioned me not to speak as he offered me his torch. Meanwhile Holmes tentatively stretched out to examine the floor before he gingerly rose to his tiptoes to inspect the ceiling. Next he scrutinized each wall, Nathaniel Hayes's coffin, the heavy bronze door with a relief of a lion, and finally the exceptional lock. I had long ago grown accustomed for such activity to be accompanied by grunts and hums of curiosity or satisfaction, but Holmes remained strangely silent. At last he waved for us to leave, at which point I noticed he was hobbling. I returned my torch to Nightlinger and followed Holmes, who thanked the constable before starting down the avenue. Holmes remained in the throes of some vexatious problem even after we had walked a suitable distance for me to inquire, "Where is Nightlinger?"

"I'm right here." The big man was strolling beside me. "My apologies but the constable would have been less obliging to you if he had seen me, so I entered and exited the mausoleum while Mr. Holmes distracted him. Mr. Holmes couldn't warn you what we were up to without the constable overhearing."

"I'm sorry, my dear fellow," Holmes murmured in a preoccupied voice.

"Did you find anything, Mr. Holmes?"

Several seconds passed before Holmes muttered, "Perhaps." He inhaled deeply. "Is he safe?"

The question elicited no reaction from Nightlinger but left me perplexed. "Is 'who' safe?"

Neither man spoke until Holmes at last answered, "Nathaniel Hayes."

"He is alive?"

Nightlinger admitted, "He is."

"Where is he?"

"The Scheherazade. I am pledged not to divulge exactly where, but I promise you that all the King's horses and men could take the place apart brick by brick and never find him."

Holmes asked, "What do you mean you are pledged?"

"That's honestly all I can say."

We were less than thirty yards from the cemetery's entrance at Old Brompton Road when Holmes stopped. "I can't say I approve of this situation."

With a resolute mien Nightlinger said, "I swear Nate will leave his sanctuary when I am positive any danger to him has passed. Can I ask how you deduced for certain Nate is under my protection?"

"I wasn't certain until you confessed."

Nightlinger gawked for an instant before bursting into lively laughter that put any owls and urchins in the vicinity to flight. "You'd be a wonder in bluff poker, Mr. Holmes! Surely, though, you deduced something from Nate's tomb."

"Very little. When I examined the lock I found scratch marks on its pins that demonstrated it had been picked. No key or Kate was used. You are a renowned locksmith, but so are at least five superlative cracksmen who currently reside in London; however, whoever picked the lock did so after the mausoleum had been sealed, which put this cracksman in a most perilous predicament. This suggested the fellow's motivation must have been very great and he was either arrogantly confident or he had been forced to react in haste." Holmes gazed in the direction of the domed chapel. "One thing I was unable to infer is why the mausoleum is designed to prevent its occupant from leaving."

"Bartholomew confided to me before Nate's funeral that he and Jorun believed their son had fallen under the influence of a bokor[177] or shaman, and they were terrified that Nate was going to rise as a slave. A zombie. The mausoleum was designed to prevent that."

I scoffed, "That's preposterous! Who could think such a thing?"

The big man smirked. "Good old Watson." The smirk dissipated. "The Hayeses watched what was happening to their only boy and not one man of science could explain much less prevent it. Circus people and the like live on the outlands of civilization, which leaves them vulnerable to encounters most normal folk only experience in dreams or nightmares, and after a while that affects the way you perceive the world. Surely you can appreciate that after some of your adventures. A vampire in Sussex.[178] A man transforming into an ape in Camford.[179] A hellhound in Dartmoor.[180] The Devil striking down four people in Poldhu."[181]

"All of which had rational explanations."

"Speaking of rational, did you notice the pentagram over the mausoleum's door?"

I cautiously nodded.

---

[177] A Voodoo witch for hire.
[178] See "The Adventure of the Sussex Vampire."
[179] See "The Adventure of the Creeping Man."
[180] See *The Hound of the Baskervilles*.
[181] See "The Adventure of the Devil's Foot."

"Pythagoreans looked at the pentagram and extrapolated the Golden Ratio, but ancient Greeks also used it as a symbol of protection. How you perceive things makes the difference. Ask any magician. West African conjure-men use an ordeal poison like *radix pedis diabolic* to drive a man insane, but it looks like they've imprecated him. Or they use a deadening brew concocted of a neurotoxin like tetrodotoxin from puffer fish to make a man susceptible to aboulia, but it looks like they've robbed him of his will and then resurrected him to do their bidding."

"You're talking about poisons. Nathaniel Hayes's doctor would have noticed if his patient had been drugged."

"Maybe. If he knew what to look for. But I had to make sure that hadn't happened to Nate and there wasn't time to debate it with Bartholomew and Jorun. They were doing what they thought was best for their son, but if they were mistaken than they were murdering him."

Holmes said, in a soft voice, "You might have been entombed."

"Call me arrogantly confident. A lock may be impassible but never impossible. Concealing me inside the mausoleum and then transporting Nate's 'cadaver' to the Scheherazade was much more challenging. In any case, my concerns were correct. Nate is being subjugated."

"How can you be certain?"

"I'm risking everything on it."

"I see." Holmes gazed again towards the mausoleum. "I wish you had imparted all this to me sooner."

"Would you have believed me?"

Holmes leveled his sights upon Nightlinger. "I am not certain I believe you now." Holmes looked towards the cemetery's entrance. "Still, eliminate all other factors --"

"'-- and the one which remains must be the truth.'"

In a preoccupied voice: "Perhaps."

I asked Nightlinger, "How did you conceal yourself while the mausoleum was being sealed? The inside can't be nearly so dark during the day, and, small as it is, there is no place to hide."

"That was no harder than prestidigitation. I just made sure never to stand where the caretaker was looking."

This sounded infeasible and I gave Holmes a dekko to see if he felt the same way, but Nightlinger's explanation elicited no reaction from him.

When I glanced back towards Nightlinger the man was gone.

"Oh, for heaven's sake."

I swiveled around, expecting to catch Nightlinger behind me, but he wasn't there.

I turned again, but he was still gone.

Holmes chuckled and I glanced his way, then looked around again but to no avail.

"All right, you've proven your point. You can come out now."

"I'm right here."

I turned once more.

Nightlinger was standing beside me.

Holmes chuckled some more. "Please forgive me, Watson, but it was a most entertaining exhibition."

"I'm afraid it probably looked as if I was playing peekaboo to Mr. Holmes."

"I'd say you are far more agile than the average dodger, Mr. Nightlinger."

"I hope so, considering how I make my living." Nightlinger's manner turned serious. "So what do you suggest we do now?"

"A pipe or two could prove useful in sorting out this problem." Holmes put a hand upon my shoulder. "It is short notice, Watson, but may I impose upon your hospitality for the night?"

"Mr. Holmes, I can make arrangements for you at The Scheherazade. At my expense, of course, and for as long as you require."

"That is most generous, but I am a man of habits of which the good doctor is familiar, as he is with my rheumatism, which I aggravated in the mausoleum."

I assured Holmes that he was always welcomed, and after we retrieved his valise and he autographed Nightlinger's edition of *Practical Handbook of Bee Culture* we commissioned a cab to take us to Queen Anne Street. Along the way we made a detour to the telegraph office so Holmes could send a few more messages and leave instructions to forward all responses to my address.

* * * *

IV. *The Knight and the Dragon*

Those responses began arriving with the next day's first delivery and continued past noon. Once in the morning and again in the early afternoon Holmes took his leave, only to lug more responses back with him. Judging from my friend's limp he was in considerable discomfort, however the game was afoot and the old sleuth hound had picked up the scent, although he evidenced little of the passion that generally consumed him. Experience had taught me that my friend preferred solitude during these times, but by late afternoon I could no longer suppress my curiosity and poked my head into his room. I found Sherlock Holmes sitting on the floor amidst a clutter of mail, telegrams, papers, notes, and almanacs borrowed from my library, resolutely reading while absently rubbing his knees. I thought my intrusion had gone unnoticed when he said, "It is times like these when I feel my years." He went on speaking as he thumbed through the replies, but it was directed more towards himself than me. "Wiggins and the Baker Street Irregulars have left the nest or flown the coop. Langdale Pyke[182] and Walter Simonson have left the stage and only the Fates know what has become of Shinwell Johnson.[183] A few *confrère* are left like Jones, Tuson,[184] Champion Harrison,[185] and Pollock,[186] who has grown into his own at the Yard, and while it has been heartening to see my methods

---

[182] See "The Adventure of the Three Gables."
[183] See "The Adventure of the Illustrious Client."
[184] See "The Adventure of the Stockbroker's Clerk."
[185] See *Dracula: The Suicide Club.*
[186] See "The Adventure of the Stockbroker's Clerk."

gain acceptance among the current ranks of professionals, it has simultaneously rendered me obsolete. Oh, I mustn't forget my American muckers such as Wilson Hargreave,[187] Leverton,[188] and my old colleague with the Continental Detective Agency.[189] Judging by their responses the fire hasn't been extinguished in their bellies." Holmes grew quiet as he continued perusing the replies, but the more he read the more the throes from the cemetery seemed to envelope him.

"What have you discovered?"

"Nothing! Nothing of use anyway."

"Surely not all your inquiries are proceeding so badly."

"My old rival Barker[190] might beg to differ. I enlisted him last night to search The Scheherazade for Nathaniel Hayes, but if the young man is there then Nightlinger was not boasting. Barker is keeping watch in the event Nightlinger attempts to transfer Hayes elsewhere, but as far as Barker can tell Nightlinger has never left his flat since we parted ways last night."

"Then Hayes must be in Nightlinger's rooms."

"He might be, but I took the precaution of examining the flat while you and Nightlinger exchanged introductions yesterday. I'm confident my rummaging would have revealed if a person had happened to be concealed there. Of course, Hayes could have been shifted in after we departed for Brompton Cemetery, but that would be out of character for

---

[187] See "The Adventure of the Dancing Men."
[188] See "The Adventure of the Red Circle."
[189] As of this writing I have been unable to verify the identity of this person.
[190] See "The Adventure of the Retired Colourman."

Nightlinger, a man not known for employing associates or collaborators. He does not even engage a business manager or stage assistants." Holmes let any papers he was holding drop into his lap. "I cannot recall meeting Sheridan Nightlinger before, but there is something peskily familiar about him. How about you, Watson?"

"No, I can't say I feel that way. He is not a man one is likely to forget."

"No, he is not. One comment Nightlinger made buzzes in my brain. He mentioned knowing the Hayes family since their circus started making winter camp in Minnesota. What age would you put our client?"

"Certainly no more than thirty-five. More likely a year or two younger."

"The Hayes Circus made its first winter camp in Minnesota in 1888. That continued until the Panic of 1893 necessitated it perform year-round. The circus toured the American Southeast between September and April through 1899, at which time it began spending winters in Minnesota once more. Since then the Hayes Circus has enjoyed remarkably good fortunes, including the birth of Nathaniel Hayes in New Orleans in August of 1900."

"Nightlinger could have misspoken. Or he might have forgotten the earlier bivouacs or is unaware of them."

"Perhaps." Holmes's tone suggested that there was more he was contemplating but was not ready to share.

"What troubles me is we have only Nightlinger's word that Nathaniel Hayes is alive. I am loath to say it, but the longer this goes on the more it strikes me as some perverse practical joke or hoax gone awry."

"That remains a possibility, but everything I've learned points to a deliberate plot implemented by a creature of infinite patience and craft."

"You mean Dr. Hell?"

"I do, but I have no proof, and therein lies the rub. At times I've felt as if Moriarty has returned to thwart me." Holmes steepled his hands and propped his chin on his fingertips. "I have contested evil in my own feeble manner during my career, but I am not the law. All I can do now is represent justice and my only recourse is a direct confrontation."

"So be it. I shall go with you."

Holmes shook his head. "You've never abandoned me, Watson, but it may be more prudent for you to remain here."

"I insist on accompanying you if there is the slightest chance of danger."

Holmes presented a rueful smile. "'The one fixed point in a changing age.'"

"Some things should not change."

"Yet they do and they shall." Holmes scanned the clutter. "So be it then. Time to put what I have to use." He collected several telegrams and folded them into his grip. "Lend me a hand, please, and commission us a cab."

Before long we were heading to Farringdon Within. Grey clouds spanned the sky and a drizzle began to fall as we drove into the heart of the city. Along the way Holmes instructed, "It is of paramount importance that you do not interfere in anything that happens unless I say differently. Understood?"

I agreed with some misgivings, after which Holmes fell into a brooding silence. A few minutes later our cab turned on to Cloth Fair and soon after parked in front of an Elizabethan townhouse with bay windows.

"Here we be, Watson."

Holmes led us to a thick wooden front door with iron ornaments. As he knocked the bells at Great St. Bart's[191] began tolling and my friend recited Samuel Butler[192] in time with the peals: "He that complies against his will is of his own opinion still."[193] Upon the sixth toll the door was opened by a robust Cajun footman in his late fifties. The footman accepted our cards and guided us down an ill-lit corridor into an equally gloomy sitting room where we were to wait for his mistress. The small chamber's oak panels were black from age and the only light came through the diamond-paned casements that reached almost level with the floor to the ceiling. Outside the clouds were darkening as the Scotch mist transformed into a downpour that tapped against the glass. The wind picked up and cried in the chimney, but there was neither fire in the fireplace nor wood in the fire-dog, its brass front pieces molded with masks of Pan. Scant furniture and decorations stood about the room, all of it exhibiting an ancient Grecian flavor, the most beautiful being a lonely chryselephantine statue of Cybele on a metal trapezai table with

---

[191] The Priory Church of St. Bartholomew the Great.
[192] 1613 – 1680. English poet and satirist.
[193] *Hudibras* (1678)

animal legs. Footsteps descended from the floor above, the tread becoming daintier as they approached, until a captivating barefoot woman entered carrying our cards.

"Mr. Holmes. Dr. Watson. Welcome to my home. Scarp told me you were calling."

Dr. Ianthe Hell appeared to be in her late twenties. Petite, precise, pretty, and pale—almost albino—her white hair was in a chignon and she was dressed in Bohemian attire that consisted of a purple high-collared shirt with flowing sleeves, a mauve tie in a Double Windsor, a dark green waistcoat with purple stripes and matching pajama pants. She also wore a pair of tinted glasses with emerald lenses, but whether it was for fashion or a condition such as photophobia I could not tell. Her accent was American and formal, but I sensed something of a spieler about her and I had little doubt that this was the woman I spotted in the cemetery.

"Do you gentlemen require refreshment? Beaune, perhaps?"

"That will not be necessary. We apologize for calling unannounced."

"That doesn't mean you were unexpected." Hell sat in a cathedra.

Holmes stood quite still. "I appreciate you seeing us nonetheless."

"You have questions for me." Hell waited.

Holmes shook his head. "You connived to trick Bartholomew and Jorun Hayes into murdering their son. If it were not for Sheridan Nightlinger, I am uncertain if you not would have succeeded."

Hell waited to hear more.

266

"You're familiar with Detective Brian Donahue of the New Orleans Police?" Holmes withdrew the folded telegrams and riffled through them until he pulled one out. "Donahue favored me by going through the Orleans Parish birth records for Nathaniel Hayes's birthday: August 13, 1900. He found a certificate for Acantha Hayes, born six minutes before Nathaniel to the same parents. Unlike her brother, who was dusky, she was abnormally dusty."

Hell cocked her head.

"Donahue also informed me that Bartholomew Hayes contracted yellow fever while in New Orleans in 1899. According to parish rumors Hayes was near death until a local Voodoo King offered his services, but demanded a child as payment. What is for certain is that the Hayes family travelled to Minnesota ahead of the circus soon after the birth of their twins, and the Minneapolis Police verified with the Minnesota Indian Agency that the following spring the family reported that Acantha had succumbed to influenza on Epiphany[194] and was buried in the Shakopee Mdewakanton Reservation."

"A pretty tale."

"A very pretty tale, since Acantha Hayes never died. She sits before me."

Each end of Hell's lips curled up. "What proof can you offer?"

"None at all, but I am prepared to publish these reports to lay bare your scheme."

"That would be seditious libel." Hell sounded disappointed.

---

[194] The Feast of Epiphany is celebrated on January 6.

"I have no idea why Acantha Hayes was abandoned or why you chose this moment to extract your vengeance. Perhaps the news of your brother's nuptials with Miss Ivy Forrester goaded your actions. She was coming into a fortune that should be shared with you. Or perhaps you felt if a Voodoo King could purportedly ask for a child in payment from your parents then you deserved the same. Given time I might find all that out, but time is not our ally. Not when a man's life and your reputation hang in the balance."

"And yours."

"I am a man of nearly seventy. Such trifles no longer concern me. Besides no man in my profession should shirk from falling upon his sword if the circumstance dictates."

"Reputations are as much the lifeblood of your profession as mine."

"And once tarnished they are impossible to completely restore. Worse, while the high-born and well-bred can make beneficial clients, they can be harpies towards outcast men. Fortunately for me I am retired." Holmes patted the telegrams. "Several suicides and untimely deaths of persons purportedly acquainted with you intimately have occurred. I cannot prove even one of these sordid allegations, but the 'truth grows stale as soon as a Lye,'[195] and when taken *in toto* they suggest if not reveal a definitive pattern." Holmes leveled his sights upon Hell. "Release Nathaniel Hayes from whatever thrall you have him in by sunrise tomorrow, or I shall provide the public with these accusations and let the chips fall where they may."

[195] From Butler's "Characters."

I started to protest but remembered Holmes's orders and caught myself.

The woman simmered but eventually stood and stepped towards the casements to gaze outside. "How little remains of what was. Two millennia ago a basilica sprawled not far from here covering two hectares and standing three stories high in places. Its ruins now lay buried alongside Roman conquerors, their temple to Mithras, and the River Walbrook whose banks the temple was built beside. Even the massive city wall that reached for two miles from Tower Hill in the east to Blackfriars Station in the west has been all but swallowed by relentless Gaea."

Holmes tucked away the telegrams. "'My name is Ozymandias.'"[196]

"You are an educated man, but it's a poor sort of memory that only works backwards."[197] Hell turned and smirked my way as she removed her glasses, unveiling blazing eyes blacker than the onyx of the *Coupe des Ptolémées*. For a moment my soul seemed to sway and I almost felt translucent as I imagined or heard Hell recite, "'O my brother, such a dream I had last night.'"[198] I recouped my bearings as Hell said, "'And two knights-errant to the rescue.'" I recalled Mary describing Holmes and I this way[199] and I worried what sort of heart this grinning face and radiant eyes concealed.

* * * *

---

[196] "Ozymandias" by Percy Bysshe Shelley (1818).
[197] Hell is paraphrasing the White Queen from Lewis Carroll's *Through the Looking Glass* (1871).
[198] From *The Epic of Gilgamesh* (c. 2100 B.C.).
[199] See *The Sign of Four*.

V. *The Garden*

Holmes telephoned Nightlinger when we returned to Queen Anne Street to parley over our meeting with Hell. I passed this time hunting through my library, determined to identify the source of Hell's enigmatic citation, and was still rummaging when Holmes informed me, "Nightlinger will apprise us of any updates in Nathaniel Hayes's condition. I say, Watson, is something troubling you?"

"Yes. That quote Hell tossed off before we departed."

"That was pert, appropriating Mrs. Watson."

"No, the one before that. I'll be deuced if I can remember where it comes from."

"Lewis Carroll, if I'm not mistaken."

Actually it was from "The Epic of Gilgamesh" where Enlil strikes down Enkidu with a wasting disease. *A rather obscure allusion to Nathaniel Hayes*, I thought. The hour was now somewhat late, but Holmes had resolved himself to waiting up in case Nightlinger telephoned. I offered to see about some dinner as well as stand watch with him, but Holmes declined both, insisting that I get some rest in case there was a call to action before sunrise.

I suspect I soon fell asleep and at some time may have dreamt that I was walking through a mist to Tannhäuser Gate.

I heard no sounds. Not even my footsteps.

When I reached the mansion I sensed dangerous eyes scrutinizing me as fog-wreaths curled around the home and reeled into a white sea upon which the upper stories drifted like a phantom galleon. I somehow passed through the dense fog and the mansion into an immense landscape garden. Broad lanes of thick grass green and even as velvet were bordered by luxurious clusters of wildflowers sprouting between blossomy stones. All lanes emptied into a wheel-route with a Grecian fountain that steered into a towering yew alley. At the far end of the alley I saw flames flickering in a brazier and the silhouettes of a frail man and Dr. Hell standing near a life-size statue of a satyr. I started to walk down the alley when a dramatic tenor voice said: "Watson, come here. I want to see you."

The mist vanished as night sounds reignited and I was tugged back into the wheel-route.

Nightlinger had changed into a dark blue bib shirt with ivy green military slacks. A Mauser pistol was holstered on his hip.

"What are you doing here? Why aren't you watching Nathaniel Hayes?"

"I am." Nightlinger pointed down the alley.

"Why aren't you with him?"

"Because I don't belong down there right now and neither do you."

"What do you mean? And where's Holmes?"

"I tried to telephone but no one answered and Nate practically dragged me here after that. It's a good thing for you we arrived when we did, though."

"Because of where I was walking?"

"Yes, that, but also because people in Wapping are protective of the Hayes family. I negotiated your safe passage on our way in." Nightlinger smiled. "It was rather nice playing the psychopomp, actually."

"You knew I'd be coming here?"

"It seemed likely. Tell me, did you ever feel wobbly while looking into Hell's eyes this afternoon?"

I had, of course. "You want me to believe she mesmerized me to come here? Without Holmes realizing what she was doing? That's —"

"'Preposterous?' I suppose it is. It could be that you're safe in bed and this is all a dream. The world will be a better place if that turns out to be true."

Which was the more logical possibility, but I asked, "Why would she entrance me?"

"Because Mr. Holmes threatened her as well as her best laid plans. What better way to chasten him than to smite you?"

The *Gilgamesh* quote suddenly took on new relevance as Enkidu is stricken after he and Gilgamesh defy Enlil and slay the Bull of Heaven. "I see."

"I was afraid of something like this if Mrs. Forrester brought you into the matter."

"A noble sentiment, however we have never shirked from danger." At the other end of the yew alley the black figure of a willowy man appeared. "Hullo? What's going on down there?"

"Nate's moment of truth. If this is Tannhäuser Gate, then that is Venusberg."

I did not understand.

"You're a literary man. You've read the ballads of *Tannhäuser* and *Thomas Rhymer*? Nate must decide whether to remain under Hell's sway or return to Ivy Forrester, and that's not an easy choice when you're enchanted."

"But if Holmes is right, then Hayes and Hell are twins."

"Hell is a trickster. You're a man of the world, Doctor. You must have heard the Aborigine tales of Waa and Bamapana when you lived in Ballarat. The Sioux talk of Iktomi and Mica while in New Orleans they whisper of Ti Malice and Tonton Bouqui. Tricksters are the same wherever they may be. They are all the multitude of Pan, who will commit any transgression to satisfy their wants." Nightlinger patted my shoulder. "I am not saying that Dr. Hell has no justification, but tricksters can go too far and some boundaries should never be crossed. The reason we don't belong down there is because Hell's moment of truth has arrived."

An inexplicable shudder rattled my spine. "Who is that new man?"

"Hell's judge, jury, and executioner. Every enterprise has its shadows and I am obliged not to divulge his name, but he understands tricksters better than most. God is not partial to princes, and the devil, depend upon it, can sometimes ... hold it!"

The frail man was starting to make his way towards us, lumbering at first but gaining confidence with each step, apparently oblivious to the shadow play that transpired behind him between Hell and the willowy man.

273

The woman's posture was frightened but defiant, like a cornered animal, as the willowy man gestured in my direction. She appeared to spit upon the ground. An instant later the fire in the brazier flared and when it tapered only the satyr's silhouette remained.

By this time the frail man had escaped the shadows of the yew alley. In his late twenties with a dark complexion, charcoal hair, and chestnut eyes, he looked unsure of himself or his surroundings until he recognized Nightlinger. The friends embraced as Nightlinger me to introduced Nathaniel Hayes, who asked, "Have I been sleepwalking again?"

"In a way, but this gentleman is a famous doctor. If you'd let him examine you, I have a hunch he'll confirm that you've just been cured." Nightlinger winked at me before glancing down the yew alley, whereupon his countenance darkened. "There will be a fee to pay, but let me worry about that." I followed Nightlinger's gaze, and, while it could have been my imagination, it appeared that the statue had swiveled so it was facing our direction. An instant later the fire flared again and then went out.

* * * *

The next thing I recall it was morning and Holmes was waking me and holding up a letter from Nightlinger. "This just arrived. Once I have confirmed matters for myself I will be returning to Sussex, but Dr. Hell has ostensibly agreed to my demands. Are you all right, dear fellow?"

I glanced about my room. Like Scrooge on Christmas morning, I found everything as I remembered leaving it when I retired. "Did I leave my room during the night?"

"I don't believe so. I did take a short constitutional as you've recommended to relieve my joints, so I can't vouch you were here the whole time."

"You left? What if Nightlinger called?"

"I saw no purpose in disturbing your slumber merely to inform you I was stepping out for a walk, and I assumed you would hear the telephone if it rang and answer it." This was so out of character for Holmes that I again felt there was more to his story that he was keeping to himself.

"Fine. What does the letter say?"

In a nutshell Scarp had delivered a counteractive to the neurotoxin which took affect shortly before dawn, but before Nightlinger could advise anyone of this Dr. Hell had fled to the Continent.

"I fear Nightlinger may have provided her with a head start out of some misguided concern for my welfare. The lady still has much to answer for, but, given the public's fascination for scandal, it would not surprise me if some particularly resourceful muckraker does not eventually expose her ignoble past."

Something in Holmes's attitude made me suspect this expose might be forthcoming sooner rather than later. "But why did she risk everything to strike at the Hayes family? Was vengeance the whole of it?"

"There we delve into the murky waters of the family's past, and in Dr. Hell's absence only Bartholomew, Jorun, or Nathaniel Hayes can answer those questions. Only time will tell, but I doubt even Nightlinger will be able to conjure much less salvage anything from those depths. I have said before that education is a series of lessons with the greatest for the last,[200] but there are occasions when men seem destined never to learn the whole truth behind their labors, and I believe this to be one such time."

Considering the circumstances I could not help but agree. Holmes returned to Sussex that afternoon and I considered the business finished, but a few days later a letter from Nightlinger arrived in the post:

November 1, 1920

Dr. Watson,

I wanted to pass along the glad tidings that Nathaniel Hayes and Ivy Forrester were married at the Sacré-Cœur on Montmartre soon after midnight. It was extremely short notice; however the Rector of the Basilica was most accommodating (especially considering the Solemnity) in reciprocation for recent services rendered and a generous though unusual ex-voto for The Crypt from Nathaniel's parents. An official announcement is forthcoming soon from Bartholomew and Jorun, but it was the wish of both bride and groom not to wait any longer and for an intimate ceremony.

Can we blame them?

Both newlyweds appear happy and grateful yet cautious, making them wiser than most at their age. I am also happy, grateful, and cautious to report no sightings of Dr. Hell nor any black figures lurking in the background during the ceremony. Hopefully this remains true throughout Nate and Ivy's lives, but all of us are at the mercy of His omnipotent finger and can only try to live well and pray for the best.

Please pass this news to Mr. Holmes along with my gratitude and appreciation. You once wrote that he is the best and wisest man you have ever known, but after our adventure I believe it would be more appropriate to amend this to "friend." Please

---

[200] See "His Last Bow."

276

forgive the liberty, but when I think of all Mr. Holmes risked I can honestly say that in all my years I have rarely seen and never known such fealty or Fóstbræðralag.[201] It reflects well upon you, Doctor, and it has been an honor to know you both.

With the fondest wishes for you and the memory of Mrs. Watson,
Nightlinger

---

[201] Icelandic term for a pact of foster blood brotherhood.

CONFESSIONAL

The original concept for *The Adventure of the Coal-Tar Derivative* was as a series of Great Hiatus radio adventures. "Mea Gloria Fides," "The Case for Which the World is Not Yet Prepared," and "The Case of the Unparalled Adventures" were first written as audio scripts. "Mea Gloria Fides" was broadcast in 2014 on the Imagination Theatre radio program *The Further Adventures of Sherlock Holmes* as "A Case of Unfinished Business." The incomparable Lawrence Albert and John Patrick Lowrie portrayed Watson and Holmes, just as they had six years earlier when IT produced "The Tragedy of the Petty Curses" as "The Case of the Petty Curses." As of this writing "The Case for Which the World is Not Yet Prepared" and "The Case of the Unparalleled Adventures" have not been produced, but over time I adapted all four scripts into short stories that were published in different MX anthologies. It did not take Wile E. Coyote, S-u-p-e-r Genius, to finally figure out what had been meant for radio was turning into what Ray Bradbury coined as an accidental novel.

In telling these Great Hiatus adventures I incorporated some historical figures and events as well as a number of fictional characters and situations, perhaps most prominently from Sir Arthur Conan Doyle's non-Canonical stories "The Story of the Lost Special" and the "The Terror of Blue John Gap." I not only borrowed the scoundrel Herbert de Lernac from "Lost Special" but its 1890 Parisian trial, itself inspired by the real-life Panama Canal Scandal trials that began approximately two years later. As for "Blue John Gap," I took considerable liberties with the fate of its protagonist Dr. James Hardcastle, not the least of which was changing his cause of death and moving his date of death from 1908 to 1893.

The Adventure of the Coal-Tar Derivative also presents some explanations to a few of the controversies in "The Final Problem" and "The Adventure of the Empty House," such as why Colonel Sebastian Moran uses stones instead of an air-gun to try to kill Holmes and why Holmes uses such a public persona like Sigerson while on the lam. I leave it to the reader to decide upon the merits of my explanations as well as the merits of my take on the apocryphal giant rat of Sumatra and Holmes's encounter with the serial killer Jack the Ripper.

For you completests I should mention that *The Adventure of the Coal-Tar Derivative* integrates every Sherlock Holmes pastiche I have written to date. Most of these stories appear here in updated forms. All of the missing adventures are graphic novels: *The Adventure of the Opera Ghost*, *The Strange Case of Dr. Jekyll & Mr. Holmes*, and *Dracula: The Suicide Club*. *Opera Ghost* and *Dr. Jekyll & Mr. Holmes* are Holmesian pastiches, but Holmes and Jack the Ripper are limited to supporting roles in *D:TSC*. You can also find more Nightlinger adventures in the graphic novel *Nightlinger: Creature of the Night*.

ACKNOWLEDGEMENTS

My lifelong gratitude and admiration goes to Sir Arthur Conan Doyle.

My appreciation likewise goes to Gary Reed, a fellow Sherlockian and the finest publisher it has been my privilege to work with. You are missed, my friend.

My thanks to Steve Emecz and all the other wonderful folks at MX Publishing.

Kudos to friend and fellow Iowan Paul Huenemann of Right Purdy Animation for his marvelous work on the book trailer for *Adventure of the Coal-Tar Derivative*. A tip of the hat also to voice actors Jens Peterson and David Harnois of *iamlostwithoutmyboswell.com* for bringing Watson and Holmes to life, and to Sherlockian extraordinaire Monica Schmidt for her support.

I find myself happily indebted to the late Jim French of *Imagination Theatre* and its current torchbearers Lawrence Albert and John Patrick Lowrie. Ditto to writer extraordinaire Matthew Elliot.

Respect, regards, and big fat hugs to David Marcum, Paul Growick, Derrick and Brian Belanger, and John Linwood Grant, not a bad writer or editor in the lot.

I want to once again express my gratitude to Professors J. Kenneth Kuntz and Jay Holstein of the University of Iowa's Department of Religion for teaching me so much about writing, including that most important of writer skills: how to read.

Never to be forgotten are my family, Lisa, Katie, and Jayden, who remind me every day that there truly are more important and wonderful things in life than books and writing.

Lightning Source UK Ltd.
Milton Keynes UK
UKHW020202101221
395393UK00004B/124

9 781787 058408